PRAISE FOR
JANE DOE AND THE CRADLE
OF ALL WORLDS

"The quick pace and witty voice make this a good
fit for adventure fans."
—*Booklist*

"Speeding trains? He's got them. Forests with
something unnerving about them? Those too,
and so much more: a girl seeking missing kin;
booby-trapped ruins; and whip tricks worthy of
Indiana Jones."
—*The Guardian*

"A fantastic, fast-paced, exciting adventure."
—*Readings Kids*

"Fast-paced adventure and numerous escapes move
forward an abundance of episodes and shifting
narratives."
—*School Library Journal*

JANE DOE

AND The

KEY OF ALL SOULS

JEREMY LACHLAN

CAROLRHODA BOOKS
MINNEAPOLIS

First American edition published in 2021 by Carolrhoda Books®

Text copyright © 2020 by Jeremy Lachlan
First published in 2020 by Hardie Grant Egmont

Carolrhoda Books®
An imprint of Lerner Publishing Group, Inc.
241 First Avenue North
Minneapolis, MN 55401 USA

For reading levels and more information, look up this title at www.lernerbooks.com.

Cover illustration by Alessia Trunfio.

Main body text set in Bembo Std.
Typeface provided by Monotype Typography.

Library of Congress Cataloging-in-Publication Data

Names: Lachlan, Jeremy, author.
Title: Jane Doe and the key of all souls / Jeremy Lachlan.
Other titles: Key of all souls
Description: Minneapolis : Carolrhoda Books, 2020. | Series: The Jane Doe chronicles | "First published in 2020 by Hardie Grant Egmont." | Audience: Ages 10–14. | Audience: Grades 4–6. | Summary: "Jane Doe races to save her imprisoned father and to stop the villainous Roth from achieving ultimate power, while every soul in every world hangs in the balance" —Provided by publisher.
Identifiers: LCCN 2019057166 (print) | LCCN 2019057167 (ebook) | ISBN 9781541539228 | ISBN 9781541599406 (ebook)
Subjects: CYAC: Prisoners—Fiction. | Adventure and adventurers—Fiction. | Soul—Fiction. | Fantasy.
Classification: LCC PZ7.1.L214 Jar 2020 (print) | LCC PZ7.1.L214 (ebook) | DDC [Fic]—dc23

LC record available at https://lccn.loc.gov/2019057166
LC ebook record available at https://lccn.loc.gov/2019057167

Manufactured in the United States of America
1-45124-35939-5/28/2020

FOR
MUM
AND
DAD
ONCE MORE,
BECAUSE THE
ADVENTURE
AIN'T OVER YET.

"TAKE HEED CROSSING THAT **OTHERWORLDLY** THRESHOLD.

WHAT **EVIL** LURKS IN THE SHADOWS? WHAT **DARKNESS** LIES WITHIN?"

—*Winifred Robin and the Pilgrimage of Thieves*

THIS IS NOT THE
BEGINNING

THE LAST IMMORTAL

He stands on a balcony before a lake of liquid fire, entranced by the roiling lava, the lashes of flame. The stone pillars of this once grand Manor hall glow red. The ceiling is ash-stained, crumbling. A lavafall flows from an upstairs gallery. There is a weakened gateway to an Otherworld up there. A world of fire.

The lava has surrounded his lair, creeping down corridors, burning through doors, but he doesn't mind. There are volcanos in his home world, too. The dying, desert world he left behind. The lava reminds him of the sacrifices he has made. The flames remind him of her. Besides, the lava cannot harm him. Nothing can.

He made sure of that long ago.

The balcony is covered in a rough patchwork of rusted metal. So are the walls and floor behind him. Protection for the stone: not from the lava, but from his bitter, tainted breath. It ripples from the porcelain lips of his half-mask. A slow, rolling growl. His eyes burn with reflected fire.

Where is the third key going?

The question has plagued him since the incident on the train. He was so close—the child was almost his—but thanks to the traitor Hickory and the girl with the knife, she got away.

Not for long. Soon, he will have all the answers he needs.

Two Leatherheads march onto the balcony behind him, dragging a beaten man between them. His brown eyes are bloodshot, weeping tears. Some call him John Doe—others, Charlie Grayson—but Roth knows the man's favorite name is Dad. The Leatherheads release him, stand to attention, and salute.

"Another chat so soon?" John coughs and wheezes. "You're getting desperate, old man."

The Leatherheads *click-clack* their throats and snarl into their gas masks, level their rifles at John's head.

Roth takes another deep, death-rattle breath.

"You know, you might want to consider a nice mint tea now and then," John says. "Get that breath under control." He coughs again. Spits at Roth's feet. "Go on, then. Do your worst."

Roth would smile if he could. *I always do.*

He grabs John by the neck, lifts him to his feet, and peers into his pitiful eyes, just like he did on the train. And just like on the train, John's feet start to jitter. He can't breathe. He is choking.

Roth is reading him, invading his mind.

He wants to know everything. The location of the Cradle. Where John's beloved Elsa might have taken the second key. The third key's strengths, fears, and weaknesses: every little thing that makes the girl tick. He can feel John fighting back, scattering his thoughts, but Roth will uncover the truth soon enough.

Everybody breaks eventually.

A fresh trail of blood seeps from John's nose. A red tear rolls down his cheek. Roth cannot push too far if he wants to keep the man alive, so he severs the connection and steps back. John collapses, but no matter. Roth has discovered something new.

The child doesn't know.

"You're right," John wheezes. "I didn't tell her she's the third key. I couldn't. But she'll find out sooner or later, and when she does she'll become more powerful than you could possibly imagine." He grins. "You can't win, Roth. You won't. Jane's brave. Smart. She has friends and a head start. With any luck, she's stepping into the Cradle right now."

This time, there's no warning. Roth pins John to the steel-plated floor and forces his way into his mind again, growling into his mask.

I will find the girl. She cannot run forever.

PART
FOUR

THE VOICES IN HER HEAD

Here's another thing: I guess I'm old. Really old. Technically, I'm older than anyone I've ever met.

I'm older than Winifred, with her scars and wrinkles. I'm older than Hickory, who was trapped inside the Manor for two thousand years. I'm older than Roth, who could be nearing his millionty-first birthday for all I know. I guess I'm as old as the Manor itself—I just spent the first gazillion-odd years of my life as a baby, locked away in the Cradle of All Worlds, drooling on the foundation stone at the center of the nefarious Sea.

But surely *this* isn't what the Makers had in mind.

Surely I wasn't supposed to be stuck on Bluehaven for fourteen years without a clue as to who or *what* I am. Surely Dad wasn't supposed to disappear. Surely my adventure through the Manor—that endangered place-between-places—wasn't supposed to be so difficult. The snow, the booby traps, the carnivorous forest and the runaway train. Hickory's lies. Violet's pretty eyes. The raging river and the vicious, overgrown tadpoles. The Tin-skins and the Leatherheads and Roth. One calamity after the next.

Surely I'm not supposed to be *here*, now, stuck in a dying Otherworld. Arakaan, of all places.

Roth's home world.

Deserts are the worst. The heat. The glare. I've been sweating and staggering under the twin suns all morning with no food, no water, no idea where I am, and I haven't seen a thing. No camp, no well, no horses, no Arakaanians. Just the scorched sky and this never-ending plain of salt. Even my shadow's trying to escape the heat, cowering beneath me as the suns hit high noon.

At this rate, I'll be dead by nightfall.

There's a mirage on the horizon. A fool's lake splashed across the desert, winking at me, teasing me. To think, just yesterday I was inside the Manor, surrounded by rapids and whirlpools, literally drowning in water. I lick my cracked, salty lips. The desert seems to tilt and sway, but I've gotta stay sharp, keep walking. Gotta get back to Violet, and find Hickory too.

The upside to all this walking is I've had plenty of time to untangle the mess in my head. All in all, I reckon I handled the situation pretty well last night. Sure, I threw up, caused a brief, minor quake, ran into the desert and screamed till my voice cracked, but I didn't pass out or break down sobbing, so that's something. Not bad for a girl who just found out her entire life's been a lie.

Then the sandstorm came, devouring the desert, eating up the stars. Blasted thing swallowed me in seconds, spun me around. I tried to run back to camp—could've sworn I heard Violet shout my name—and that was my biggest mistake. Once I started running I couldn't stop. I ran and ran through the howling dark, shivering, choking, crying. Wasn't till my legs gave out that I realized it wasn't the storm I was running from. By the time the twin suns rose, the gale had moved on, and I was stranded in the middle of nowhere with nothing but the voices in my head.

My god. You really don't know.

They had a baby boy. He died, Jane.

They found you. They took you from the Cradle.

I'm the third key. I'm the third key. I'm the third key.

I'm the third Cradle key. How the Makers made me is a mystery. I don't even wanna know. It's the *why* that's important. I'm the Makers' Plan B, the secret weapon they left behind in case an immortal maniac ever invaded the Manor, their oh-so-hallowed—now dying—creation.

Two regular keys to open the Cradle.

One key of flesh and bone to control it.

Me.

But what does that mean? What am I supposed to do in there? Heal every gateway? Protect every Otherworld? How can I save the Manor when all I've done so far is tear it apart?

I can't believe he didn't tell you.

Dad. John Doe. Charlie Grayson. The Man with Too Many Names. Part of me wants to shout at him, shove him, tell him I hate him just to see what he'd do, because this is the thing I keep coming back to, the thing that cuts deepest: he isn't really my dad, after all. He's just a man. A stranger who plucked an amber-eyed baby from the Cradle and paid the ultimate price. A man who was stuck in a realm of nightmares for fourteen years—gripped by a Specter, a guardian of the Cradle—unable to talk, barely able to walk, while that baby grew into a girl. A girl who cared for him day in and day out because she didn't know any better.

Because she never learned the truth.

"No," I say.

I looked after him because I love him, simple as that. He's the only family I've ever known. I can't blame him for not telling me the truth right away. I think he was about to tell me on the train.

Yes, Jane, you were born in the Manor, but . . .

Dad sacrificed his freedom on the spiral road so we could get away. He told me he loved me, but what happens when this is over? Where do we go? What do we do? He doesn't need me anymore. He can make his own meals, put himself to bed, read his own stories. What if he wants to return to his home world, Tallis, without me? And what about Elsa? Would she go with him?

The old lady who I'd mistakenly thought was my mom couldn't stand the sight of me last night. I still don't know anything about her life here in Arakaan, or what happened to her inside the Manor after she was separated from Dad. You'd think she wouldn't be able to shut up about it—about *him*—after all these years, but no.

I can't do this, she said. *I thought I was strong enough. I'm sorry.*

I'll have to talk to her as soon as I find my way back to camp. Or as soon as they find me—because they're out there, surely, combing the desert right now.

I wanna get my key back, too. The real key.

"Thieving jerks," I grunt.

Gotta be nice about it, though. Elsa's the only one who can take us to the Cradle, after all. The only one who knows the location of the true second key.

Where did she say it was hidden?

An ancient city to the west. A canyon hideout the people of this region fled to long ago.

I've already lost the dummy key she gave me last night, meaning I threw the useless piece of trash as far as I could during the storm. Elsa'll be angry, but that's the least of my worries right now.

The air in this world tastes off. Bitter. Smells like burning coal, even though the sky is clear. I feel like I'm trekking through invisible fire. My bare feet are red-raw, crunching over the hard crust of salt.

Note to self: next time you run off into the desert, take appropriate footwear.

I stop walking. Scan the barren wasteland with binocular hands. No birds. No flies. Not a breath of wind. The silence of the desert closes in.

Strange. In the Manor I was surrounded by walls and out here I'm surrounded by nothing, yet somehow they feel the same. Thick with heavy, suffocating quiet.

How is it possible to feel so confined in such an open space?

"Keep going," I tell myself. "Forward is the only way."

I can't die here. There's too much at stake.

I'm the third key. I'm the third key. I'm the third key.

It explains everything, Violet said. *The quakes. Your dreams. Your connection to the Manor.*

The reason Roth wants to capture me.

It all makes sense now. Roth wants to rule the Manor. Reckons he can do it by getting inside my head, controlling me, possessing me. Sure, I stopped him from doing it on the train, but how long could I keep that up? What if he tortures me? What if he tortures the people I love? Roth could break me in seconds. Invade my thoughts. Dangle me over the foundation stone like his personal plaything. Through me, he could open any gateway and unleash the Cradle Sea.

Through me, he could conquer any world.

I swear I can feel his hands around my neck. His rotten breath on my skin. I can hear him laughing at me through his porcelain half-mask, just like he did on the train.

I bet Roth knew I was the third key all along.

He must've caught up to Dad and Elsa soon after they took me from the Cradle. Must've seen me in their arms. He would've been furious they'd snatched his prize—even angrier that they slipped out of his clutches again moments later—but at least he knew. The Cradle had been found. The third key was out there, and he'd stop at nothing to track me down. He'd spend the next hundred years scouring the Manor for us, but he had no idea Dad and Elsa were separated, no idea Dad and I had made it outside. And while a hundred years passed for Roth inside the Manor, only fourteen passed for us on Bluehaven.

All those years of anguish and pain.

Roth's to blame for them all.

I clench my fists and grit my teeth as a jolt of pain shoots up my left arm. The gash in my palm's gone crusty and gross. Understandable, really. It's been slashed three times in, what, less than a week? By Mayor Atlas back on Bluehaven, at the base of the Sacred Stairs. By Violet on the runaway train. By me in the jelly-egged corridor near the river, when I nearly killed us all. I really shouldn't have ripped off the bandage last night.

"A hundred more steps," I say. "Two hundred. Then you can rest."

My skin's already turning browner from the suns. Not quite as brown as Violet's, but a deeper, darker olive than the pale, basement-blanched olive I had, living with the Hollows. The glare of the salt's so bright it hurts. I walk with my eyes half-closed, lashes splintering the light.

But wait. "What the . . ."

There's something out there. A shadow on the plain, rippling in the heat-shimmer.

Is it the camp? A house? Another mirage?

I walk a little faster and the shadow on the plain gets bigger, far too large for a house. It's a hill, I reckon. Maybe a mountain. I jog, stagger and stumble for a while. Stop and stare.

It isn't a house or a hill or a mountain.

It's a shipwreck.

THE BOY WHO NEVER WAS

The wreck looks like the rotted-out carcass of some ancient beast. It's about ten stories high. Rusty metal marred by long, jagged cracks. A red sand dune's heaped against its side. I've never seen a ship this big. Did it run aground before the ocean dried up? Sink in a battle or storm? The empty portholes stare back at me like hungry spider eyes. Watching. Waiting.

"Creepy," I say out loud.

I swing around the stern, into the shade. There's a tear in the base of the hull. A makeshift door. Could be supplies inside. Barrels of water. If I can get to the top, I reckon I'll be able to see for miles.

"Hello?" I shout. "Anyone in there?" The silence of the desert closes in again. "I'm coming in," I say, and in an almost-whisper, "Don't shoot me."

It's dim inside. Cavernous. Some kind of cargo hold, probably. The air's only slightly cooler—more like an oven than a raging furnace—but the change is welcome. Tiny shafts of light beam through the rusted-out holes in the hull. A carpet of sand has trickled through. It's littered with half-buried crates and barrels, all of them broken. There's a towering wall to my left, dotted with landings, hatches, and a zigzagging metal staircase.

I head up the stairs, armed with a plank of wood in case someone or some*thing* is hiding in the shadows.

The hatch on the first landing is ajar. I step through it, plank ready to swing, but there's nobody there.

"Hellooooo?"

I find a storeroom down the corridor. There's a massive hole in the middle of the floor, and a hole in the ceiling above it, too. Scratch that—a dozen holes, floor after floor of them. A shaft soaring all the way up to a patch of sky at the top of the wreck. It's as if something came crashing through the ship long ago. There are wires, too—taut, like strings on a harp—rising up through the shaft and branching off onto each deck in a vast, metallic web. All of them stem from the room below, which is so dark I can barely see inside it. I flick one, and the web rattles.

I sink to my knees and peer into the hole. "You've gotta be kidding me."

The room's filled with explosives. Bubbly old sticks of dynamite. Open barrels of gunpowder. All these rusty, mini-pineapple-looking things, which I'm pretty sure are called grenades. The shipwreck's one big powder keg. I stare up at the web of wires again.

Tripwires. The whole place is rigged to blow.

"Nice and easy, then . . ."

I back away slowly and continue up the stairs. The top deck's just as messed up as the cargo hold. The heat hits me like a wall when I step outside. I've climbed to a dizzying height. The peak of the dune heaped against the wreck is several stories below me now. The salt pan stretches out as far as I can see. No camp. None of Elsa's Arakaanian pals. Far to my right, a ridge on the horizon. A mountain range.

The canyon city must be in there, somewhere.

I pick my way toward the front of the ship and find what must've been the control room. The place is a dive. A giant ship's wheel is snapped in half on the floor. The control panels are covered in broken levers and flyaway springs. Far as I know, we've never had machines like this on Bluehaven. I've only read about them in books. Otherworldly contraptions. Foreign devices. Who were these ancient sailors? *What* were they? Human, Leatherhead, or something else? What was it Dad said about Roth's people?

I think his was a handsome race. Strong and proud, now all but extinct.

Could they have built this? Abandoned this? Hell, Roth could've stood right here, once upon a time. I shudder at the thought and scan the salt flats on the other side of the ship. Still nothing.

"Don't panic," I tell myself. "You're okay. Think."

Wood. Kindling. Signal fire.

The ship's wheel could work, though it won't burn long enough on its own. I look for something else to use, but all I find is the top of the trip-wired shaft in a big, empty room. I'm about to spit down it when I hear something— at least, I think I do—out in the desert.

Someone calling my name? I spin around, hope flaring in my chest. I've been found. Rescued at last.

But I stop when I see the markings all over the wall, scratched into the rusted metal. Tally marks. Wavy lines and circles. Hundreds of nonsensical scribbles. The floor's littered with broken glass and torn scraps of old, wrinkled parchment inked in symbols I can't decipher, words I can't understand. Over in the corner, three dusty bottles of booze, still corked.

Elsa.

She told me she wandered the desert for days after she was brought back to Arakaan. Maybe she took shelter here for a while. But what about the paper scraps and booze? No, she's been here more recently than that.

I'm so thirsty, I uncork one of the bottles and consider a swig, but the smell alone burns my throat. I'm about to put it back when I notice an image on the wall. A drawing she clearly spent time on, etched with care.

A baby—her baby—wrapped in a blanket.

I squat and run my fingers over the boy's face, and I *know*. It clicks. This is Elsa's private place. Her secret hideaway. A spot she visits to remember the boy she lost. The boy Roth took from her. He's everywhere, I realize. On the other walls, a patch of floor, above the hatch I stepped through moments ago. I suppose the boy would be a man now, if he'd survived and come here, to Arakaan, with Elsa. I guess he'd be fourteen if he came to Bluehaven with Dad and me. I wonder if they gave him a name.

And suddenly it hits me. This is the nightmare Dad's Specter would've preyed upon. While I was plodding around the basement, whining about my life and singing him stupid songs, he would've been watching his little boy die, over and over again.

"I'm sorry," I whisper, to Dad, to Elsa, to the boy who never even had a chance.

I swear to myself I won't tell anyone I've seen this. Not Violet, not Hickory, certainly not Elsa. This is her secret, and that's how it'll remain. Anyway, the shipwreck's so big I could've wandered right past this room and never noticed a thing. Nobody'll know any—

"*Ow!*" There's that voice outside again, louder now. "*Ow-ooo!*"

Wait a second. Not a voice. Not even human.

A yelp from some kind of animal.

And that's when I hear the other, more terrifying sounds echoing up through the wreck. Howling. Whimpering. Frenzied barking. I've been found, all right. But not by Elsa's Arakaanian crew.

Tin-skins.

I dash outside, lean over the railing. Count six of them down there on the salt and sand, barking at the tear in the base of the hull, bolting inside. Wild Tin-skins. Untamed. They look just as big as the ones we encountered in the Manor, but they have eyes and ears. They're tin-less, covered in fur and bristles, like a pack of wolf-boar hybrids.

And they've definitely caught my scent.

I swear at the sky and stumble back to the shaft. I can hear the pack raging through the wreck, their claws scraping steel. My head spins. My vision blurs.

Steady, Jane. Think.

It won't take them long to find me. Should I barricade myself in a cabin? Dive over the side and take my chances on the dune? What would Violet do? What about Hickory? I'm too tired. Can't think. I can see the Tin-skins' shadows, darting up the shaft through a haze of light. They could trip one of the wires any second now, which would be very, very bad.

Or very good, I tell myself, and almost laugh. It'd kill them, at least. Make a decent signal fire, too. Like, a *really* decent signal fire, visible for miles.

Oh, crap. I have to blow up the ship.

I ditch my plank of wood, grab one half of the ship's wheel and lug it down the corridor. The sucker weighs an absolute ton. Every muscle in my body screams, but I can't stop.

"If anyone else is hiding in here," I shout, "you'd better get out now!"

I heave the ship's wheel right up to the shaft, tip it over the edge and sprint for the door.

But then I freeze, breath held, and wait. There's no *twang* of tripped wires. No big bang. All I can hear are the Tin-skins coming to eat me, and the pounding of my heart.

"Seriously?" I stumble back to the shaft. The half-wheel wasn't heavy enough. It's dangling on top of the wires. "Oh, *come on!*"

More Tin-skin shadows, darting round the shaft. Higher now. Way too close.

Take two, then. I drag the other half of the wheel toward the shaft, huffing and puffing, panic snapping at my heels. It's bigger than the other one. Heavier, too. I pull it. Push it. Heave the stupid thing with white-knuckled hands, then drop to my butt and kick it.

"Come . . . on . . . you stupid piece of—"

A rumble outside tells me the Tin-skins have made it to the upper deck. One of them leaps at a porthole and shoves its big, ugly head into the room, gnashing its teeth.

I kick the wheel again. It tips over the edge, out of sight. I stagger to my feet and head back to the control room, sprinting, swearing, hoping against all hope it's done the trick.

CRASH! TWANG! TWANG! TWANG!

"Yes!"

Now I've just gotta hope the tripwires actually make the bomb—

KA-BOOM!

The explosion's so loud my ears burst. So powerful I'm launched through a grimy window. I hit the forward deck in a shower of glass. A Tin-skin snaps its jaws right beside me—too close—but another explosion tears through the wreck just in time. The deck lurches, tilting violently to one side, away from the dune. The Tin-skin scratches for purchase with its claws, slips away. I manage to scramble up the steepening slope and throw myself over the side. I hit the dune two seconds later, roll and tumble, flip and slide, screaming, "Ugh—crap—argh!"

Debris rains down around me. Clumps of metal. Shattered crates. A flying toilet. I skid to the bottom and keep running, covered in cuts and bruises, coughing up sand. The wreck groans behind me and collapses onto the desert floor. A third and final explosion obliterates what's left, and a giant fireball soars into the sky. A black mushroom cloud.

I fall to my knees once I'm a safe distance away, utterly spent. Breathing hard.

Talk about a signal fire. If the Arakaanians don't see this, I'll—

A growl to my left.

Turns out I wasn't the only one to get out of the wreck. A Tin-skin's snarling at me, thirty paces away, crouching low, licking its chops.

I'm too tired for this.

"Don't even think about it," I say.

And wouldn't you know it? The mutt blinks at me. Cocks its furry head to one side. Even sits and stares at the burning wreck for a while before it trots off into the desert. Off to find another pack, I suppose.

It isn't long before I hear the thunder of hooves on the salt. The signal fire worked.

The Arakaanians have found me at last.

THE WOUND

Violet keeps staring at me. It's getting annoying, to be honest. I know she just wants to make sure I'm okay, but so many people have been staring at me since the explosion, I might as well be back on Bluehaven. They're not unkind stares. Nobody's shaking their head or muttering prayers of salvation. I even catch the occasional nervous smile. But it still feels weird, like I'm some sort of rare gem.

I shouldn't be surprised. They've been waiting for me out here a long time. Maybe I'm not the hero they were expecting, but I'm still the girl with amber eyes. Jane Doe, formerly Cursed One. Now something altogether different.

"Here." Violet hands me her waterskin. I've already finished mine. "Keep drinking."

I take a swig. "Thanks." Despite the water, my voice is still raspy. I've barely spoken since we sat down. Can't bring myself to look Violet in the eye, let alone tell her what's on my mind.

"I'd grab you something to eat, but rations are low," she says. "I think there was a cache of food, water, and supplies hidden in the shipwreck they were counting on, but—"

"I blew it up."

"Yep." Violet keeps gaping at the smoldering wreck. We've set up camp a short hike away. "I can't believe you blew something up without me." She flashes me a smile. "But it's fine. You're alive. That's all that matters."

"Not sure everyone agrees with you," I say, nodding across the camp.

Elsa hasn't stopped ranting: at the horses for munching too loudly on their hay, at her waterskin for being empty, at the poor chump who spilled a drop of booze when he refilled it, and the suns for taking too long to set. She didn't say a word when the Arakaanians found me. She just looked me up and down with her watery eyes. Face weathered, unreadable. Skin like tough, tanned leather, cured by the suns. Then she leapt off her horse and started barking orders. Understandable, really—I'd just blown her secret place to pieces. All those etchings of her baby boy are lost now, buried under a mountain of metal.

"She hates me," I say.

Violet screws up her face. "Actually, I think she hates everyone. Except maybe him." She nods at Lazy Eye, the guy who grabbed me out by the gateway yesterday. Bald head. Dark skin. Permanent scowl. He's sitting on a mat near Elsa, staring at us. "His name's Yaku. Elsa's right-hand man. Doesn't say much, but he can understand us. I think she's taught him our language."

I nod at the rest of the Arakaanians in the group: twenty-odd men, women, and children. Some are black-skinned, some are brown-skinned, some have skin almost as white as the salt and wear long, hooded robes to shield themselves from the blazing suns. Some are bald, like Yaku. Some have shags of flyaway hair or fancy braids.

"And them?"

Violet shrugs. "Scavengers. Warriors. Survivors."

Similar to the folk of Bluehaven, I guess. People from all corners of a ruined world.

A few of them are assembling makeshift tents of ragged cloth. Others are lounging back on the salt, using their saddles as pillows, enjoying this sweet spot between day and night, oblivious to Elsa's ranting. They seem peaceful enough, but can we trust them?

"Reckon they're telling the truth about Hickory? They didn't . . . you know. Kill him?"

Violet hugs her knees to her chest. Frowns at Yaku. "He's the one who tortured him. Nearly broke both his arms. And Elsa just sat there, asking questions about you and the key. It was terrible, but . . . well, I guess they couldn't take any chances." She shakes her head. "I may not like them, but we're still on the same side, right? Elsa told me Hickory's alive. Promised. She said they sent him ahead to some kind of outpost at the edge of the mountains, to get his wounds looked at by some healers. We're stopping there tomorrow, on our way to the canyon city."

I look to the west. In the Manor, I told Hickory I'd banish him from the group when we found Elsa, but now that we're here? Now that we know she isn't my mom? Now that we've seen what she's become? At this rate, she's gonna drink herself to death before we make it back to the Manor.

"I don't think we can win this without him, Violet."

"I know," she says softly. "We'll get him back."

The salt pan glows a vibrant pink as the setting suns hover above the horizon, not to the west but to the south. Different world, different rules.

"I'm sorry you had to go through that," I say. "Last night, I mean. And I'm sorry I ran off."

"Elsa said the storms can get so bad out here the sand can tear flesh from bone," Violet says. "I wanted to head out and find you right away, but she wouldn't let me. Had to tie me up again to make sure I stayed put." She looks down at her knees. "I thought I'd lost you, Jane."

I stare at her, heart hammering away in my chest.

She stares right back.

Then she punches me in the shoulder. Hard.

"Ouch!"

"Don't ever do that again. This is a big, old world, and it's just as dangerous as the Manor. Who knows what's out there?"

"I said I'm sorry."

"Not good enough." She points at me. Pretty much jabs her finger into my nose. "No more running. Unless we're being chased or something. Then you can run. But you have to make sure I'm with you. At all times. Deal?"

Even though my shoulder's killing me, I smile. "Deal."

"You should probably apologize to Elsa, too."

"Yeah," I say, "I know." On the other side of camp, Elsa shouts a final insult at her horse and passes out. "Maybe once she sobers up a bit."

I yawn. Desperately need some shut-eye, but my head's pounding, and the gash in my palm's packed with grit from my tumble down the dune. I scratch at the skin around it and wince.

"Here," Violet says, "let me take a look."

"It's fine."

Violet tuts at me, grabs my hand. "We should clean it at least."

Her grip's firm but soft. She's concentrating so hard she chews on her tongue, and for the briefest of moments the desert disappears. We could be anywhere, sitting side by side in a perfect Otherworld of our own. No salt pan, no Arakaanians, no dangerous mission. It's nice.

Violet blows gently on my hand and brushes a few specks of sand away. "Looks infected. Don't worry, I bet there's some sort of special cactus out here that can heal wounds. Desert folk are all over that stuff, from what I've read. We can ask Hickory's healers tomorrow."

Assuming they really exist.

Violet grabs her waterskin and douses my hand. When she wipes some of the dirt clear, her skin brushes mine. This time, an electric fuzzy-buzz darts up my arm, across my chest and deep down into my gut. It's strange and thrilling, and it makes me feel safe—protected—for the first time since I don't know when.

Before I can stop them, the words come spilling out. "How am I gonna do this, Violet? It's all so . . . big."

"You do it step by step," Violet says. "Eat your elephant in small pieces."

I look around the camp, horrified. "Wait, we're having *elephant* for dinner? I didn't know there were elephants here—"

"It's a saying, doofus. Means don't look at the big picture. Tackle things bit by bit, one problem at a time. First, we get to this outpost and find Hickory."

"And then?"

"We head to the secret canyon city—whatever it's called—and grab the second key."

"And then?"

"We cross the dune sea to Roth's gateway and get back inside the Manor—"

"Somehow bypassing an entire army standing in our way."

"—*and then*," Violet pushes on, "we find the Cradle, which should be much easier now that we have Elsa. After all, she's the one who found it before."

I swallow the lump in my throat. "Then I just have to stand on the foundation stone in the center of the Cradle Sea, somehow heal the entire Manor before Roth destroys it completely, defeat Roth, *and* save my dad." I shake my head. "What if we get inside the Cradle and I still don't know what to do? Or what if we figure it out, but I mess it up and kill everyone?"

Violet dabs my hand dry with a corner of her robe. "You're not going to kill everyone."

"How do you know?"

"Because despite what people say, you're smart, capable and definitely *not* evil."

"I lost control yesterday, Violet. Back in the Manor . . ."
I bite my lip. I still haven't told her about the Specter. How
it found me in the water and wrapped its tendrils of light
over my hand. How I asked it to help me, and it did. At
least, I think it did. It didn't Grip me, anyway. But why?
Because the Makers left the Specters behind to protect me?
Because they're bound to me, just as they're bound to the
Cradle? I suppose Violet figures I simply got away from the
thing, and that's fine by me. The Specters are monsters. If
I'm connected to them, what does that make me?

"I tore that corridor apart," I say. "If the gateway hadn't
been there, we would've drowned."

"But it was there," Violet says. "And *you* opened it. You
saved us, Jane."

I remember it all so clearly. Almost drowning after the
Specter fled. Waking up to see Violet leaning over me.
I grabbed her knife, sliced open my palm and slammed it
onto the stone. That was when the power got away from
me. When everything fell apart. I can still feel it: every
crack, every tremor. It was terrifying, and it hurt, but—as
odd as it sounds—for a second there it felt incredible. Part
of me liked it, part of me wanted *more*, and that's the scari-
est part of all.

I shake my head. "We got lucky. I'm telling you, I'm
not ready for this."

Violet tears a strip of material from her robe and wraps
it around my palm. "Think about it this way. What do we
know about the Makers? Who are they? How did they create the Manor?"

"I'm tired, Violet. I don't feel like rehashing every little—"

"Trust me," she says. "It'll help, I promise. Go on. Tell me."

"Well," I rattle off the story as it comes to mind, "long, long ago, the Otherworlds were violent, chaotic places. Then Po, Aris, and Nabu-kai met. The Gatekeeper, the Builder, and the Scribe. The Makers. Po could travel between worlds, Aris could create and shape stone, and Nabu-kai could see into the future. He was sort of like the grand architect, I guess. He foresaw it all. The Manor's halls and booby traps. The corridors and gateways, and the paths of everyone who'd walk through them. Together, they brought his vision to life—they created the Manor—and it bound and stabilized the Otherworlds."

Violet nods, and ties the bandage off. "But in order for life to truly begin . . ."

"They had to clear the Otherworlds of the old Gods of Chaos. So they tricked them. Told them about the Manor, opened every gateway, and let them into the Cradle, the enormous chamber at the core of it all."

"And once inside, their combined energies clashed and swirled and formed the Cradle Sea, a source of terrible, unmatched power that could raze entire worlds if unleashed!"

"Really not helping the nerves, Violet."

"Sorry," she says. "But it's true. And what happened next?"

"Well, the Makers knew they'd have to join the Gods

of Chaos, but instead of becoming part of the Sea, they poured their energy, their life force, into the foundation stone—the first stone laid down by Aris—sitting in the center of the Cradle, to bind and protect the Sea."

Violet nods. "But before they did that?"

"Well, they left two keys in the Manor to open the Cradle—"

"And a third—you—inside the Cradle to protect it," Violet says. She smiles, soft and reassuring. "See? As weird and daunting and scary as it sounds, you're part of the Manor, Jane. You were literally made for this. Born for this. Trust that. Trust *them*."

I huff out a breath. "Trust the Makers."

"They gave you this connection to the Manor for a reason. You said it yourself. The Makers poured their life force into the foundation stone." She nods at my wounded hand. "If you get to the stone and make the connection, maybe it'll *amplify* your powers. Focus them. Open up a direct line between you and the Manor. Between you and the Makers themselves."

I trace my thumb over the bandage. "You reckon I'll be able to . . . talk to them?"

"Well, I doubt you'll have a lengthy chat over a cup of tea, but maybe they'll be there for you. In essence, spirit, whatever you want to call it. Maybe they'll guide you."

"That's a lot of maybes."

"I know everything seems overwhelming, Jane. I know it's unfair. We're outnumbered. Outgunned. Out-*side*. The fate of all worlds shouldn't rest on the shoulders of a fourteen-year-old girl, but it does." Violet pauses. "Well, technically, you're not fourteen."

"Technically, I'm not a girl. I'm a key."

"The point is, you'll find a way. *We* will find a way. How do we find the Cradle? How do we save the Manor? How do we rescue your dad? Answers will come, and when they do?" She smiles at me. "You'll be unstoppable."

And there it is. The word that frightens me more than any other.

Unstoppable.

THE NEW NIGHTMARE

I'm back in the Manor, whirling through black water, lungs on fire. My same-old, same-old nightmare. Good times.

Again, I see Dad and Elsa suspended in the dark. Again, I hear the eerie underwater moaning and that soft, whispered voice.

Let go.

I used to think it was Elsa's voice. Now I know I was wrong.

The tide changes, and I'm pinned to a wall. The current eases. The Specter looms before me, white and blinding; a wisp of horns, eyes like white-hot embers. Tendrils of light stream from its sides, curling with the ebb and flow of the water. I take the Cradle key from my pocket.

If you want to save the Manor, I think, *help us. Let me go.*

But this time, it doesn't help us. This time, the Specter turns against me. Roars so loud every bone in my body aches and my teeth feel like they're about to crack. The tendrils of light reach out to grab me—*Grip* me—drag me kicking and screaming to that realm of waking nightmares.

But someone pulls me out of the water just in time.

"No!"

The porcelain half-mask. The veiny, mottled skin. Roth's rotten stench blasts my throat dry. He leans over me and growls, rippling the air between us with his rancid breath. My skin itches and crawls. He stares into my eyes, trying to turn me inside out, trying to read me.

I know exactly what he's thinking. *You're mine.*

I cry out, kick him, slip from his grasp and scramble to my feet.

When I spin around, the water has disappeared. I'm sprawled in a black-sandy corridor, surrounded by glittering crystals of pale blue and rose. I can still smell Roth, still hear him breathing somewhere down the corridor, so I turn and run. The crystals crack, tremble and grow, sprouting and stabbing from the walls. I sprint for an open door, dive through the shrinking gap, and land in a puddle of blood-red sludge.

I'm back in the forest now, surrounded by red-leafed trees, snaking vines, and those glowing spores floating through the air like miniature moons. I feel lightheaded, woozy, like I could lie down and sleep forever, but I can still hear Roth, still *feel* him—he's coming for me—so I pull myself out of the sludge and run. The red leaves flap. The vines whip around and try to snag me. Tree roots burst from the leaf- and bone-litter, tripping me up. But when I hit the ground it isn't sludge I land in.

"What the . . ."

This time, I'm bathed in candlelight, lying in a mound of snow. I've been here before. It's the first hall I entered after I left Bluehaven. Roth has vanished. I scan the frosted balconies. The icicles. The columns adorned with stone-carved faces. The doors on this lower level are almost completely buried in the snow.

There's the hole I burrowed through when I first arrived, so clueless, so lost.

There's my trail of footsteps.

There's *me*—past-me—however-many-days-ago-Jane—trudging through the snow.

"*Dad*," she whisper-shouts, clinging to her lantern. "*You there?*"

I have to stop her. Have to save her. "Wait! You're going the wrong way!"

She can't hear me. Can't see me. She's already stepping into the black archway at the other end of the hall, swallowed by the dark. I move through the snow as fast as I can, but when I finally step through the archway, past-me has already fled. The Specters are here instead—the two that escaped from the Cradle all those years ago—looming before me, reaching out with their tendrils of light.

"P—please," I stammer. "You're supposed to help me. W—we're on the same side."

They shake their heads, slow and menacing. They've been waiting for me. I can feel it. Waiting for this moment ever since I stepped into Arakaan. Ever since I found out I'm the third key. Their tendrils seep into my eyes, up my nose, down my throat, infecting me with that white-fire light, Gripping me at last. And then—

Poof! They're gone, along with the snow.

I'm kneeling on the foundation stone in the center of the Cradle Sea now. I've made it. Somehow I've beaten Roth and my bleeding hand's pressed to the trembling stone. I can feel the power of the Makers flowing through me, stronger than ever before. But something's wrong. A bad feeling, deep inside. A dark and endless void. It hurts. It hurts so much I'm crying, screaming, and I don't know what to do because Dad and Violet are dead. How they died, I've no idea. All I know is they're gone—lost forever—and it's all my fault.

Someone, somewhere, keeps shouting my name. Elsa, I think. She's pleading with me, telling me to stop, but I can't feel the Makers anymore, just that gaping void in my chest.

"No," I gasp through gritted teeth. "Please, no."

I can't stop it. This is the end. The foundation stone cracks. The Cradle Sea surges and glows, white and blinding like the Specters.

Return, the voice that isn't Elsa's whispers.

And I wake with a start, gasping for air, twisted in my blanket under the stars. I shudder with relief. Violet's snoring softly beside me. Everybody's passed out, by the look of it. But I'm not the only one having nightmares. Elsa's tossing and turning on the other side of camp.

"No," she calls out. "Please."

I creep over to her as quietly as I can, blanket wrapped around my shoulders, stepping past saddles and smoldering campfires, over splayed legs and spears. Illuminated by this Otherworldly night sky, the salt pan is an ocean of silver, dead calm. The moon's small and sickle-shaped, dangling over our heads like one of Roth's blades.

"Charlie," Elsa whispers. "Charlie?"

She's dreaming about Dad. I kneel beside her. Grab a corner of my blanket and dab the little beads of sweat from her wrinkled brow. "He's okay," I whisper. "Roth needs him. He'll keep him alive."

I need to hear it as much as she does. I never want to feel that void in my chest again.

We'll save him, I want to tell her. *I don't know how, but we will.*

"No," Elsa mumbles. "Roth . . ."

She's trembling, just like Dad used to tremble in the Hollows' basement. I hold her hand, just like I held his. I tell her, "It's okay, I'm here, go back to sleep." When she settles, I uncork her waterskin, toss it aside, and let the booze bleed into the salt. Then I stand up and freeze.

Yaku's awake, watching me, the moonlight glinting in his good eye.

I nod hello and hold up my hands to show him I'm unarmed. He frowns, goes to say something—*Buzz off,* I assume—so I beat him to it. "Don't worry," I mutter, "I'm going."

Violet stirs when I curl up beside her. "Another nightmare?"

"No." Liar. "Go back to sleep."

"Okay," she yawns, closing her eyes again. "Just make sure Hickory saves me some pancakes."

"Will do," I say, and watch as a shooting star streaks across the sky.

SOME OTHER REASON

The Arakaanians ride single file, supplies tethered to their saddles, weapons slung round their backs. Rifles, mostly. Wooden staffs, clubs, a couple of swords. Elsa's nursing a crossbow near the front of the line, sleeping in her saddle. Her speckled horse keeps breaking formation, wandering left or right till Elsa wakes up, swears loudly, yanks the poor beast back in line and passes out again. I may have spilled her stash of booze, but that didn't stop her from nicking someone else's.

She hasn't even looked at me all morning.

We set off before dawn, when the suns started draining the northern sky of stars.

"*Novu,*" Yaku spat at me from his horse, jabbing a meaty finger in the directions of the compass. "*Novu, torru, pillai, raan.*" North, south, east, west. "We're going *raan.*"

West to the mountain range, to the outpost, to Hickory and, beyond that, the secret canyon city. Asmadin, they call it. Resting place of the second Cradle key.

It's midmorning now, and I'm already baking. The desert's shimmering so much it looks like the world's about to wrinkle in on itself. The salt pan ended ages ago, giving way to a blistering landscape of sand and scree. Everyone's on edge, scanning the desert for who knows what. Another sandstorm? More Tin-skins? Some other deadly Arakaanian beast?

I'm sweating in my saddle near the tail end of the line. The hooded robe I was given this morning stinks so bad it reminds me of Roth. My goggles, fashioned from an old Leatherhead gas mask, are lopsided and too tight, but at least they cut the glare. I'm still trying to figure out how this horse business works. We have 'em on Bluehaven, but I've never had the chance to ride one. I'm pretty sure this one's broken. He keeps trying to head-butt the other horses, and whenever I yank on the reins to stop him, the jerk tries to bite me. He's dirty. Ugly. Irritating. Nobody told me his name, so I've decided to call him Scab.

Violet's riding beside me, cloaked and goggled, too. She named her horse Rex, and he's perfect, of course. Calm. Polite. Keeps his teeth to himself. "Are you sure you didn't have a nightmare last night?"

I still haven't told her about the dream, for the same reason I didn't tell her about the Specter in the water, back in the Manor: I'm afraid. Afraid of what I am, what I can do, what could happen if I lose control again. The Specters in my nightmare could sense it. I reckon that's why they Gripped me. They think I'm gonna fail, which makes me as big a threat to the Manor as Roth. If I mess this up, we're all doomed. Every Otherworld. Every soul. What if they're right?

I can still feel and see it all. That void in my chest when

I knew I'd lost Dad and Violet. The cracking stone. The surging, glowing Cradle Sea. That voice.

Return.

Back in the Manor, the voice was a comfort. It gave me hope when the river creatures were closing in, told me what to do. Now it terrifies me, not least because I have no idea whose voice it is. The Manor's? One of the Makers'? Po's, perhaps. And return to what? The Cradle?

Great tip. What do they think I'm trying to do?

"If I did have a nightmare, I can't remember it," I lie.

"Hmm," Violet says. "It's a shame, really. I know your nightmares are no picnic, but I was hoping we might get another hint of what's to come. Maybe a nudge in the right direction, like we had inside the Manor. Even you have to admit, they're handy. They're a gift."

"A *gift*? Uh-uh."

All those nightmares I had growing up. All those never-ending stone corridors. All those times I was drowning in the Cradle Sea. They were a twisted glimpse of my past, but what about the others? Those people I saw running for their lives. The children screaming and dying. Were they terrible but regular, run-of-the-mill dreams? Or were they things that *have* happened? Things that are *going to* happen? Things that *are* happening, right now, inside the Manor and out? How am I supposed to tell the difference?

"I'd rather dream about pancakes, like you."

Violet scrunches her face at me. "What?"

"Never mind. Point is, I hate the nightmares, just like the quakes."

"And, like the quakes," Violet says, "we need them, whether you like it or not. The Manor's been calling to you, Jane, all your life. Showing you things. Telling you things. You just weren't aware of it. But this power inside you—it's awake now. There's no going back. You can't ignore it. Next time the Manor calls, you have to listen."

"I *did* listen, remember? The Manor showed me the path to the river and the hall of waterfalls. I followed it— *we* followed it—the path that led us here."

"Yeah," Violet says to herself, looking out at the desert, "here."

We ride and we ride, and the mountain range doesn't seem to get any closer. When the suns get too high and the temperature soars even higher, Elsa—having slept off her hangover at last—orders everyone to get off their horses and walk. Luckily, I've been given a pair of sandals, but even so it's too much. All of it. The sweat. The aching legs. The growling hunger and throat-wrenching thirst. I barely even have the energy to swear at Scab anymore. Violet, on the other hand?

"I've been thinking," she says out of nowhere. "Why are we in Arakaan?"

I wipe a trail of sweat from my cheek. "Because the Manor wanted us to find Elsa."

"Yeah, but why did it bring *her* here?"

"Because this is the world Roth left for dead." I glance over my shoulder at Yaku. Guy's been riding behind us all day. "It's the last place he'd ever think to look for the second key."

"There must be more to it than that," Violet says. "Roth hasn't returned to Arakaan, but that doesn't make it safe. This is still enemy territory. Roth's kept the Manor gateway by the dune sea open all these years, which means he can always return. He doesn't *want* to, but he could. The Manor bringing Elsa back here—bringing *us* here? It's too risky. I mean, why not seal Elsa off in a nice, green, peaceful world and let her wait for us there instead?"

"Because the Manor's a jerk?"

"Because there's something else we're supposed to do here." Violet leans in a little closer, lowers her voice. "Think about it. After we get to the Cradle and you heal the Manor, we still have to deal with Roth. If he really is immortal, how do we stop him?"

"No idea."

"Do you think the Cradle Sea could destroy him?"

"Maybe. Everyone says it's the most destructive force in all the worlds." I scratch my head. "Then again, Dad and Elsa swam in it. I did, too, when I was a baby. Nothing happened to us."

Violet chews her lip, nodding. "The foundation stone binds and protects the Sea, thanks to the Makers' life force. Stands to reason that the Sea only becomes activated—dangerous and deadly—once it's separated from the stone. Once the Sea's *released* from the Cradle. But unleashing that kind of power is exactly what we're trying to avoid."

"Yep," I say. "Okay, so using the Cradle Sea isn't an option. Next."

"Well, we can't bury Roth under a mountain of rock inside the Manor. He'll just keep rotting away at the stone and claw his way out, generations after we're all dead and buried. We can't doom the future like that. And we can't turf him back here and let him rule over Arakaan again. These people have suffered enough as it is." Violet shakes her head. "Everyone says he's invincible, right? But something or someone hurt him. And it must have happened here, in Arakaan. Before he captured John and Elsa. Before he entered the Manor. I mean, it's almost like something's eating away at him from the inside. Some kind of sickness. Maybe a disease swept across Arakaan and wiped out his ancestors, like the Unspeakable Plague nearly did to mine back home. Maybe Roth found a cure just in time and . . . and kept it for himself."

For an Unspeakable Plague, Bluehaven folk sure do speak about it a lot: the plague that swept across the Dying Lands thousands of years ago and sent the lucky survivors on a voyage across the seas. They were the founders of Bluehaven. Hickory was one of them—just a kid when it happened.

"I dunno, Violet," I say. "We could throw around theories all day, but Elsa's been here for ages. If she hasn't figured out how to stop him, what chance do we have?"

"Who knows? Maybe she started searching for answers but gave up because it was too hard. Or maybe she *has* found out something." Violet cocks an eyebrow at me. I can see my reflection in her goggles: two distorted, bug-eyed Janes. "Maybe she needs our help . . ."

"I know, I know," I say. "I have to talk to her. But

something tells me she'd sooner shoot me in the butt with her crossbow than give me a history lesson."

Violet groans, a look of desperate longing plastered over her face. "Don't talk to me about crossbows. I miss mine so much. I'd have brought it with me if it weren't for the second law."

We enter the Manor unarmed. "But what kind of four-teen-year-old *owns* a crossbow?"

"The recovering pyromaniac kind," Violet says. "Win-ifred started drilling me on target practice after I . . . *accidentally* set the Great Library on fire. She said it'd help me focus. Every time I got the urge to burn something, I went to Outset Square for some target practice instead. I became a crack shot in no time." She perks up, struck by an idea. "Hey, you could ask Elsa if I could borrow hers for a bit! And make sure you ask about the Cradle, too. If we're going to find it before Roth does, we need details—how she and John found it, what the entrance looks like, everything."

"That's all, huh?"

Violet shrugs. "Wouldn't hurt to know more about these Arakaanians, I guess."

"Okay, okay," I say. She's right. I may be the third Cra-dle key, but Elsa's the key to unraveling everything else. I hand Violet Scab's reins, adjust my goggles, and glance at Yaku again. Surprise, surprise, he's scowling at me. "Be careful," I whisper. "I'm not sure we can trust him."

"Your horse or Yaku?"

"Both," I say, and set off up the line.

ELSA

The Arakaanians gawk and whisper as I pass them. Not even their hoods and goggles can hide their fascination. The kid leading Elsa's horse stares up at me when I overtake him, mouth gaping. My hand itches. Those all-too-familiar evil wasps swirl around my gut. This is my chance to get all the information we need. If I play my cards right, Elsa might even tell me about my dad. What he was like before they opened the Cradle and all. Before he was Gripped.

"Get back in line," she says when I'm still three paces away.

Or not.

"Will do," I say, falling in step beside her. "I just want to apologize first. For running off the other night. I didn't mean to get lost, I just . . . it was a lot to take in. And I didn't mean to blow up the shipwreck. Actually, that's a lie. I *did* mean to, but only because of the Tin-skins."

Elsa hefts the crossbow onto her shoulder, stares out at the desert and sighs. "Taw-taws. Out here they're called Taw-taws."

"Oh. Okay. Anyway, I was lucky the bomb was there. I assume you folks rigged it up? It saved my skin. Truly. That and the sand dune."

Elsa stiffens a little. "You jumped from the upper deck?"

Uh-oh. "Um, yeah, but—"

"Did you find anything up there?"

Just your secret place. Your scribbles on the wall.

The etchings of your baby boy.

"No," I lie. "I didn't have time to look around. I was kinda running for my life, you know? I'm just glad you found me. Really. So thank you."

Elsa lowers her goggles for a moment and looks at me. Her eyes are baggy and bloodshot, crusty with sleep. I can tell she doesn't trust me. She nods at my bandaged hand. "You should let that breathe."

"I will," I say. "Thanks." I glance back down the line of horses. Violet's leading Scab and Rex a little out of formation so she can watch us. Yaku's yelling at her but keeping an eye on us too. Closer to hand, the kid's swiveling his head from me to Elsa and back again, like he's watching a game of catch. I clear my throat and push on. "Um, why *was* the bomb there?"

"Roth's Gorani," Elsa says. "Leatherheads, I believe you call 'em. They wander through these parts sometimes. Deserters. Gotta protect what's ours."

I frown. "If they're deserters, doesn't that mean they're against Roth, too?"

"Maybe. But that doesn't make us friends."

"So that's why everyone's on edge, huh? They're worried about a Leatherhead—I mean, Gorani attack?"

Elsa nods. "Not to mention the sandstorms, the Tawtaws, the Boboki . . ."

"Who are they?"

"Rival group. They've never been keen on my presence here. Always feared I'd lure Roth back to Arakaan. They used to attack us regularly. Kidnapped Yaku when he was a boy, just to get to me. Wasn't easy, but I got him back. They've kept their distance since then, for the most part. But if word gets out that *you're* here? Let's just say it's best we get you in and out of Asmadin as quickly as possible. The Boboki are a bunch of thieves and murderers."

Perfect. More people who want to kill me.

"So when will we get to Asmadin?"

"Late tomorrow." Elsa nods at the mountain range lurking ahead, stretching from north to south. It looks closer now, come to think of it. At long last. "In a few hours, we'll reach Orin-kin, an outpost at the edge of the Kahega Range."

"That's where you sent Hickory, yeah? To some healers."

"Indeed. Asmadin's about a day's trek from there, westward through the Mulu Pass."

"Right." I take a deep breath. Here goes nothing. "Elsa—"

"You have questions," she says with a sigh. "I know. Ask away, then."

"Well, how about we start here? How'd you find these people?"

"I didn't. They found me." She waves a hand at the desert. "Couple of nomads, way out there somewhere. I was near death. Driven mad by the suns. Stumbling. Rambling. They took me to Asmadin, their ancestral home. Healers brought me back. I can't remember it all, but I know the Elders questioned me. Pieced my story together before I came to."

"The Elders?"

"Leaders of Asmadin. Eleven women and men elected by the people."

"Are you an Elder?"

A bubble of laughter escapes Elsa's gob. "Gods, no."

"They understood you, though? They actually talked to you?"

"One of 'em did, yeah. Masaru. He's a healer. An Elder now, too. Good man. Very good man. You'll meet him in Asmadin. He helped me find my strength again, slowly but surely."

Elsa stops there, as if that's all I need to know. That, or she's forgotten I'm here.

"Um . . . and then?" I ask.

She swears under her breath. "*Then*, I started learning their customs, their language. They knew the legend of the Cradle keys, and agreed to help me return to the Manor. When I was strong enough, they took me back out to the flats. We found the gateway again, but it still wouldn't open. So we built a well and set up camp. Waited and watched. After several weeks, supplies and morale were running low. Everyone would've left if it weren't for the Taw-taws."

"You were attacked?"

Elsa kicks at a stone. "A whole pack picked up our scent. I saw them first, raised the alarm. Killed half-a-dozen myself. Saved Masaru and the rest of the Asmadinians. That changed everything. From then on the people trust me, respected me as one of their own." She sniffs. "They said I swooped in like Hali-gabera."

"Hali-ga-what-now?" I'm gonna have to start writing all these names down.

"Hali-gabera," Elsa says. "Local legend. Died hundreds of years ago. She's buried on the eastern side of Asmadin. Lovely tomb. Point is, I'd earned the people's trust. That's when Orin-kin was set up as a sort of half-way point. It started small, but it's grown over the years. People wanting a change from Asmadin. Families devoted to the cause."

"What cause?"

"Waiting for you, of course. Roth left a hundred years ago, sure, but these people know their lives are still in danger. They figure destroying Arakaan is right at the top of his to-do list once he claims the Cradle. Common theory is he'll use it as a testing ground. Unleash the Cradle Sea and wipe this world from existence once and for all."

"No offense, but it doesn't look like there's much left to destroy."

Elsa nods slowly. "This is an old world, yes, but there's life here—beauty, also—and it's worth saving. Even I forget it sometimes." She glances back at the Arakaanians behind us. "I'm not the woman I used to be, Jane. I've been here so long I'm more Arakaanian than Tallisian. These people would do anything to protect this world, and so will I. They're my family now."

My heart breaks when she says this.

How many times has Dad replayed their reunion in his head over the years? How often has he dreamed of holding Elsa again, kissing her, hearing her voice again, her laughter? He has no idea the woman he knew has lived a whole other life.

Still, I think I'm starting to understand Elsa. After all these years—*forty-seven* of them, she told me the other night—how could she not change? Escaping to that room on the wreck. Scratching away at the wall. Feeling her old life slip further away from her, day by day, decade by decade, just like Hickory trapped in the Manor. The jungles of Tallis, Dad, their baby boy: they were all reduced to the stuff of dreams. I feel like I should apologize again—for running away, for blowing up the wreck, for making her wait out here so long most of all—but I can't.

Sorry is too small a word.

"That it, then?" Elsa asks. "No more questions?"

"No," I say. "I mean, yeah. So many."

"Wonderful."

"Can you tell me about the Cradle?"

"Ugh."

"Maybe if you start at the beginning—"

"Boring." Elsa waves a hand at me. "We found the Manor gateway on Tallis, made our way through to Arakaan, and got caught by Roth at the edge of the dune sea. He threatened to cut me. Charlie opened the gateway again and let Roth and his army in. They started building his fortress inside the Manor and threw us in a cell. End of story."

This is gonna be trickier than I thought.

"Well, it wasn't exactly the end, was it?" I scratch at my ear. Gotta tread carefully. "You were . . . pregnant, right? When you were caught." Elsa clenches her fists, but I can't stop now. "Roth left you there for ages while he tried to find the Cradle, but he had no luck, so he went back to see you when you were giving birth, and . . . and . . ."

And something went wrong.

They had a baby boy. He died, Jane.

And here comes the *sorry* at last, quick and hot and dripping in shame. "I'm so, so sorry, Elsa. I can't even imagine—"

"Don't," she says. "Don't imagine it. Don't speak of it. Not a word. Ever again."

Another awkward silence hangs in the stifling air.

"How did you escape?" I ask after a while. "What did the path to the Cradle look like—the room where the path began? What does the entrance to the Cradle look like, exactly?"

"Too much talking." Elsa hangs back till the kid with the horses catches up. Starts rifling through her saddlebag, one-handed. "The path, the spike pit, the Cradle—blah, blah, blah."

Wait a second. "What spike pit? Is that where the—"

"I'm sick of it. Told you. Boring."

"I know this is tough, Elsa, but I need details. You have to tell me everything."

"I don't *have* to do anything. Ah-ha." She plucks a bottle from the saddlebag, pops it open with her mouth, spits out the cork, and takes a long swig. "Oh, that's good."

The kid twitches his head, warning me to leave.

I nod at Elsa's bottle instead. "Maybe you should stick to water, huh? I don't—"

"*Enough.*" Elsa stops walking. The rest of the group stops, too. "Let's get something straight. Three things, actually." She holds up a finger. "First, you may be destined to save the Manor, but while we're in Arakaan I'm in charge, and I'll drink *what*ever, *when*ever I want."

"Okay," I say, but—"

"Second"—up goes finger number two—"there'll be a celebration at Orin-kin tonight, to honor your arrival. I'd rather focus on the journey ahead, but the Arakaanians have their traditions. Their rules and rituals. We must respect them. Remember, you're a guest. Smile. Wave." She glares at me. "*Don't* do anything stupid. I've worked too hard and waited too long to have my position here jeopardized by a couple of schoolgirls."

Wow. "Okay, technically, I've never even been to school, except that one time I hid in a classroom cupboard, so that comment doesn't even make sense. And in case you've forgotten, Violet and I brought one of the Cradle keys all this way—"

"Which brings me to my third point. You still got the fake key I gave you?"

"Um, no. I kinda"—chucked it away—"lost it."

Elsa sighs and fishes the true Cradle key—*my* key— from her pocket. I reach out to take it, but she closes her fist. "Uh-uh. I'm keeping this one for now."

"But it's mine."

"You're not responsible enough to carry it. You lost the fake one almost immediately. And you've lost the real one twice since you left Bluehaven. Your friends told me all about it."

"Oh, you mean when you interrogated and tortured them?"

"They told me you let the bounty hunter take it, after he pulled you from the forest."

"I didn't *let* him take it. The forest nearly *ate* us. I could barely even move and—"

"You also let us take the key the moment you got here."

"You were holding me at gunpoint. You shot me with a dart!"

"Exactly." She slips the key back into her pocket. "I can't leave something so important in the hands of someone so easily subdued."

"*Easily subdued?*" Now she's crossed the line. "Excuse me, but over the past week I've been half-frozen, almost squashed, semi-digested, and very nearly skewered, shot and drowned. I pushed Roth off a speeding train. Violet shot a bazooka at him." I point at her. "A *bazooka*, lady. Then we derailed the train. Together. Roth would've gotten his stinkin' hands on the key ages ago if it weren't for us. Hickory, too, actually."

"Hickory is an agent of Roth's."

"He *was* an agent of Roth's. You better not be lying about those healers, Elsa. Hickory knows Roth's lair and the Manor better than any of us. If you want to get Dad back—" It just slips out. *Dad.* Elsa goes rigid, as if the word has given her an electric shock. I wish I hadn't said it, but it's too late now. "Elsa . . . you haven't seen him in forever. I know you had to make a new life here, but don't you even want to know how he is, or—or what he's *like?*"

She whips off her goggles and glares at me. "I'll ask when I'm ready." For a moment, she looks so old, so sad, but it's quickly overshadowed by something else. Something dark and grim that hardens the lines on her face. "I'll give you the true keys once we're back inside the Manor. Not a second before."

I feel like I've been punched in the gut.

Now would probably be a bad time to ask if Violet can borrow her crossbow.

"Go back to the end of the line," Elsa says. "And if you even think about running off again, a pack of Taw-taws'll be the least of your worries. I promise you that."

THE OUTPOST OF ORIN-KIN

We ride slowly through low-rolling foothills, past wandering dunes and towering columns of stone. The curtains of heat-shimmer have parted at last, unveiling the Kahega Range in all its glory. We're headed for the tallest peak, a sheer cliff riddled with caves. It kinda looks like a crusty slab of cheese. If I crane my neck, I can just make out a few staircases and balconies carved into the cliff about two-thirds of the way up. Some crimson banners, too. We're supposed to reach them via a steep, zigzagging path.

Orin-kin.

"*Schoolgirls*," Violet mutters again. "I'll show her just how dangerous a schoolgirl can be. And yeah, I let slip that Hickory used to be a bounty hunter, but I told Elsa ten times he wasn't working for Roth anymore. Also, what rules and rituals was she talking about?"

"No idea." I give Scab an awkward pat. He's getting more and more skittish the closer we get to the mountains. "Easy, boy." He tries to bite me again.

"This spike pit she mentioned, though," Violet says. "It could be near the Cradle entrance."

"I thought so, too," I say, "but it doesn't really help us that much. There are probably loads of spike pits inside the Manor."

"It's a start, at least. I'm sure Hickory's seen a few. If the entrance is small and secret, he could've passed it dozens of times and not even known."

Music drifts toward us, quiet at first. A low rumble of tribal drums.

"Hopefully we'll get the chance to ask him soon," I say.

Elsa blows a horn. We pick up the pace. I'm not sure who's keener to reach the shadow of the mountains, the Arakaanians or their horses. A cloud of sand billows from the base of the cliffs: a bunch of riders galloping out to meet us. They circle us in no time, whooping and hollering. Ten or so jumped-up boys and girls. The kid who was leading Elsa's horse shouts at them, pointing back at us. They halt their horses and stare.

I share an uneasy look with Violet.

Closer still and the mountains loom above us, blocking out the suns. We breathe a sigh of relief and start up the steep cliffside path. I try to ignore the long drop, the clattering pebbles, the very real possibility that Scab could turf me over the edge just because he feels like it. Thankfully, the drums are so loud now, nobody can hear my constant swearing.

The path levels out near the top. We ride onto a wide ledge—an entrance to a massive cave. The rock around it has been chiseled into smooth columns capped with ornate designs. Swirls and weathered faces, stone flowers in bloom. Stairs branch off from the landing, scaling the cliffs to other, smaller caves. The crimson banners hang from tall wooden posts, utterly still. A crowd's gathering. A few people rush over to hug their loved ones the moment they dismount. The others just stand there, slack-jawed, staring at Violet and me. Soon, we're the only ones left on our horses. The drums stop with a final *BADA-BOOM*.

Smile, I remind myself. *Wave*.

Slowly, carefully, I raise my good hand. Sure enough, one guy gasps. Another grips the handle of a machete strapped to his waist. A woman grabs her kid, holds him close. Standard greeting, in my experience. I should feel right at home.

"*Choo-nah!*" Elsa shouts. "*Da linga pador*," something-something, "*du Jane Doe!*"

She points up at me, strides over, and snatches Scab's reins, blabbing on and on to the crowd, probably telling them the story of our arrival. The crowd hangs on her every word, expressions changing from shock to awe to joy. When she shouts something that kinda sounds like "cheese-bits," everyone cheers. Elsa smiles, broad and winning, but when she turns back to us, she frowns and gestures for us to dismount, so we do, fast.

Well, Violet does. My foot gets caught in the stirrup. I topple over in front of everyone. The cheering falters. A few people laugh as Elsa yanks me back to my feet.

"I'm okay," I say loudly, brushing the dirt from my butt. "Pfft. Horses, am I right?"

"Just . . . stop," Elsa says. "Shut up and smile."

I do as I'm told. Elsa points at me, says something that makes everyone go wild. The drumming starts again—a lively, celebratory beat—and Violet and I are swarmed by a bunch of older women. They touch our shoulders, our ratty robes, our mangy hair. They gawk at my eyes—stunned by the color, I guess—and whisper things as they shepherd us through the crowd and into the cave. It's huge. A dome decorated with more intricate carvings of flowers and faces.

"Whoa," Violet whispers.

Five tunnels branch off from the dome, delving deeper into the mountain, all of them lit by flaming torches. The horses are led down the tunnel dead ahead. Scab glances back at me as they go. More people stream from the other tunnels, probably drawn here by the hullabaloo.

I can see the drummers over by the entrance. People dancing, sharing bottles of booze. Elsa getting her fill, and Yaku—our constant shadow—watching us, oblivious to the celebration. But no Hickory.

"Our friend," I ask the women. "Have you seen him? Lean guy, looks a few years older than us. Shaggy black hair? Kinda smells?"

They just smile and hand us mugs of water. I chug mine as we walk. We pass baskets filled with strange-looking fruit, and people don't throw them at me, they *offer* them to me, as if they're glad I'm here, as if they *like* me. One little girl even hands me a desert flower, pink and papery. She giggles and runs away before I can thank her. Nobody's ever given me a flower before.

Down a tunnel we go, into a small chamber with windows carved into the far wall. There's a table laden with food in the corner. In the center of the room are two metal tubs, filled with water, divided by a long, scrap-metal partition. Violet and I are each directed to a tub. Yaku tries to step inside, too, but a tiny, brown-skinned woman with flyaway hair slams the door in his face, mid-protest.

"*Ku-tai*," she shouts, "*calabanai!*" and the women laugh.

They add salts and powders to the tubs and, before we can say a word, we're helped out of our clothes and plonked into the cool, sweet-smelling water. The women scrub and brush, chatting and laughing, wincing at the state of my nails and the knots in my hair.

There's a woman with red-feathered earrings. Skin the color of old parchment. Emerald eyes. She reaches for my injured hand, nods and smiles, and I let her take it. She unravels the bandage and studies the wound, gently prodding the skin around it. A healer, I guess.

"Is it infected?" I ask.

"*Lon*," she says, with a reassuring smile. "*Lon*."

After my hand's cleaned and dried, she grabs a ceramic pot filled with a reddish paste and dabs a few globs over the cut. It stings, but quickly mellows to a dull buzz. Next, she wraps a fresh bandage around my hand and nods at her handiwork, jiggling her earrings.

"Thank you," I say, nodding and smiling.

"Hey," Violet snaps behind the partition. "Don't . . . fine. You can't—ouch. Stop that!"

The women around me chuckle and roll their eyes.

"She's nicer than she seems," I tell them.

"I heard that," Violet says. And to the women, "Hey—listen, I—ugh!"

Before long, I'm whipped out of the bath, toweled down, and slipped into a fresh long-sleeved tunic-thing that's soft and airy and actually feels super comfortable. After making sure Violet's decent, I step out from behind the partition, fighting a hot flush in my cheeks. She's dressed in the same kind of tunic-thing as mine. Looks so lovely it kills me.

The women brush and braid our hair. Give us new sandals, too. Finally they clear out as fast as a whirling sandstorm and slam the door behind them.

"Um," Violet says, "did that just happen?"

"Yep." I run my fingers over my braids. I've never felt so fancy in my life. Kinda wish we had a mirror. Violet's hair looks amazing, like some sort of small, elaborate bird's nest. "I like your head," I say. "Your hair. It's pretty." Crap. There's that word again. "Good!" I add, a little too loudly. "I mean, pretty good. You know. For you."

Violet fights back a smile. "Um, thanks. How's the hand?"

"Not bad, actually," I say. My palm doesn't hurt anymore. The dull buzz is almost pleasant. The paste must be doing its job. "So what are we supposed to do now?"

It sounds like the crowd's filing past our room. The drummers are on the move, too.

"We wait, I guess," Violet says. "And eat."

We turn to the table. Behold the baskets of fruit and nuts, the platters of flatbread and strips of dried meat, the jugs of water.

"Shouldn't we"—I lick my lips, my stomach growls—"look for Hickory first?"

"Oh, definitely,' Violet says, but we're already walking toward the table. "We really need to find him. As quickly as possible. Make sure he's okay."

"Get some answers."

"Prepare for the journey ahead."

We look at each other. Back down at the food.

"On the other hand, we need our strength."

"Hickory would *want* us to eat."

Violet grabs a piece of fruit that looks like a lumpy papaya, digs into the pink flesh with her fingers, and slurps the innards down. I shove half a melon-type-thing into my face before diving into the nuts.

Violet downs a handful of berries. "How do they even grow anything out here?"

I gnaw at a meat-strip. "Don't know, don't—"

The door slams open. Yaku's back, scowling as always, flanked by a couple of guards.

"—care," I finish. "Um, can we help you?"

Yaku flicks his head. "Come. Now."

We head down the tunnel, toward the echoing drums. There's a rusty metal door ahead. The drums are *thump-ba-dump*ing so loud on the other side I can feel it in my bones. The crowd's cheering and clapping.

"What's happening?" I ask Yaku.

He frowns at the other guards, opens the door, and shoves us through to a small landing. Violet rounds on him, ready to snap at him, but I quickly grab her arm.

The crowd's packed into a second, smaller dome. Elsa's standing on a podium, soaking up the applause. There's a dirty great pit in the center of the chamber.

And Hickory's standing near the edge of it with a gun to his head.

HICKORY'S PENANCE

He's barely able to stand. Pale skin sunburned and blistered, covered in fresh cuts and bruises. They've stripped off his clothes and replaced them with a loincloth. Hacked all his hair off, too. He doesn't flinch when a sandal flies from the crowd and smacks him in the head. Doesn't so much as blink when the guy with the gun nudges him closer to the pit.

"Hickory!"

Yaku knows what I'm thinking. He tries to stop me from running off, but Violet grabs his wrist with one hand, jabs him twice with the other, rounds on the two guards and shouts, "Go, Jane—I've got this!"

And I'm off, leaping down from the landing, ducking and weaving through the crowd.

It's bananas. Everyone's clapping, stomping, trying to get a good view of the pit. I catch glimpses of Elsa through the flailing arms and jostling bodies. I can't understand what she's shouting, but I catch "Roth" in there a few times. She keeps pointing at Hickory, too.

"Elsa," I shout, "stop!" But she can't hear me, can't see me.

"Roth, *ku-nah!*" she yells, and the crowd roars.

I squeeze between two big guys, fighting my way closer to the pit. Catch a glimpse of Hickory just standing there, swaying slightly on his feet.

Why isn't he fighting back?

"Hickory!" I shout again.

I force my way through the crowd, trip over and land on my hands and knees at the edge of the pit. It's at least ten feet deep, as wide as the Hollows' basement, and scattered with bones: a leg, an arm, and several broken, not-quite-human skulls. And there, crouched in the far corner—

"Oh, crap."

A Leatherhead—a *Gorani*—but one I've never seen the likes of before. It has no suit, no gas mask, no gun. It's dressed in a loincloth, same as Hickory's, and its black-beady eyes are sunken and wild, its waxen skin covered in burns and scars. This is no foot soldier. This is a pitiful, desperate creature, which makes it all the more dangerous.

I get up, take a deep breath and shout, "*STOP!*"

It works. Elsa holds up her hands. Everyone falls silent. The people around me take a step back.

"Let him go," I say. "Right now. You can't do this."

Elsa forces a smile. She's trying to remain calm, in control, but I can tell she's angry. Or is she scared?

"Please," I say. "You know this is wrong."

Hickory looks even worse close up. His bottom lip's swollen, bleeding at the corner. He's taking shallow breaths, like maybe he has a broken rib or two. Worst of all, he doesn't seem to know who I am. He's looking at me, *through* me, like I'm just another person in the crowd.

The Gorani's even more terrified now that everyone's gone quiet; little eyes darting around, three-fingered hands clinging to the rock wall at its back.

"Jane Doe." Elsa holds her arms out wide. "In honor of your arrival, we present you with this gift." She gestures at the pit like it's the grandest birthday cake in all the worlds.

Yaku pushes his way to the edge of the pit with Violet struggling in his arms, a hand clasped over her mouth.

"Not just a confirmation of faith," Elsa continues, "but a demonstration of our commitment to end Roth's reign of terror, and bring all who serve him to justice!"

Yaku translates for everyone. The crowd goes wild.

Violet's clearly rattled but nods at me all the same. *I'm okay. You've got this.*

I take a few steps around the edge of the pit, closer to Hickory. Yaku yells something at the people near me. Two guys try to grab me, but I slap their hands away and glare at them.

Elsa gives me a subtle headshake. A warning.

Don't do anything stupid? Clearly, she doesn't know who she's dealing with.

"First," I shout, and wait a second for the crowd to settle, "you folks really suck at gift-giving. Second, I already told you: Hickory doesn't serve Roth anymore."

"I'm sure that's what he wants you to think," Elsa says.

"He saved our lives!" How do I explain this? "He *used to* be a bounty hunter, but he's on our side now. Tell her, Hickory." He stares down at the pit, doesn't say a thing. "Hickory, tell them you don't work for Roth!"

65

He closes his eyes, hangs his head.

This isn't the Hickory I know. The guy who faced Roth atop a speeding train and used a whip to snag him on a passing chandelier. The guy who stabbed a river creature in the back seconds before it was about to eat us alive. The guy who always has a plan.

"What's wrong with you?" I ask him. "After everything we've been through, you can't just—"

Elsa nods at the guy with the gun. He nudges Hickory till his toes are poking over the edge of the pit.

The crowd stirs again, jostling for better views.

"Wait! Elsa, don't. You know we need him. You kill Hickory, you kill our best chance of stopping Roth and getting Dad—John—Charlie—whatever you want to call him—back." It's risky, bringing him into this, but I have to get through to her somehow. I think it works, too. I can see her eyes narrow from all the way over here. "Look," I say, light and breezy, "we got off on the wrong foot here. How about we all calm down, back away from the creepy death pit and talk, huh?"

The crowd's growing impatient. Whispering. Fidgeting. Elsa steels herself. "You're wasting your time, Jane. Even if he has renounced Roth, the laws of our land dictate that he must be punished. We captured this Gorani months ago, fleeing Roth's army." She nods at the creature in the pit. "A deserter, true, but guilty of unimaginable atrocities nonetheless. Hickory is no different."

"He was *caught* by Roth inside the Manor. Roth *forced* him to—"

"Kill innocent people? Lead them to their doom?'

"Yes! Wait, no. I mean—"

"Listen to me, Jane." Elsa glares at me again. "He has a chance. He has a choice."

"Fight or die? Some choice! And I hate Leathereads—I mean, Gorani—as much as the next girl, but if this one fled Roth's army then it isn't really a threat anymore, is it? Just let it go!"

"I have to uphold the law," Elsa says, teeth gritted, fists clenched.

"Screw the law," I shout, and point at Hickory. "He. Can't. Fight."

"*Kaida nu*," someone shouts. Elsa holds her head high, tries to ignore them, but everyone's joining in now, shouting louder and louder. "*Kaida nu. Kaida nu. Kaida nu!*"

"What are they saying?" I ask.

She calls for silence. The crowd obeys. "They're saying . . . death."

The guy with the gun shoves Hickory. He topples into the pit. I shout, "No!" but I'm drowned out by the crowd as they clamor and haggle around the pit, waving copper coins in the air. I can't believe it.

They're actually placing bets.

Hickory's gasping on the pit floor, clawing at the dirt, winded from the fall. The Gorani tries to scramble up the wall, rattling its throat and screeching as it slips back down. Obviously, it doesn't want to fight either, but it could turn on Hickory any second.

"Hickory," I shout, "get up! Arm yourself." He gets to

his knees, looks at the bones scattered around him. "Yes," I shout, "grab a big one! A leg bone or—*what are you doing?*"

The chump just sat back down.

Violet kicks and squirms in Yaku's arms. Shakes his hand away from her mouth and shouts, "If Hickory dies, John dies," but I can barely hear her over the roar of the crowd. Elsa doesn't move, doesn't blink. I can tell she's torn, though, and that's all that matters.

Problem is, a guy near Violet and Yaku can see it, too. A weedy white man with a long blade strapped to his waist. A blade he's unsheathing.

"No, no, no," I say.

The Gorani's pacing up and down the far wall of the pit now, growing more panicked by the second, and Hickory's just sitting there, doing nothing.

The weedy man's getting ready to toss the blade.

"Elsa," I shout. "Stop him—that guy there!"

But it's too late. The blade flies through the air and falls down, down, down, landing right between Hickory and the Gorani in the center of the pit. The crowd roars. The Gorani glances from the blade to Hickory and back again, calculating the distance, assessing the risks, crouching low, getting ready to pounce. Hickory stares at the blade, too, but doesn't move a muscle. And that's when I really get scared. When it really sinks in. He isn't even gonna try for it.

Hickory Dawes wants to die.

INTO THE PIT

I'm not sure when I get the bright idea to jump into the pit. One second I'm standing on the edge, shouting at Hickory, and the next I'm leaping, dropping, hitting the ground hard and rolling, diving for the blade before the Gorani gets there first. Somehow I make it, too. Snatch it up, spin around, and skid to a halt with the blade held high. Piece of cake.

Or maybe not.

I haven't thought this through. The Gorani may be weak, but it's still twice my size.

The Arakaanians wave their arms and shake their fists. They're so loud I can barely hear myself think. Even the kids are joining in.

"What do you think you're doing?" Hickory croaks.

"Saving your skin," I say. "Get up." My hands are shaking. The blade's heavier than it looks. I keep it aimed at the Gorani's chest, higher and higher as it stands as tall as it can. "Feel free to help me out, by the way." The Gorani takes a step closer. "Anytime now." I scramble back by Hickory's side. The Gorani bares its teeth and shrieks at us, and that's when something snaps. I *hate* this place. I'm sick of these people, this world. I've come too far to die in a stinking hole. "Ugh, screw it . . ."

I shift my stance, hold the blade high above my head, and scream my guts out.

And it actually works.

The Gorani backs down and cowers against the wall, head shaking in its three-fingered hands. The crowd cheers, and before long they're clapping as one. Chanting something, too. I can't understand what they're saying, but I don't need to. They were promised blood.

This is a battle to the death.

The Gorani stares at me, bony chest heaving. I should want to kill it, even if it did flee Roth's army. How many of its kind chased us through the Manor? They put us in chains, would've killed us if Roth told them to. It's a monster. Nothing more, nothing less.

Hickory shrugs at me. Elsa has this fascinated, hungry look on her face. Yaku's scowling—big surprise. Violet's no longer struggling in his arms. She's just standing there, watching me.

Do it, her eyes are saying. *You don't have a choice.*

I walk toward the Gorani, hands trembling. Adjust my grip on the blade. This should be easy. One swing and it's done. One fell swoop and we're free.

But it isn't easy. This isn't like the time on the train, when we were fighting and fleeing for our lives. This is up close and personal. No masks. No guns. I can see the fear in the creature's eyes. It's so helpless, so weak. It just wants to get out of here, like me.

What if it just wants to go home?

Clap. Clap. Clap. Kill. Kill. Kill.

Hot tears prick my eyes. I cry out and bring the blade down as hard as I can, and it finds its mark, straight and true: lodged into the dirt by my side, blade-first.

The crowd goes quiet. I step back, breathing hard.

Everyone's staring down at me, wondering what I'll do next. Elsa's wide-eyed, exhilarated. Had a change of heart. She glances around the dome, but doesn't tell the guards to let us out. Instead, she nods at the guy who shoved Hickory into the pit, and he aims his gun at me. A few others in the crowd do, too. Four guns in total, locked and loaded, ready to fire.

"Fine," I yell, "you wanna test me?"

I yank the bandage from my wounded hand.

"Jane?" Hickory mutters behind me. "Bad idea."

"What do you care?" I mutter back. "You were happy to die two seconds ago." I hold my hand up so everyone can see the gash in my palm, and shout, "You want blood? Let us go, *right now*, or I swear to the gods I'll tear this place apart."

An uneasy murmur ripples through the crowd. Maybe by now they know I derailed a train. Maybe they know about the Manor corridor I tore apart to stop the river creatures.

"Let us go. All of us. Hickory, Violet, me . . ." I glance down at the Gorani. Feel responsible for the stupid thing now. "It, too. You help us get the second key, you get us back to the Manor, and you don't lay a finger on us ever again."

I should probably cause a little quake to show them I mean business, but I'm exhausted and afraid. Hickory's right. This is a bad idea. We're surrounded by rock. If the power gets away from me, I'll crush us all. I can't do it. But the crowd doesn't know that.

I clench my fist and stand as tall as I can. Bold. Confident. Like someone who negotiates their way out of death pits every week. "I'm the third key, which means you have to do what I say." I nod at the men with guns and glare at Elsa. "All of you."

The ghost of a grin curls the edges of her lips. She translates what I said. Hams it up a little, too. Points at the pit and the dome, makes a few crumbling, tearing gestures. When she's finished, the crowd stares at me, and I wonder if they're about to flee for their lives.

But one by one, they smile.

"Child of the Makers," Elsa shouts, "welcome at last," and as soon as she translates it the crowd erupts into applause.

The Gorani looks from me to the blade and back again, confused. Yaku releases Violet. She kicks at a bundle of wood and rope sitting on the edge of the pit, and a rope ladder unfurls down the wall. I slip the bandage back around my palm, wincing, and turn back to Hickory.

He looks weird with his hair chopped off. His skull's covered in nicks where the shears cut too close. His black eyes are glazed. I don't know what to say. *Why didn't you fight? Nice loincloth?* I settle on a simple "You look terrible," and reach down to help him.

"Get away from me," Hickory says, swiping away my hand. "I'm done. We're through."

He tries to stand. Staggers, sways. And hits the floor like a sack of yams, out cold.

AKI

If you told me a week ago I'd end up stranded in a world of exploding shipwrecks, desert-dwellers, and dirty death pits, I'd have suggested you have a nap. If you told me a couple of days ago I'd save a stinking *Leatherhead*, I'd have laughed in your face.

But here we are.

We tried to get rid of it—took it out to the top of the cliffside stairs and told it to run—but it wouldn't leave my side. Just blinked down at me and *click-clack*ed its throat, softly, like a purring cat. Can't say I blame it, really. The Gorani knows the score. Saw all the people keeping their distance as we made our way through the tunnels. It knows they won't hurt it so long as I'm around, but if it set off down the path alone? Who's to say Yaku or some other chump with a gun wouldn't get an itchy trigger finger?

Thing's got smarts, I'll give it that.

I've decided to let it stay.

"I'm just saying," Violet says now, "maybe you didn't think this through."

We're standing in our new quarters while the healers

take care of Hickory in the next room. This main chamber's kinda nice. Pillows. Rugs. An open cliffside balcony looking out over the desert. The suns must be nearing the horizon because the light's gone deep gold. The torches in here have already been lit. The Gorani's bent over a table overflowing with food, chowing down on three-fingered fistfuls of cured meat and flatbread.

"I was stuck in a pit surrounded by a bloodthirsty mob, Violet. Of course I didn't think it through. I just—"

"Decided to adopt one of Roth's minions."

"I didn't *adopt* it. And it's an *ex*-minion, remember?"

"Oh, that's okay, then."

The Arakaanians are still celebrating all through the tunnels and up in the main dome: pounding drums, singing songs, making the mountain thrum. They may have missed out on a bloodbath, but at least I gave them a good show. Predictably, Elsa disappeared into the crowd before we'd even clambered out of the pit. I keep expecting her to show up, hoping she'll apologize and spill the beans. Deep down, I know better. She's probably drunk or passed out in a corner somewhere. If I want answers, I'll have to get them myself. And I will. Soon.

But first, our grubby new roommate.

"It's only for one night," I say. "Once we're back on the road, I'm sure it'll go . . . wherever it was going when it got caught. Besides, I don't think it wants to hurt us."

"Yeah? What are you basing that on, exactly?"

I shrug. "It would've done it already." *He*, I correct myself. *He* would've done it already. The skimpiness of the Arakaanian loincloth leades me to conclude that this Gorani is a guy.

The Gorani swipes a fruit platter to the floor.

"Hey!" I shout, "stop making a mess." He freezes, black-beady eyes fixed on mine, a strip of meat dangling from his mouth. Slowly, he sucks the strip into his mouth like a wriggling worm, swallows it whole, and backs away from the table. He's so tall his head nearly scrapes the ceiling. I step closer, ignoring a grumble of protest from Violet. "If you're gonna stay the night, you have to be quiet. And you're not allowed to eat us. Okay?"

The Gorani blinks at me.

"You realize it can't understand you, right?" Violet mumbles.

"Maybe not," I say, "but I'm sure he can read my body language." I take another step forward. "You're not gonna hurt us, are you?"

He *click-clacks* his throat.

I force a quick smile. "I'm gonna assume that was a no. Um. You got a name?" I hold a hand to my chest. "I'm Jane." I point at Violet. "That's Violet." I repeat the motions over and over. "Jane, Violet, Jane, Violet." I point at the Gorani. "And you? What's your name?" It works. He rattles off a string of clicks and clacks and these strangled little gargles that make me want to clear my throat. I can't make head or tail of it, but I do catch one sound at the end that's different from the others. "Aki," I say. "Can I call you Aki?"

The Gorani tilts his head.

"I'll take that as a yes. Nice to meet you, Aki." I point at the corner. "Now, would you mind just . . . standing over there for a while, please?"

Amazingly—without a single click or clack of protest—he stands in the corner.

"There," I say to Violet, "see? He's okay."

"I can't believe you gave it a name."

"Him. I gave *him* a name."

Violet points at Aki. "You stay there. I mean it. Come any closer and I'll toss you over the balcony." And to me, under her breath, "We'll have to sleep in shifts tonight."

Aki just stares at us. At me.

"Probably a good idea." I nod at the curtain. "We have to keep watch on Hickory anyway."

It took three men to lug him from the pit. Two to carry him in here. Elsa must've given everyone strict instructions to look after him before she split. Sure, I caught one of the healers spitting into his water before we were shooed away, but apart from that they've been swell.

"Reckon he'll be okay?" I ask Violet.

"He'll live," she says.

"That's the thing. I'm not so sure he wants to."

Feels strange to admit this, but the idea of losing him scares me, and not just because we need him. Truth is, I've come to think of him as a friend. A crappy, lying, backstabbing friend, sure, but I don't want him to die.

That look he gave me in the pit, though. *I'm done*, he said. *We're through.*

"He didn't fight," I say. "He didn't even try. Why?"

Violet wanders over to a heap of pillows in the corner, plops down and sighs. "Because he finally knows the truth. You weren't there the other night, when Elsa interrogated us. When she told us about what—I mean, *who* you really are. Hickory looked like he'd had his heart ripped out. At the time, I thought it was shock, but now I wonder . . ."

"Wonder what?"

Violet sighs. "I think he was upset because he'd found out his big plan to destroy the Manor was never going to work. He can't claim the Cradle for himself. The third key isn't waiting for him on the foundation stone. There's no ancient machine in there that just anyone can use to channel the Sea. He's given up because the power lies within *you*, and he knows he'll never be able to control it. It proves that . . . well—"

"He was always gonna turn on us," I say, "in the end."

You're wrong about me, he told me on the river, back in the Manor, but we were right all along. He isn't our friend. He isn't on our side. He was only ever helping himself.

"I know you think we need him," Violet says, "but we can't trust him. If he wants to stay here and die, I say we let him. Leave him behind."

I feel sick. Sure, I'm angry with Hickory. Part of me wants to drag him out of bed, kick him in the nuts, and toss him off the balcony. But leaving him behind just doesn't feel right.

"The guy was trapped inside the Manor for two thousand years, Violet. Do you really think it kept him alive all that time just so he could give up now?"

"He helped us get here," she says. "Maybe that's enough."

"I know he has a bigger part to play in all this," I say. "I can feel it."

The hustle and bustle in the next room intensifies. Clay pots rattle, medicine bottles chink. The curtain's swept aside and the women hurry from the room, eager to rejoin the party. Most of them stare at Aki as they go, tutting under their breath. The woman who fixed my hand shoots me a quick, kindly smile before the guard outside closes the door. We're all alone at last.

"Stay there," I tell Aki, pointing again. "Um. Please."

He *click-clacks* at me but obeys.

Violet and I step into the next room and pull the curtain closed behind us. Hickory's sprawled on his back in bed, out cold: sponged down, bandaged up, wheezing with every breath. The healers have done a good job on his wounds. His bedside table's scattered with pots of oils, pastes and powders. A few wooden spoons to stir them. There are two more beds in here, too. Another open balcony and a few flickering torches. It's cozy. Outside, the golden light's turning a deep blood-red.

I'm not sure what to say, what to do. I swear I can hear the cogs ticking over in Violet's brain, weighing up the pros and cons of letting him stick around.

"I can't imagine how terrible it was for him," she says, "stuck inside the Manor all those years. But wanting to tear apart the very foundation of the Otherworlds? Wanting to destroy everything and everyone in existence? What could drive someone to do that?"

An image pops into my head. Hickory, sitting behind me in the boat, staring down at the water. He looked so lonely, humming that sad, sad song.

A song about a girl.

"Love," I say, surprising myself as much as Violet.

"What?"

A cool breeze blows through the balcony door. I pull Hickory's blanket up to his chest and feel his forehead, just like I used to do with Dad. At least he doesn't have a fever. "When Hickory and I were in the forest—before it tried to eat us, I mean—I started singing about coconuts, and—"

"Why were you singing about coconuts?"

"Um, because they're delicious and nutritious, and—look, the point is, while *I* was singing about coconuts, Hickory started singing about a girl called Farrow. He told us he can't remember anyone back on Bluehaven, but I think he *can*. I think that's why he wants to destroy the Manor. He blames it for taking him away from her."

"Forgive me for not weeping," Violet says. "And if that's true, it just makes him even more dangerous." She puts her hands on her hips. "I'm telling you, the guy's a ticking time bomb."

"Maybe," I say, and sigh. "Look, we can ditch him when all this is over, but until then, we've gotta keep him close. He's coming with us, Violet."

"Fine," she huffs. "But we're going to have enough trouble as it is dealing with Elsa. The woman's lost it."

That look on Elsa's face when I held out my hand.

That ghost of a smile.

"No," I say. "I think she knows exactly what she's doing."

"How do we know she's telling the truth about the second key?" Violet asks. "What if she's stalling? Taking us on a wild goose chase because she lost the real key years ago?"

"She's pretty determined to get to Asmadin." I fight back a yawn. Sit on the bed next to Hickory's and gaze out at the reddening sky. "I'm sure the key's there."

"Either way, we'll find her first thing in the morning and make her talk. Together. And if Yaku or anyone else tries to stop us, I'll shove a torch down their throat." Violet nods at my bed. "Sleep. I'll take first watch and make sure your new pet back there doesn't try to eat us."

"He's already scarfed down his body weight in snacks, Violet."

She arches her eyebrows and pulls the curtain to the other room aside. Aki's back at the snack table—*on* the snack table—shoveling food into his gob. He freezes, beady eyes fixed on us, but can't resist. Inch by inch, he raises another handful to his mouth.

"Point taken," I say. "Wake me in a few hours."

THE SEA UNLEASHED

I wake from another nightmare, gasping and sweating. It was the same as last time. Roth hunting me through the crystal caverns and the forest. The Specters Gripping me in the snow. The same gaping void in my chest as I knelt on the foundation stone at the center of the Cradle. The same terrible knowledge that Dad and Violet were dead and it was all my fault. The same terror as the power got away from me and sparked the Cradle Sea. That same whispered voice.

Return.

But this time, the nightmare kept going. I saw a world of ice, a world of water, a world of misty mountains, a world on fire. I saw dark swamps and bustling Otherworldly villages. Foreign cities and peaceful temples. I saw Manor gateways opening in caves and cliffsides—on mountain tops and under enormous, ancient trees—and the Cradle Sea bursting through them all in tidal waves of shining, white-fire water. I saw the townsfolk of Bluehaven running for cover as the Sea poured down the Sacred Stairs and decimated everything in its path. I saw Winifred Robin, wrapped in her crimson cloak, staring down the deluge as it swallowed Outset Square. I heard the screams of the people. Felt nothing but despair when they were gone.

This time, I saw Dad sinking in the dark. Dead.

It's a wonder I didn't cause a quake while I was sleeping.

I'm shivering. The torches have burned out. I can see the sickle moon through the balcony door. Violet's fast asleep on the bed to my left, clutching a chair leg as a weapon. Hickory's still sleeping on my right. Apart from Aki's soft rattle-snores in the next room, it's deathly quiet. No drumming. No cheering.

The party's over.

I step onto the balcony, bracing myself against the cold. Take in the flat, silver desert. The clear sky awash with stars. Ledges and balconies dot the cliff-face around me. I lean over the edge a little. We're so high up, I can barely see the path we climbed to get here. It's a dizzying sight, almost as sickening as my nightmare.

The Manor's been calling to you, Jane, Violet said, *all your life.*

You have to listen.

To what? My fears? My own brain turning against me?

I rub my temples, try to clear my head, but I can't stop thinking about Dad. While we're crossing this salty sand-pit of a world, he's stuck inside the Manor at the mercy of a madman. How many times has Roth trawled through his mind? How much information has he gleaned?

We're wasting precious time.

"Hang in there, Dad." I cast the words out across the desert, through the salt pan gateway, along the winding Manor corridors, into Roth's fortress and Dad's cell. I imagine the words sneaking into his ears while he sleeps. "Hold on."

"Talking to yourself, Doe?" Hickory's lurking in the doorway behind me, eyes downcast, a blanket draped around his shoulders. I fold my arms. "What?" he says.

"I'm just waiting for my thank you. I saved your life."

"Yeah, well, nobody asked you to." He runs a hand over his shear-nicked head. Freezes when Aki rattle-snores extra loud in the next room. "Tell me that isn't what I think it is."

"It is," I say. "But it's okay. I think Aki's"—I can't believe I'm about to say this—"a good Leatherhead. Gorani, I mean. That's what they call them here."

"*Aki?* Oh, this gets better and better. You should pick up a Tin-skin while you're at it. It could sleep at the foot of your bed."

"Hickory. Look at me."

His head twitches. He kicks at a stone. Still isn't used to all this open sky. I can't imagine how strange it must be for him, the simple fact of being outside. I reach out to him. "It isn't gonna hurt you."

Slowly, hesitantly, Hickory lifts his head and looks at the stars. The moonlight catches in his eyes. He draws in a sharp breath, holds it, steps out onto the balcony and exhales. He looks like a little boy in awe of the wonders of the world. For a second, I'm sure he's gonna smile. Until he clears his throat and stares at his feet again. "So. You're the third key, huh?"

"Yeah."

"Should've seen it coming, really."

"Maybe." I rub at the bandage around my palm. "I mean, I guess it makes sense."

Hickory stares at my hand for a moment and sighs, as if that's all we need to say about it. He twitches his head at our room. "Where are we? What is this place?"

"Orin-kin. An outpost on the way to Asmadin."

"And what's in Asmadin?"

"The second key."

"I see." He turns to the door. "Well, good luck.'"

'You're coming, too, Hickory."

He stops. "You couldn't wait to banish me back in the Manor. You said once you found Elsa, you wouldn't need me anymore. Unless"—he turns back to me—"she doesn't *quite* have all the answers you were hoping for. She still hasn't told you where the Cradle is, has she?"

"We're working on it."

"But it's worse than that." He gasps, really laying it on thick. "You don't trust her. And after everything we went through to find her. That's a shame."

This guy. "What the hell's wrong with you?" I say. "I thought—"

"What? That I'd get all teary-eyed because you jumped into a pit for me? You thought I'd see the light and help you *save the worlds?* Let's get something straight here. You and me? We're not friends. I've known you for, what, a week? I'm two thousand years old, remember? You're a speck, Doe. You and Violet. A couple of blips in my life."

"Blips?" I say. "We got you out of the Manor."

"And that's worked out really well for me so far. Thank you."

"I know you care about us."

"I've been using you, Jane. I wanted to—"

"Claim the Cradle and tear the Manor apart. We know."

"So why do you want me sticking around?"

"Because I don't think you would've gone through with it. You can be a real jerk, but you're not evil. We need your help, Hickory. Please."

"Oh, you need help, all right. You couldn't be further from the Cradle, you still don't have the second key, and your only way back to the Manor's *through* the bad guy's gateway, not to mention the fact that your new sidekick's a Leatherhead and your guide's a raging alcoholic. I'd say the odds of you stopping Roth and saving the worlds are a billion to one."

That's the last straw. "First, Aki isn't my sidekick. He's just staying the night. Second . . . okay, Elsa probably is an alcoholic, but third, there's another way back inside the Manor. And we know where the second key is, so we basically kind of have it already."

"Basically kind of. That's a relief."

I step right up to Hickory. "It all comes down to this, skinhead. We need you, and you need us, whether you admit it or not. But if you mess this up—if you try to cross me again or try to get yourself killed—I swear I'll take you back to the Manor, lock you in some random, empty room and make sure nobody finds you. Ever. Again."

"Big words, little Doe." Hickory narrows his eyes. "You really believe it, don't you? You really think I'm one of the good guys."

"I'm betting my life on it. Push comes to shove, you'll be standing right by our side."

"You don't know me at all, then." Hickory turns back to the room. "I'm going back to bed. I assume you'll be leaving at first light. Don't bother waking me when you go."

Alone once more, I look at the stars and steady my shaking hands.

How do I get Hickory on our side? How can I make him see?

I'm about to head inside when something smashes on a balcony down to my left. A bottle. I lean over the edge and look up. Spot a glimmer of torchlight on the highest balcony, way up near the top of the cliff. A shifting shadow.

I step back inside, wrap a blanket around my shoulders and slip on my sandals.

I'm sick of being kept in the dark.

She still hasn't told you where the Cradle is, has she?

Hickory's asleep already.

What if she's stalling?

Violet's still sleeping, too.

I know we agreed we'd talk to Elsa together in the morning, but she's probably alone and, seeing as there's no way I'm getting any more sleep tonight, I might as well nip upstairs and grill her now.

And the truth is, I *want* to do this alone.

This is between me and Elsa.

THE WATCHTOWER

The guard in the corridor doesn't even blink when I sneak out and ask him to take me to see Elsa—just leads me through the silent, post-party chaos of Orin-kin, like he's been waiting for me all night. The drums in the main dome have been toppled over. An old man's shuffling around, tidying up. A drunken couple's slow-dancing to a non-existent tune. Everyone else is snoring and drooling, passed out on the floor with empty cups and bottles in their hands.

We head down a winding tunnel, then up, up, up a steep stone stairwell. When we get to the top, I gasp. We've climbed to a watchtower at the peak of the mountain. Torches flicker in the corners. Elsa's watching the night sky from a shallow balcony. There's one to our left and another to our right, too, on the northern and southern sides of the peak, looking out over the edge of the Kahega Range. Serpentine cliffs, jagged ridges and dark valleys wind off in both directions, clashing with the desert flats out east.

Everything's so silent, so still. A cold, crisp breeze ripples Elsa's robe. She doesn't move a muscle.

"Thank you," I whisper to the guard. I take a deep breath and cross the chamber, the anger I was feeling overshadowed by a crackle of nerves. Was coming up here a mistake?

"I knew you'd come," Elsa says at last.

And just like that, I don't feel nervous anymore. It's her tone. The way she's standing there with her hands behind her back, like she's too important to even look at me. Hell, she's already opened another bottle of booze.

'You're a real piece of work, you know that?" I say.

"If you're referring to the incident in the pit, I had no choice. I told you. The laws of this land—"

"I don't give a crap about the laws of this land." I step onto the balcony, carefully sidle up to the stone-carved balustrade, and immediately wish we could duck back inside. "You should've warned us."

"And you should've let things play out." Elsa waves her bottle my way, sloshing the liquid inside. "Jumping into the pit was a stupid move, Jane. You're lucky the Gorani backed down."

"I'm *lucky* I wasn't shot."

"Pfft, no one was gonna shoot you. You refused to fight; we needed to give the crowd a show. And anyway, you managed fine. Threatening to cause a quake? *That* was smart. I almost believed you'd do it, too." She downs a mouthful of booze. "I wouldn't have saved the Gorani, of course, but it could work to our advantage. Life debts are powerful things."

I blink at her. "I'm sorry, what?"

"Then again, it is a deserter. Might not honor the bond at all."

"Excuse me," I say. "What life debt? What bond?"

Elsa turns to me at last. "The Gorani are a curious species. There's a reason Roth aligned with them prior to the Great War. They come from an honor-bound culture. For too long, they'd been banished to the shadows of this world. Forgotten. Roth freed 'em. Brought 'em into the light, or so he led 'em to believe. That's why they serve him, generation after generation."

"Out of the shadows and into the Manor," I say. "Hardly what I'd call freedom."

"Well," Elsa says, "I never said they were smart."

"So, because I spared Aki's life in the pit—"

Elsa chuckle-huffs. "You gave it a name?"

"I gave *him* a name," I say. "So what?"

"Never heard of such a thing. But, yes, because you spared its life, it's bound to you. Sworn to protect and obey you till the debt is repaid. And that, my dear, is a very good thing. We'll need all the help we can get to sneak through the dune sea gateway undetected. He'll blend in better than any of us. And if he takes a bullet for you in the process, all's the better."

"That's a terrible thing to say."

"This is war. All that matters is getting you to the Cradle in one piece." Elsa takes another swig. "We'll have to watch him in Asmadin, of course. Most people there have never even seen a Gorani in the flesh—not a live one, anyway. Last thing we want to do is cause a panic. Not when we're so close to the end."

I picture the journey ahead: all those mountains and valleys of the Kahega Range, the canyon city of Asmadin and the sprawling dune sea. "*Are* we close to the end? Because it sure doesn't feel like it."

"We're a lot closer than we were yesterday." Elsa stifles a burp. "Look." She staggers to the balcony on the northern side of the peak and leans out so far I swear a stiff breeze could tip her over the edge. "Down there. See that path off to the left? That's the Mulu Pass. We leave at first light. It's a dangerous road, but we've trekked it many times before."

I spot a bunch of specks way down on a neighboring hillside. A pack of Taw-taws darting around under the moonlight. "Speaking of dangerous, they can't get in here, right?"

"No," Elsa says. "The lower tunnels are protected. Gates on every entrance. Two guards apiece. Don't worry, Jane, you're safe. We've got everything covered."

The Taw-taws scurry out of sight. We stare out at the mountains, standing side by side.

"If we're not on the same page," I say, "Roth's gonna wipe the floor with us when we get back to the Manor. You don't like me? Fine. But you have to trust me."

Elsa huffs out a deep breath. Turns to the guard and nods. He says something and she snaps something back. He frowns at me, nods, and heads back down the stairs. "Sometimes I wonder who's really in charge around here," Elsa says once his footsteps have faded. Then she clears her throat and straightens up. "So, where should we start?"

Okay. This is good. This is happening. I decide not to ask about the Cradle yet, though. Or the mysterious spike pit in the Manor, or exactly what happened to her and Dad. I can't have her shutting down and pushing me away again.

"The second key," I say instead. "I want to know exactly where it's hidden in Asmadin. And I want to know about the dummy keys, too. Why didn't you just keep the real one secret when you got here?"

She sighs. "I was delirious when the nomads found me. Rambling about the Cradle. Word got around quickly: one of the legendary keys had been found. The Elders decreed that nobody was to speak of it, under penalty of banishment, but we knew that wasn't enough. If Roth ever returned—"

"He could read anyone's thoughts and learn the truth," I say. "Everyone must've been terrified. I'm surprised the Elders didn't want to just destroy the key."

"One did. Tried to kill me in my sleep, too. Rena Boboki was her name. Thankfully, the other Elders sided with me. They knew the importance of the key. Rena was expelled from the council, exiled into the desert with her followers. She's dead now, but her legacy lives on."

"The Boboki," I say. "Your rivals."

"Exactly." Another sip. Another burp. "It was Masaru's idea to forge the false keys."

"Masaru," I say. "The old healer who helped you."

Elsa nods. "We forged three hundred keys. Paraded 'em before all of Asmadin. Made a show of adding the true key to the chest, mixed 'em round and divvied 'em up. I was given one. Each of the Elders, too. Trusted families, warriors, nomads and shepherds. They were all instructed to keep their key safe and secret, and sent off into the world." Elsa nods at the dark horizon. "They left to form new settlements all over Arakaan. Reclaim ruined cities of sand and stone. Far as everyone's concerned, the true key could be hidden in any one of them."

"But you tricked them, right?"

"Well, we had to be able to get to the key quickly if need be, so . . . yeah. I added a key to the chest in front of the crowd, but it was just another fake." She pauses. Swirls the booze left in her bottle. "The real key's hidden in an ancient vault. There are twelve combinations to the lock. The Elders and I each entered a number in private—another fail-safe in case Roth returned. We sent a rider to inform them of your arrival in Arakaan. They know we're coming. They'll have everything prepared."

"And they'll help us cross the dune sea?"

Elsa nods. "According to the Elders, no human has ever crossed the sea and lived to tell the tale, but we've found a way. Believe me, they'll do anything to help us defeat Roth. Anything to get revenge for what he did to this world and their ancestors."

A breath of wind makes the torches flicker and crackle.

"What *did* he do to this world?" I ask. "You mentioned a Great War—"

"The Immortal War, yes. It's a miracle anyone survived."

"Roth started it, right? So that he could be the last of his kind?"

"Yes," Elsa says, "and no. The war may have turned into a genocidal quest to conquer Arakaan and the Otherworlds, but it started with a jealous prince, a sacrifice, and an act of revenge. Stuff of fairytales, no mistake. Not one of those happy ones, either." Elsa turns to the starlit sky once again. "And it all began on a night like tonight, when Roth and his beloved partner, Neela, received some very bad news . . ."

AN INTERRUPTION

"Wait a second," I say. "Roth's *beloved partner?*"

"Blast it, Jane, you ruined the vibe. I was really on a roll there."

"He actually *loved* someone? And they loved him *back?*"

"That's generally what beloved partner means."

"Sorry, I just . . . vomited in my mouth a bit. How could anyone *love* Roth?"

"Can I continue?"

"Yeah. Sorry."

"Thank you." Elsa gazes out at the sky again. "Then I'll begin."

THE DAHAARI CULL

"Before the mask, before the army, before his quest to conquer the worlds, Roth was a simple man. Immortal like the rest of his kin, the Dahaari, yes, but ordinary nonetheless. He was a farmer, on the outskirts of a city called Atol Na. The city lies in ruin now, but according to legend it was once the grandest in all of Arakaan, populated by Dahaari and mortals alike."

Elsa leans her butt against the balcony and looks across the chamber at the mountains down south. I move closer so I can grab her in case she tips too far back.

"They lived together in peace. The mortals thought the Dahaari were gods. In turn, the Dahaari cherished the mortals—these curious, wondrous beings who lived, aged, and died before their eyes, coming and going like the wind. The Dahaari revered the natural balance of their world. Saw it as their duty to keep everything just so, including the population of their own kind. Unchecked, an immortal empire could run any world into the ground. So, every century, there was a cull to stop their population from overwhelming Arakaan. And this went on for ages, Jane. Eons. Each century, five hundred men and five hundred women were chosen at random, taken to a sacred temple in the center of Atol Na, and killed."

"Wait," I say. "I thought the Dahaari were immortal. Invincible." Unless Violet was right. "You're saying there *is* a way to kill Roth?"

"I'm saying there *was*," Elsa says, "long ago." She raises the bottle, thinks twice, and tosses it over her shoulder, unfinished. "But it's lost now."

"What was it?" I ask.

"Well," Elsa says, "weapons of rock, flame, and steel were useless against the Dahaari. But weapons carved of Dahaari *bone* could harm them, even kill them, if pierced through the heart. And there was only one such weapon. The Arrowhead of Atol Na."

"An arrow," I say thoughtfully. "Carved from bone."

"An arrow*head*," Elsa corrects me, "carved from *Dahaari* bone. It had to be attached to a regular arrow shaft, plucked out of its victims and reused again and again."

"But . . . if the Dahaari were all immortal and invincible, how was it made in the first place?"

"Nobody knows for sure," Elsa says. "Some say it was a gift from the gods. Others say the Dahaari only attained true immortality upon reaching adulthood—that the arrowhead was carved from the bones of a child."

"That's pretty grim."

"History often is," Elsa says. "Anyway, where was I? The Cull. Yes. The chosen Dahaari were taken to the sacred temple and shot through the heart with the arrowhead, one by one. It was seen as a great honor. Afterward, their bodies were taken east of the city and dropped into the fiery pit of a sacred volcano—honestly, everything was sacred to the Dahaari—whereupon their remains would sink to the core of Arakaan and fuel their world forevermore, maintaining balance. It was their duty—or so they believed—to keep the fire burning.

"The Honored were chosen from a pool of the eldest Dahaari, but the royal family were always spared—the wealthiest families, too. Funny how that works, huh? Neela and Roth were neither. According to legend, they were only ten thousand years old, give or take, when all this went down. Far too young to be considered for the Cull. But there was a prince, see, who'd always had his eye on Neela. Wanted her so bad he put Roth's name in the pot, even altered his birthing record so nobody'd be suspicious. Surprise, surprise—"

"Roth was chosen," I say.

"The prince rigged the whole thing," Elsa says, "but here's the rub. Neela offered her own life in Roth's stead. Roth protested, of course—the prince, too. Thing is, to offer one's own life was—you guessed it—a sacred pledge. Couldn't be broken.

"And so, the Honored were taken to the temple. Roth tried to stop the ceremony—it took five warriors to restrain him. Neela, on the other hand, was resigned to her fate." Another pause. An almost-smile. "I've always admired her, really." And just like that, the almost-smile vanishes. "I suppose I should pity Roth for what happened next, but I don't. Not one bit. The thought only brings me joy. Neela was his life, his everything. All he could do was watch as the archer let his arrow fly."

"Right through her heart," I say, and Elsa nods.

"Roth was enraged. The prince tried to have him killed as well, but the king and queen wouldn't have it. The quota had been met. Balance maintained. Instead, they banished Roth for trying to stop the ceremony, cast him out to the desert." Elsa shakes her head. "They should've known better. Out there in the Great Southern Wastelands, Roth swore revenge. He would kill the warriors who restrained him, the archer, the king, the queen. And last of all, the prince."

I frown. "But without the arrowhead—"

"He couldn't do a thing. Exactly. So eventually he sneaked back into Atol Na in the dead of night, broke into the sacred temple, stole the arrowhead from its altar, and fixed it to a new arrow. Bow in hand, he crept through the city and took out the first warrior. With this kill, he made a new weapon."

"Oh, gross, you mean he—"

"Carved a sword from the first warrior's left femur, yes." A brief pause. "Or maybe it was his right femur. One of his leg bones, anyway." Elsa shrugs. "Either way, it was a heinous act that hadn't been done since the arrowhead was carved."

My hands are shaking, and it isn't from the cold. I can see it all too clearly. Roth, bent over the warrior's body with the arrowhead in his fist. A splatter of blood, like red paint flicked from a brush. "So he killed them all," I say. "Everyone he blamed for Neela's death."

"Almost," Elsa says. "Roth killed the warriors and the archer, the king in his bed. He could've killed the queen, too, but at the last moment, he stopped. He wanted the prince to know something like the pain he felt. Wanted him to watch his mother die. So he dragged the queen from her bed and held the bone sword to her throat. Guards streamed in. The prince came running, too. Roth took his time—wanted to savor the moment. While he was banging on about vengeance and the like, the queen broke free of his grip and wrenched the sword from his hands. Brought Roth to his knees. The guards leapt on him and disarmed him of the arrowhead."

"Why didn't they kill him?"

"I'm sure many wanted to, but in the queen's eyes, death was too light a punishment for killing a king. She wanted Roth to suffer as no one had ever suffered before. Several days later, before all of Atol Na—a cheering, jeering crowd of Dahaari and mortals—she stabbed Roth through the chest with the sword he'd made. Not through the heart, but through the lungs. She left seven fragments of bone in there, one for each of the lives he'd taken. Then she bound and buried him deep beneath the sacred temple, so he would slowly rot from the inside out for all eternity—forever in pain, but never able to die."

I can't believe what I'm hearing. Don't know what to say.

"Life went back to normal for the Dahaari," Elsa continues. "The queen reigned for a thousand years. The prince fell in love. The Cull continued each century. Balance was maintained. For the mortals of Arakaan, Roth passed from legend to myth, his name all but forgotten. But under their feet, Roth endured, consumed by grief and rage. Trapped in the dark, he was forced to look inward, day after day, year after year, century after century, and what he found was twisted. Ugly. Eventually, he awoke within him a powerful ability long lost to the Dahaari. A dark power that would let him wreak havoc over all of Arakaan."

Another chill rattles my bones. "The power to read minds."

Elsa nods. "Roth reached outward with his mind, up through the rock, calling for someone to help him. As I said earlier, the Gorani had long been kept to the shadows of Arakaan. Most dwelled in the desert, but many were kept as slaves in the city, by Dahaari and mortals alike. According to legend, three Gorani had been charged with maintaining the sacred temple. Nobody batted an eyelid as they made their way inside, night after night. The Gorani were like well-trained dogs to the Dahaari. Obedient to a fault. Perfectly harmless, or so they thought."

"Roth was calling out to them."

Elsa nods again. "Gorani are more susceptible to Roth's power. They wouldn't have known who or what lay deep underground. All they would've heard was a mysterious voice promising freedom, riches beyond their wildest dreams. They were drawn to it. They *wanted* it. Roth was possessing them. On the fifth night, the three Gorani killed the temple guards and started digging, their hearts filled with terrible adoration. As the suns crept over the horizon—"

"Roth was free," I almost-whisper.

"Free of the temple, yes," Elsa says, "but a slave to his thirst for revenge." Finally, she quits leaning on the balcony, and turns to face the northern horizon. It's lighter out there now. "The queen had created a monster far more dangerous than the man she'd buried. The love Roth once felt for Neela was gone. Corrupted. All he knew was malice, and with his new power he would bring Arakaan to its knees."

THE WEAPONS OF BONE

"Roth's chest wound had healed, but the bone fragments remained, slowly tearing him apart day and night, poisoning his lungs. His jaw started to rot. His breath, like acid, burned those around him. Racked with pain, he fled deep into the desert with the three Gorani, went to the rest of their kin and convinced the slaves that *he* had freed *them*. Promised freedom for their entire clan, thousands-strong. The Gorani swore their fealty. The bond was made.

"They marched at once. The Dahaari had discovered Roth's empty tomb in the sacred temple and tripled their defenses, but Roth's army was too great. The Gorani swarmed the city, killing any mortals in their path. They couldn't yet harm the Dahaari, but Roth had a plan. He captured the queen's courtiers and guards. Drained their thoughts and learned her secrets. He discovered she had long since disposed of the king's body. The archer, the warriors, and the bone sword, too. She'd thrown 'em into the volcano to ensure no more weapons could be made."

"But she kept the arrowhead," I say, "to perform the Cull."

"Wore it around her neck to keep it safe," Elsa says, nodding. "The queen and the prince were about to be smuggled away, but Roth tracked them down. Grabbed the arrowhead, killed the queen, then slayed the prince at last. Roth had finally killed everyone responsible for Neela's death, but he didn't stop. He'd taken Atol Na. The world lay ahead. Warships, planes, trucks, tanks—Roth used them all to spread his reign of terror. With every Dahaari kill, his weapon supply grew. The Gorani carved swords and axes. More arrowheads, too. Atol Na was transformed into a weapons factory, forever stained with ash and blood, filled with corpses."

"Wait a minute," I say. "If everyone died, how do we know all this?"

"Because some managed to escape. Dahaari, and mortals, too. They fled across the desert to other, distant cities and villages, warning of the coming purge. Soon, the surviving Dahaari formed an army of their own. Battles were fought, won and lost, upon ancient seas and desert plains, over thousands of years. Born into a world of chaos, some mortals fought alongside the Dahaari. Most fled to the far reaches of the world. All of Arakaan suffered. The oceans dried up. The air turned rank and foul. Roth never stopped, never slept, focused all his efforts on killing the Dahaari. Clash after clash, they fell, until he was the last one standing."

"The last immortal," I say.

"Like the queen, Roth was wary of the weapons of bone, lest they be used against him. He dumped 'em into volcanos all over Arakaan to ensure no mortal could get their hands on 'em. Every Dahaari corpse. Every Dahaari weapon. But, like the queen, he kept one—the arrowhead—on a chain around his neck, just in case a Dahaari had somehow slipped his grasp. The mortals made several attempts to retrieve the arrowhead over the next few centuries. All of them failed. Like the Dahaari before them, their time on Arakaan, it seemed, had come to an end."

"So what happened? What changed?"

"*She* rose from the sands," Elsa says, a twinkle in her eyes. "Hali-gabera."

The woman who died hundreds of years ago. The legend buried in Asmadin.

"What do you mean, she rose from the sands?" I ask.

"That's the way they tell the story. Means she came from a distant village *across* the sands, but you can't blame 'em for getting creative. By all accounts, the woman was a marvel. Young, fierce, determined. There'd be no mortals left in this world it weren't for her. Back then, most had retreated to some kind of stronghold, far from Atol Na, but not far enough for Hali-gabera. She knew it was only a matter of time till Roth found them."

"She got them out?"

"Fought Roth first," Elsa says. "Hand-to-hand combat on the Cliffs of Kalanthoon, no less. Got her hands on the arrowhead, yanked it from the chain around his neck, and swung for her life. Took his jaw clean off."

"No way," I gasp.

"Indeed," Elsa says. "Then she swung again, aiming for the heart. Almost got him, too, but the cliffs gave way. Hali managed to cling to a rock. Roth fell out of sight, buried in a landslide. She wanted to finish the job, but she was badly injured, body and soul. Roth had gotten inside her head, see? Tormented her. Anyway, Hali had a companion. Inigo. Nice guy from the stronghold. He convinced her to flee while the going was good. While the Gorani soldiers worked to free Roth, she led the mortals of Arakaan on a pilgrimage north across the desert. They walked for months, until they finally reached a series of deep, deserted canyons. *She* founded Asmadin. Lived there for years, building defenses, sowing deep-shade crops, sinking wells. She was their salvation."

"Whoa." Violet'll go nuts when she hears all this. The battles, the power of the Dahaari bones, the arrowhead. It's real. And Hali-gabera took it to Asmadin. But wait—no. "You said the arrowhead was lost. What went wrong?"

Elsa stares up at the sky. It's awash with color now: burnt reds, deep purples, watery blues. Looks like a healing bruise. "Hali knew Roth would never stop searching for her—not till he reclaimed the arrowhead and got his revenge. She knew the longer she remained in Asmadin, the more danger her people would be in. One day, some Gorani scouts were spotted west of the city. Along with Inigo, Hali tracked the scouts to their camp. Discovered Roth was there, too."

"Wearing the mask now, right?" I ask.

Elsa nods. "The time had come. Hali and Inigo made sure he spotted them. Led the battalion away from Asmadin, on a desperate week-long chase through the Kahega. Hali and Inigo were so exhausted when Roth caught up to them they could barely stand, let alone fight. He dragged them to the summit of a nearby volcano, plucked the arrowhead from around Hali's neck, and destroyed it at last. He tossed the arrowhead—their last hope of defeating him—into the lava, where it sank and vanished." Elsa bows her head. "Then, according to Inigo, Roth pulled a sickle blade from his cloak and killed Hali-gabera, right there on the mountainside."

And I thought I couldn't hate Roth any more than I already do. "What about Inigo?"

"Roth invaded his mind, showed him exactly what he wanted him to do: take Hali's body back to their people and tell them the almighty Roth had won. Inigo staggered back to Asmadin days later, near death, carrying Hali's lifeless body over his shoulders, wrapped in her cloak. He wouldn't let anyone else touch her body—wouldn't even let them near it. They were in love, you see. That kind of grief . . ."

Elsa slips into that thousand-yard stare. Shakes her head and pushes on. "Inigo prepared her body for burial, chose her tomb, and laid Hali-gabera to rest at last. A time of great mourning passed. People feared Roth's return, but he never came back. With the bone weapons gone, all his rivals defeated, he'd turned his mind to a bigger prize."

"Ruling the Manor," I say. "Controlling the Otherworlds."

Elsa nods. "The legend of the Makers and the three Cradle keys had long been told by the Dahaari. The mortals of Arakaan, too. Roth decided to see if there was any truth behind the tale. Somehow, he found the Manor gateway by the dune sea. There, he posted guards and waited for centuries. Waited until two foolish explorers from a distant world stumbled into his trap and set in motion a chain of events that could very well bring about the end of all things. Me and Charlie." She shakes her head. Breathes in the cold dawn air, long and deep. "So that's it. The whole sorry tale. Feel any better, now that you know the truth?"

"Not really."

"Neither did I, when Masaru first told me."

"It's just . . . that can't be the end of the story. There were hundreds—probably thousands—of weapons that could kill Roth, and you're saying he destroyed them *all*?"

"Every single one. Trust me, I've looked. I spent years looking. I was sure there had to be a reason the Manor brought me back here. I studied. Read every book I could find. On one of my stays in Asmadin, I hiked out to the volcano where Roth disposed of the arrowhead and killed Hali-gabera, just to see it. I even broke into her tomb when I returned, to make sure Inigo hadn't left a bone weapon in her sarcophagus. It was a mess. All I found were brittle bones and a torn shroud. Masaru caught me. Kept it a secret, thankfully. Ordered me to stop. But I couldn't.

Next day, I stole a book from the Elders' library—the journal in which Inigo had chronicled the pilgrimage north. I sneaked it out to the shipwreck, kept it hidden in my room."

Her secret place on the upper deck.

A hot flush fills my cheeks.

"You're a terrible liar, Jane," Elsa says. "I know you saw it."

I shift my weight awkwardly. "I may have *glimpsed* it—"

"It's okay." Elsa shoots me a sad smile. "I'm glad you found it. Glad you destroyed it, too. I used to go there on my own, when things got a bit . . . much. The pain. The waiting. The grief. It was good for me, at first, but after I stole the journal, the wreck became a place of madness. I cut myself off from everyone. Translated and researched Inigo's journal day and night. Plotted on the walls. I became obsessed with finding Atol Na. Had to go there, had to *know*."

I gasp. The scribbles weren't random after all. "It was a map . . ."

Elsa nods. "To the city where it all began. Where the arrowhead rested for millennia. Where Roth's troops forged new weapons of Dahaari bone by the truckload during the war."

"And you found it? You actually went there?"

"Didn't tell anyone I was going, not even Masaru." She shakes her head. "There's nothing down there but rabid Taw-taws and empty ruins, Jane. I scoured the ancient Gorani forges for weeks. Entered the sacred temple, saw

Roth's tomb. I stood before the altar where Neela and the other Honored were killed, even trekked out to the sacred volcano. There were no weapons left. Not even a chip of Dahaari bone.

"I ran out of supplies. Became too weak to hunt. I started back but didn't make it far. I collapsed in the sand. Was about to give up and let the suns take me—I'm not ashamed to say it. I felt so useless. So alone. I'd failed." Elsa nods to herself, slowly, eyes so wide it's like they're about to swallow the world. "But then I saw it. A vision in the heat-shimmer. A woman with glowing amber eyes. She was walking toward me, the ground quaking and roiling in her wake. At first, I was frightened, but then the woman raised her hands, and bright golden light shone from deep inside her, and it felt so electric, so . . . *real*." She nods again. "The desert showed me. The desert made me see. It was my duty to get up, keep walking, keep going. To return to this group of Arakaanians and keep waiting for you. *That* was my purpose." She blinks, snaps out of her trance, looks me up and down. "I'll admit, I was expecting someone a little taller." Her look softens a little. "I may not show it, but I'm glad you're here, Jane."

The first sun peeks over the painted horizon, bathing us in crimson light. We watch it in silence, the whole world holding its breath as the sun morphs from a red speck to a sliver of molten gold to a bloated, watchful eye burning in the sky. The second sun won't be far behind.

"I'm glad too," I say, surprised to find I actually mean it. "I'm sorry I'm not like your vision. And I'm sorry you had to wait so long out here. I would've come sooner if I could've." I take a deep breath, take the plunge. "Dad would've, too. I mean, John—crap—I mean, *Charlie*. Sorry."

Thankfully, Elsa takes pity on me. "It's okay. You have every right to call him that. He's the only parent you've ever known." She pauses. Chooses her next words carefully. "I don't suppose he asked you to pass on a message?"

"No," I say. "But only because we were being attacked at the time."

"Oh. I understand."

"He still loves you, Elsa," I add. "You know that, right? He told me you're strong and wise—said you're the most resilient woman he's ever known."

"Did he?" Again, she tries to smile. Again, it doesn't take. "I doubt he'd even recognize me now." She rubs at a stain on her robe, wipes her nose. "I'm sorry I've made things so . . . difficult. For you and your friends.'

"Maybe just keep the death pits to a minimum from here on out, yeah?"

She chuckles. "I'll try."

I smile, too, but something's been gnawing at the back of my mind for a while now. Something about the journey ahead. "Um, speaking of difficult, you said the dune sea's really dangerous. No human's ever walked across it and lived to tell the tale?"

"According to the Elders, no."

"Right. So how are we gonna cross it?"

"Ah-ha." Elsa claps her hands. "That's the fun part. Charlie didn't tell you what I used to do in Tallis, did he? Before we set out to find the Manor."

"No, I—I don't think he did."

"Well, I was a flight engineer. A pilot, too." Elsa strides back to the stairs and beckons me to follow. "We're not crossing the dune sea on foot, Jane. We're gonna fly over it."

THE ATTACK

Elsa built a plane. Big one, apparently. Found an old wreck on the outskirts of Asmadin and spent half a decade fixing it up: tinkering, forging, scavenging replacement parts near and far. She tells me all about it as we head back down the stairs. All the strange looks she got from people, who had seen the wreckage out in the desert and considered them obsolete. Remnants of a bygone era, as ancient and useless as the shipwrecks. The plane was her back-up plan in case Roth ever returned to Arakaan and stormed Asmadin—in case she had to make a quick getaway with Masaru and the true Cradle key.

She even gave it a name. Betty's our only hope of crossing the dune sea.

"Magnificent machine," Elsa says. "Beautiful. She's parked in a canyon north of Asmadin. Made ourselves a runway and all. She'll get us to the gateway in one piece, mark my words."

"Mm-hmm," I say. "Sounds good."

"You don't believe me," Elsa says.

"No—I mean, yeah, I do."

"What's wrong, then? You look worried."

I am, but not about Betty. Actually, that's a lie. There are no planes on Bluehaven, of course—the only things that fly around there are birds, insects, and the occasional frying pan hurled by Mrs. Hollow—but I've seen plenty of drawings in books, and I wouldn't trust Elsa to pilot one of them in a million years. I'm pretty sure we'll crash and burn, if we ever manage to get off the ground in the first place.

Betty isn't the *only* thing I'm worried about.

"Elsa, you just told me the world's worst bedtime story back there. I guess I'm a little distracted." I run my fingers along the rough stone wall, careful not to snag my bandage. "I mean, I finally know the truth about Roth, but it doesn't change anything. The Dahaari weapons are gone. We still don't know how to stop him. The only other thing powerful enough to maybe—*maybe*—wipe him out is the Cradle Sea, but we can't unleash that. It's way too dangerous, too powerful. We'd end up destroying everything—the Manor *and* every Otherworld."

Elsa frowns. "How do you know that?"

"Just trust me." I nearly trip down the stairs as images from my latest nightmare scratch at the back of my eyes. All those gateways opening. Those Otherworlds consumed by the white-fire tide. "I know."

"Don't worry about the Otherworlds, Jane," she says. "We're gonna save them all."

"Only if we manage to claim the Cradle," I say, "which is a whole other thing. We still have no idea how to *find* it."

I take a deep breath. It's time. "Yesterday, you mentioned a spike pit. A spike pit inside the Manor. Is that where you found the Cradle?"

"Yes. The spike pit lies at the end of the path. Very near it, at least."

"And the beginning?" My heart hammers. "I know you and Dad picked up the path near Roth's lair after you escaped, but Violet and I figure the Manor must've shifted it far away from there by now."

"It did," Elsa says. "I checked."

"You went *back*? To Roth's fortress?"

"I was stuck inside the Manor for years. Of course I went back. Thought if I could just find the Cradle again, get back to the foundation stone, then maybe . . ." Elsa sighs, shakes her head. "It doesn't matter. The path had vanished. I'm sure Roth tried to stop the rooms from shifting after we slipped through his fingers, but all it takes is one closed door. I've thought about it a lot over the years. I think the Manor led Charlie and me to the Cradle because it knew it was in danger. It knew the time had come for you to step outside. To grow, learn, and prepare. Now, the Cradle could be anywhere, waiting for your return—for *our* return."

"But I'm not prepared," I say. "I don't know what I'm supposed to do in the Cradle. Violet reckons the foundation stone'll amplify my powers. Says the Makers'll be there to guide me. But what if she's wrong? This . . . *thing* inside me. We call it a power, but what if it's something else? What if it really is a curse?"

Elsa stops me near the bottom of the stairs. "There's nothing wrong with a bit of fear, Jane. Fear keeps us alive. You just have to make sure it doesn't control you. For what it's worth, I think Violet's theory is sound."

"But it's only a theory. What if the Makers aren't there? Or what if they *are* there? Are they gonna, like, *possess* me? Because that doesn't exactly float my boat, either."

"Jane—"

"Or what if they're expecting some sort of super-amazing quake goddess in complete control of her powers, like your vision in the desert? Because we both know that's not me."

"Hey." Elsa grabs my arm. "Take a breath."

"Sorry." I breathe. "Elephant. Small pieces."

A little smile plays over Elsa's lips. "You are one very strange girl, Jane Doe. But I have no doubt you'll shine when the time comes. You're the heir to the Manor. The avatar of all three Makers—Po, Aris, and Nabu-kai. Their power lies within you, and it *will* awaken. As far as finding the Cradle goes—picking up the path again?—I believe the Manor will help us. It'll know you've returned the moment you step inside. It'll know you have both keys. Just as it did for Charlie and me, way back when, I think it will bring the Cradle to *us*."

"Just like that? Doesn't that seem a little . . . easy?"

"Believe me," Elsa says, "the path to the Cradle is anything but easy. We barely got through it alive." She places her hands on my shoulders again. "But know this: you're not alone, Jane. I'll be right beside you. I won't stop fighting, not until we're standing atop the foundation stone, together. We'll make Roth pay for what he's done. We'll make everything *right*."

"And then we free my dad," I add quickly, just to make sure it's on the agenda. "And every other innocent person trapped in Roth's fortress. Somehow."

There's a fierce glint in Elsa's eyes. "Absolutely. We'll free them all."

Relief pulses through my veins. I could hug this woman. Really, I could. "You are gonna remember all this when you sober up, yeah?"

"Oh, please. I sobered up an hour ago." She sets off down the stairs again. "Speaking of, I'm parched. Come along! Lots to be done if we're gonna reach the Canyon of the Dead by noon."

"Okay, but—wait, did you say the Canyon of the—"

"Place is crawling with darkling beetles, but they're harmless. Pretty tasty, actually. Scorpions are the real danger. They got those on Bluehaven?"

"No, but I've read—"

"I saw plenty on Tallis. The ones they've got here?" She shudders. "They feast on the darklings, mostly, but just one of those little blighters could kill twenty people, easy."

"Is that why they call it the Canyon of the Dead?"

"What? Oh, no, that's because of all the corpses."

"*Corpses?*"

"Place is full of 'em. Literally wall to wall. Been there forever. Remnants of a lost empire, pre-Dahaari, they say. Don't worry, they're entombed. Most have probably turned to dust by now. Unless they were mummified or taken by Taw-taws. Stunning sight."

"Can't wait," I say, and gulp so hard I nearly swallow my tongue.

Why couldn't it be the Valley of Rainbows? The Valley of Sunshine and Kittens?

Yaku's waiting for us at the bottom of the stairs. He looks worried. Maybe even a little scared. He tries to play it cool as he falls into step beside us, but his bald head's shiny with sweat and he keeps fidgeting while we walk. I get the feeling he's been pacing for a while.

Elsa frowns at him. "What's wrong with you?"

"*Tanuum*," he says, wringing his big hands together. "Nothing. Elsa, *nay badda*. It's just . . . the girl is not supposed to be out of her room."

"She's with me, and perfectly fine."

"Yes, *oda min. Nay badda.* I just wanted to—"

"Make sure Jane didn't toss me from the balcony?" Elsa says with a smile. "Honestly, you worry too much. *Sah-ha de mundaya.* We're all on the same side here."

"Yes, *oda min*," the big man says again, but his eyes linger on me a fraction too long.

Still, blessed relief pulses through my veins, calming the wasps in my gut. I love this: walking, talking, plotting the path ahead. I may not be able to call Elsa *Mom*, but I'm pretty sure I can call her a friend.

"Nourishment," she says, "that's what we need. Food and wine—I mean, water. The stable hands should be getting the horses ready as we speak. We leave within the hour."

"You sure about that?" I ask. "It's so quiet around here."

"Hmm." Elsa stops. Looks up and down the deserted tunnel, concerned, and mutters something to Yaku. He shrugs and mutters something back, as if he hasn't noticed a thing. Something isn't right, though.

His reaction feels too forced.

"Go to the kitchen, *oda min*," he says. "Eat. Drink. I can take Jane back to her room."

Why is he being so helpful? So nice?

Elsa waves him off. "Stay close, stay quiet."

The people in the main dome are still passed out. The old man's gone to sleep right in the middle of his clean-up. The dancing couple have, too, as if they collapsed mid-stride. I hurry over to make sure they're okay, and that's when I see them. Darts. Lodged into their necks.

"Elsa—"

"I know." She plucks a dart from the old man's shoulder. Stands bolt upright and scans the surrounding tunnels. "Jane, head back to the watchtower. Right now."

"What is it? Who'd do this? Why?"

"Boboki," Elsa says.

And that's when Yaku strikes.

He lunges at me. Elsa pushes me clear just in time, and they fall in a heap by the fire. Yaku pins her down, wraps his hands around her neck, and squeezes. I leap on his back. He bucks me off. I spin around to try again, but Elsa's already grabbing a half-charred log from the fire.

She swings hard and clocks him right in the head. Yaku hits the floor like a bag of bricks.

"Jane," Elsa wheezes, ditching the log, sucking down air, "you okay?"

"Am *I* okay? What the hell's going on? I thought he was your friend."

"So did I." Elsa shoves her boot into Yaku's side. "Clearly, I was wr—"

A muffled *crash*, somewhere down the tunnel.

Coming from our room, I'm sure.

"Jane, no," Elsa shouts, "it's too dangerous!" But I'm already sprinting across the dome, desperate to get back to Violet.

The tunnel's deserted. No—almost deserted. Our guard's facedown on the floor, legs akimbo, weapon gone. There's a dart in his neck, too.

"Violet! Hickory!" I skid to a halt in front of the door. It's locked. "Hey, somebody open up!" I jiggle the handle, pound my fist.

The sound of a scuffle inside. Another loud crash. Violet grunting, Aki screeching, and a man who definitely isn't Hickory shouting at them both.

"Violet!" I shove my shoulder into the door. "Aki, let me in!"

"Jane," Violet shouts, "don't—" but the rest of her words are muffled.

"You let her go," I shout at the man, whoever he is. "If you hurt her . . ."

Elsa's by my side now. We shove the door together. This time it bursts open.

The table's been flipped, the food platters flung far and

wide. A black-cloaked man's unconscious on the floor. Aki has two more pinned to the wall. Violet's fighting a bald guy twice her size over by the balcony. She jabs a quick one-two, ducks, weaves, kicks one of his legs and brings him to his knees. She goes to kick him again, but he spins around and grabs her foot, and before I know it I'm dashing across the room, grabbing a platter, leaping over an upturned chair and smacking the chump square in the face. He releases Violet's foot, groans and sways.

"I said," I huff and puff, "let her go."

The guy's eyes roll back into his head. He topples over like a felled tree.

Over by the table, Aki tightens his grip on the two men, smashes their heads together and drops them in a heap. After that, he waves at me like I've just popped in for some tea.

"Hey, Aki." I ditch the platter and smile at Violet. "Just in time, huh?"

But Violet isn't smiling back. "Just in time?" She unsheathes Platter Face's blade from his belt. "After I wake up beside an empty bed with some guy's hand over my mouth and a knife at my neck? I can't believe you left! Again!'

"I didn't *leave*." I jab a thumb at Elsa as she steps into the room, wide-eyed. The woman's in shock. "I was just talking to Elsa, and then Yaku—"

"You don't go anywhere without me," Violet says. "That was the deal."

"I'm sorry, Violet, but I had to—"

"Save it. We've got bigger problems right now."

"We do indeed," Elsa says, her voice trembling. She nudges the black-cloaked guy on the floor with her foot. "They're Boboki raiders, all right. They've come to kill you, Jane."

"Kill her?" Violet says, staring down at the blade in her hands. "But . . . they didn't use their weapons."

"Yes, well," Elsa grunts, "they rarely do. Boboki prefer hand-to-hand combat."

"And they're loyal to Roth?"

Elsa unsheathes a Boboki blade for herself. "They're loyal to Arakaan, or so they claim. They want to stop us from reentering the Manor. Yaku must've been working with them for years, ever since . . ." She shakes her head in disgust. "I guess I didn't rescue him. They *let* me take him because they'd already turned him. He was just a boy." And she snaps. Spins around, screams, and slashes at the wall till it's cracked and scarred.

She stops. Smooths down her robe. Tucks her flyaway hair behind her ears. "Apologies. I just had to—"

"Kill the wall," I say. "Hey, no judgment here. I'd be angry too."

"Where's Yaku now?" Violet says.

"He just attacked us in the main dome."

"He must've let them in through one of the lower gates," Elsa says, nodding at the black-cloaks. "There could be more out there. Other traitors, too. Orin-kin is no longer safe."

"Wait, where's Hickory?" I say, rushing to the next room.

His bed and side table have been upturned. He's lying between them, tangled in a sheet, doused in the oils, pastes, and powders from the healers' pots. There's a fifth black-cloaked Boboki sprawled beside him, dead. Guy's got a spoon sticking out of one eye.

"Heeeeey, you're back." Hickory grins up at me and sniffs his overly oiled hands. "I dunno what this stuff is, but I like it. Smells like . . . purple."

"Oh." I turn back to the others. "Yeah, he's fine."

"Praise the Makers," Violet mutters, and turns to Elsa. "So what do we do now?"

Elsa strides over to the door, checks the tunnel left and right. "We leave. Make for the Mulu Pass before it's too late."

That's when a gunshot echoes through the mountain. Somebody, somewhere, screams and a rumble of angry chanting echoes through the tunnels.

More Boboki are coming. The battle's only just begun.

"Stay close," Elsa tells me. "Keep your head down. Anyone sees the color of your eyes, they'll know you're the one they're here to kill." She nods at the next room. "Hickory stays."

"Not a chance. I told you, we need him."

"We can't carry him, Jane. He'll only slow us down."

"ARRGGHHH!" Out of nowhere, Platter Face leaps to his feet by the balcony door, ready to charge at me and Elsa. Violet leaps forward to take him down, but Aki gets there first, vaulting over the table, springing from the floor, kicking the man square in the chest with both feet and sending him flying backward, out over the balcony and into the morning light.

We stare at Aki, stunned. He stands up straight, nods at me and rattles his throat. *Click-clack-click-click.*

"Um," Violet says, frozen mid-attack, "what the—"

"Life debt," I say. "Apparently, he's kinda . . . bound to me now."

"Leatherheads have an *honor code?*"

"Who would've thought, huh?" I say. I turn to Elsa, struck by a brilliant idea. "We don't have to carry Hickory." I point at Aki. "He can."

SLIDE AND RIDE

"He's gonna hate us for this," I say to Violet as we run.

Hickory's slung over Aki's shoulders, bouncing up and down in front of us as we sprint through the tunnels, humming a merry tune. Every time Aki swings around to check on me, Hickory's head smacks into a wall, but I'm pretty sure he can't feel a thing. "Ouch," he mutters, then chuckles and starts humming again.

"He should be grateful we're bringing him at all," Violet snaps back.

Orin-kin is in chaos. Woken by the gunshot and chanting, half our group is sprinting through the tunnels with us, so panicked they don't seem to notice or care that a seven-foot Gorani's running alongside them. Others are charging back toward the action with clubs and blades in hand, ready to battle the Boboki.

I keep expecting Yaku to burst through the crowd. No wonder he was annoyed I'd gone to see Elsa. I was supposed to be with the others, grouped together for an easy kill.

"Through here," Elsa shouts.

She plucks a fire-lit torch from a bracket on the wall and dashes down a thin, deserted tunnel. Aki does too, scraping Hickory along the stone as he goes. Violet shoves me in after them. The ceiling's much lower in here, the walls less than three feet apart. We run single file.

More gunshots echo behind us. Another chorus of Boboki chanting.

"Where are we going?" Violet hisses.

"Shortcut down to the stables." We all skid to a halt as Elsa stops suddenly. She reaches into one of several small holes cut into the rock wall, shoulder-deep. "Step aside as soon as you get to the bottom, Jane. Stay put. The rest of us'll be coming in fast right behind you."

"What are you talking about?" I ask. "The bottom of what?"

"Move forward a bit. Half a step."

I obey. "Here? Why?"

"Arms in tight."

"Like this?"

"Perfect," Elsa says. "Have fun."

She tugs a lever or something in the wall and the next thing I know I'm falling, slipping, sliding down a secret trapdoor chute, swearing my guts out. The darkness is thick and cool, the stone worn smooth by centuries of sliding butts. The wind rushes through my ears. Close behind me, I can hear Violet sliding, Aki *click-clack*ing, Hickory cackling, crying, *"Whoopeeee!"* The slide banks left and right, corkscrew twirls.

A flash of light, and I shoot across the hay-strewn floor

of a storeroom, slam into a wall. Before I can roll to the side, Violet crashes into me. Leaps to her feet and scans the junk scattered around the room. Crates. Saddles. Bales of hay. A rack of shovels and rakes.

She grabs a shovel. "Better than nothing."

A second later, Aki and Hickory slip across the floor and slam into me, too. Hickory shoots me a dopey grin. "Let's do that again." Seems the effects of the healers' oils haven't worn off yet.

"Get up, all of you," Violet whispers, creeping over to the door. "And keep it down."

Elsa slides into the room nice and easy, like she's out for a morning jaunt. Hops up and rummages around behind the bales of hay, looking for a weapon or something, I guess.

"A little warning would've been nice," I say, nodding back at the chute.

"And miss the look on your face when you fell? *Pfft.* Ah-ha!" She pulls out a dusty bottle of booze, uncorks it with her teeth, chugs a mouthful and sighs. "Lovely."

"Question," Hickory says, staring at his hands. "Did I just kill a guy with a spoon?"

"Can we focus, please?" Violet hisses. She eases the door open a crack to see if the coast is clear. It isn't, of course. "I count four hostages. Kids. Three hostiles, all armed. On the plus side, most of the horses are already saddled."

Elsa joins Violet by the door. "Those kids are the stable hands." She opens the door a little wider so I can look, too.

"The gate down there's still closed. Yaku must've let the Boboki in through a different one. Ungrateful little—" She swears and takes another swig.

The place is big. Horse stalls and hay bales line the far wall. Torches flicker in every corner. To our left, three tunnels wind up into the mountain. To our right, a much shorter one leads to the stable gate. Two Boboki raiders are guarding it, spears and machetes at the ready. The stable hands—four terrified kids—are on their knees in the middle of the room. The third Boboki raider's pacing around them. Guy's a walking brick wall, white skin inked in swirling tattoos.

Violet pokes her head out to get a better look, ducks back, and eases the door shut. "There's a wagon loaded with barrels to the right of the exit tunnel . . ."

"Supplies from Asmadin," Elsa says. "Salted meat. Flint. Oil."

Violet's eyes light up. "For the torches? Flammable oil?"

"Don't even think about it, Violet," I say.

"But—"

"You're not blowing anything up. You could kill the horses. Not to mention yourself."

"Hey," she snaps, "I'm still mad at you for leaving, so don't lecture me."

"I told you, I didn't *leave*."

"Oh, sure," Elsa says, "let's settle this now. Not like we're in a hurry or anything."

"Fine!" Violet wrings her hands on her shovel. "No

explosions. You all stay here. As soon as I step outside, you close the door behind me, count to twenty, and then get to the horses. Jane, stay close to Aki and Hickory. Aki, I know you can't understand a word I'm saying, but on the off-chance you can—kill anyone who tries to hurt Jane. Elsa?" Violet snatches the bottle from her hands, tosses it onto a pile of hay. "Stop drinking for two seconds. Honestly, you're a mess. I'll take down the Boboki, free the stable hands and open the gate."

Elsa blinks at her. "How old are you again?"

"Fourteen,' Violet says. "You got a problem with that?"

"Not at all." She salutes Violet. "Off you go, then."

"What? No!" I whisper-shout. "You're not going out there alone, Violet."

But she's already slipping through the door, Elsa's already closing it, and when I try to open it again, Aki grabs my wrist. I try to shake him off, but his grip's too tight.

Elsa starts the countdown—"One, two, three"—and holds her ear to the door—"four, five . . . Interesting girl, by the way. Real firecracker. I can see why you have a crush on her."

"*What? I*—"

"Jane called her pretty,' Hickory says. 'Back inside the Manor."

"Shut up, Hickory."

"Did she now? Nine, ten, eleven—"

"Mm-hmm," he says. "Remember, Jane? Remember when you called Violet pretty? Jane's never kissed anyone

129

before, though," he tells Elsa. "Told me so in the forest. It's a secret."

"I hate you so much right now." I've had enough of this. I slap Aki's hand off my arm. "Fourteen, nineteen, twenty—let's go."

By the time I shove Elsa aside and open the door, Violet's already taken down the raider in the center of the stable. The stable hands have scattered. Now Violet's charging at the other two Boboki with her shovel in hand. They throw their spears. She dives clear, leaps up and sprints again, barely missing a step. The men twirl their machetes, ready to fight.

We stick to the plan and head for the horses. They're all spooked by the commotion, stomping hooves, flaring nostrils. All except Scab, that is. He's munching on some hay.

"Stay down, don't move," Elsa says, pushing me into a corner. Aki squats beside me. "Soon as Violet has the gate open, hit the road and head for the Pass. Don't stop. Don't look back."

"Wait, wh—where are you going?"

"Essential supply run." She winks, barks an order at the stable hands, and slips off between the stalls. They immediately lead Rex over to the wagon by the exit, tugging frantically at his reins as he rears.

Violet smacks one Boboki with her shovel, kicks off the wall, leaps onto the other's shoulders and whacks him, too. She rolls clear when they collapse, storms toward the gate.

I think I love her.

"Jane," Hickory calls, "come look! What *is* this stuff?"

The chump's swaying in the middle of the stable, staring at a pile of horse crap on the floor like it's some kind of miracle sent by the gods, completely oblivious to the Boboki girl darting from the shadows, charging at him with a spear.

"Hickory, *move!*"

I sprint over and crash-tackle him clear. The Boboki girl skids past us—a near miss. We hit the ground and roll. I spin around first chance I get, and the girl does, too, raising her spear again. So much for Boboki not using their weapons.

"Please"—I hold up my hands—"we don't have to fight."

She's only a few years older than me. Brown-skinned. Covered in elaborate tattoos like the other guy. They wrap around her arms and legs in swirls and spikes, and curl right up to her neck. She gasps when she sees my eyes. "*Tu bai,*" she cries, scanning the stables for her kin. "*Tu bai!*"

She knows I'm the one they've come to kill.

But if she wants to kill me, why is she lowering her spear? Why are her hands shaking?

"*Cabagu-nai,*" she says. "*Cabagu-nai, de—*"

BAM. She's wiped out by a flying saddle, hurled by Aki. Her spear clatters to the ground. She sinks to the floor, out cold. I stand over her, mind racing. What was she trying to tell me?

131

Aki rattles his throat at me, no doubt telling me to hurry. It's time to go.

I kick Hickory's leg. "Get up. Now."

"Nah." He stretches out on the straw-scattered floor, tucks his hands behind his head. "I already told you, Janey. I'm done. You go, though. Say hi to Roth for me."

I narrow my eyes. *Janey?*

"Aki," I shout, and point at Hickory. "Get him."

Hickory tries to crawl away, but Aki scoops him up and hauls him back to the horses, just as an almighty horn bellows through the stables. Another Boboki in the shadows, calling for reinforcements.

"Crap." I grab a nearby bucket and throw it at him. Miss by a long shot. He goes to blow the horn again when—*BLAMO!*—it's blasted clean from his hands.

Elsa's back, striding from one of the tunnels with a bulging sack slung over her shoulder and a pistol in her hand. She aims at the guy again, but he's gone.

"This place'll be overrun by Boboki any second," she shouts. "Everybody out!"

I take a final look at the Boboki girl and wonder who she is.

"Jane!" Violet's cranking the gate down the exit tunnel now, flooding the place with pale morning light. "You waiting for a spear to the gut or what? Get on a horse and ride!"

Girl's got a point.

I make a beeline for Yaku's horse. Almost get my foot into the stirrup, too. Unfortunately, Elsa nabs me at the last second and pushes me toward Scab, of all the options.

While I try to protest, Elsa heaves me up into the saddle, not that Scab seems to notice. I consider jumping off, picking another horse—literally *any* other horse—but the Boboki have arrived. Dozens of them storm into the stables with their weapons drawn.

Yaku's with them, black-cloaked now, holding a bloodied rag to his face. "Elsa," he screams, "*dahna de nai!*"

I give Scab a little kick. "Move it, you stupid animal!"

Aki slings Hickory over his shoulder—"*Put me down, you overgrown toad!*"—hops into the saddle of a silver mare, and canters off with a swift kick and throat rattle.

"Move it," I shout again. "Go! Onward! Um. Hey presto?" I kick Scab, shake the reins, bob up and down, but nothing works. "Elsa, how do I make him go?'"

I shouldn't have asked. She slaps his rump with a sharp "*Hey-yah!*" and Scab whinnies, rears back and bolts through the stables so fast I nearly crap my pants. We leap over the fallen Boboki, rocket past the stable hands tethering Rex to the wagon, blast down the tunnel, and overtake Aki and Hickory. Before I know it, we're bolting into the light, and Violet's yelling at me, reaching out a hand. I grab it, grit my teeth and swing. Somehow, she twists around and lands right behind me in the saddle, swift as a goddess of the wind.

"Go, go, go," she shouts into my ear.

I crack the reins. Scab steps up the pace. The road's dead straight, cutting across an upward-sloping plateau, leading to a thin cleft between two craggy peaks. The Mulu Pass. The road to Asmadin.

The wind whips our hair, flaps our tunics. Violet wraps her arms around me, and even though she's mad at me, even though we're fleeing for our lives, my guts get all giddy.

"Hey, I'm really sorry I went and talked to Elsa," I shout.

"This is hardly the time," Violet shouts back.

"I know I promised I wouldn't go anywhere without you—"

"Jane—"

"—but I saw her up on her balcony, and I just *had* to go see her! And it worked! She told me all about Roth!"

"Would you please shut up and concentrate!"

"Relax," I tell her, "we're home free!"

"I think they'd disagree."

"Who?"

"*Them*. Behind us!"

I lean a little to the side, risk a glance back. Aki's close behind, squatting awkwardly atop his horse with Hickory fish-out-of-water-flopping over his shoulder, hurling abuse. Elsa's farther back, riding Rex, hauling the wagon of supplies and guzzling from another bottle of booze. It'd be a comforting sight, really, if it weren't for the dozen bareback Boboki riders galloping from the stable gate behind her. Yaku's leading the charge, black cloak flailing.

"Oh, *come* on!" I scream. "Don't these jerks ever give up?"

"Focus, Jane! As soon as we're through the Pass, you're gonna have to bring it down!"

"*What?*"

"The Pass," Violet shouts. "You need to block it! Stop the Boboki from following!"

"No way," I shout. "I can't!" I'm not ready. My hand still hurts. I can't feel the furious tide. "You know I can't turn the quakes on and off like that!"

"Find a way! Make it work!"

The peaks loom above us, crested with morning light. The Mulu Pass looks like an angry snarl in the rock. And now we're there, darting into the cool shadow, the towering walls a wicked blur. Ahead, a patch of light. A rocky clearing.

I close my eyes, clench my injured hand, grit my teeth against the pain and picture that Manor hallway again, the river creatures coming to get us, the broth of white water. What did I do? I grabbed Violet's knife and thought about Mr. and Mrs. Hollow, Mayor Atlas, Eric Junior. Everyone who made my life miserable back on Bluehaven. Mainly, I thought about Roth. I stoked the fire, *became* the rock, felt every crack and tremor. But then I lost control. The power got away from me. Just like it did in my nightmare.

We've cleared the Pass. Violet reaches around, pulls on the reins, and slips off Scab's rump before we've even stopped. She beckons me to do the same. "Bring them down, as soon as Elsa's clear."

Aki bolts into the clearing and waves an elongated arm

at us, urging us to keep riding, oblivious as Hickory hits him repeatedly with a "Let. Me. *Go!*"

"Get back on the horse, Violet," I plead. "We have to get out of here."

"No." She's glaring up at me now. "You can do this, Jane. You have to *try.*"

"I told you, I can't!"

"You're not scared enough, is that it?' She points at Elsa and Rex rattling through the Pass with the wagon, and the stampede of Boboki gaining behind them. "The Boboki won't stop until they kill us all!"

My nightmare. The gaping void. All those gateways opening. Those Otherworlds consumed by the Cradle Sea. "Look around," I say. "We're surrounded by rock. *I'll* kill us all!"

"You won't," Violet says. "Just reach out and let go. It's the only way!"

Elsa thunders into the clearing, jerks Rex to a halt, leaps onto the wagon and starts scattering her sack of "essentials" around the barrels of oil. Bottles of booze. Boxes of ammo. A dozen sticks of dynamite.

"No," I say to Violet. "It isn't."

"A little help, please?" Elsa shouts at us.

Violet beholds this mobile bomb-to-be and gasps. "I stand corrected."

I leap off Scab and we dash over to help. Elsa tosses me a machete, and I slash at the wagon straps, untethering Rex. Violet grabs a rifle stashed under his saddle, checks that it's loaded. Elsa pockets a fresh bottle of booze and jumps down.

"Clear?"

I cut the final strap and slap Rex on the rump. He whinnies and trots over to Scab. "Clear!"

Pebbles clatter down from the cliffs and bounce around our feet. The whole mountain's trembling, but not because of me. Yaku and the Boboki have entered the Pass. They'll be on us any second.

"Aki!" I point at the wagon and mime a shoulder-barge. "Ram it!"

He dumps Hickory on the road—"*Ouch! You lanky son of a . . .*"—storms across the clearing and slams into the wagon so hard it careens back down the Pass.

"Take cover!" Elsa shouts, diving clear.

Aki scoops me up and leaps beside her.

Only Violet stands her ground, chewing on her tongue in concentration, raising the rifle. Slowly, carefully, she takes aim and fires.

I can't actually see the blast, but I can hear it all right. I can picture the wagon exploding in a great ball of fire, the Pass collapsing, Yaku and the Boboki wheeling their horses around to escape the billowing cloud of debris.

Violet dives clear just in time, avoiding a shower of stones, grinning because she got to blow something up at last. Maybe she's still mad at me, but right now I don't care. I'm just glad there's more than one way to bring down a mountain pass.

"Everyone okay?" Elsa asks.

"Peachy," I say as Aki sets me down.

Violet rolls onto her back and sighs, utterly content.

"Okay, so that was pretty amazing," Hickory says, still back down the road where Aki dumped him. "I'll give you that." The cloud of dust from the explosion envelops him. "But I still hate you all," he coughs, and with that, projectile vomits and passes out once more.

THE ROAD TO ASMADIN

We've been on the move for hours, winding our way along sharp ridges, skirting ravines, heading deeper into the Kahega Range to put as much distance between us and the Boboki as we can. Apparently, there's another road to Asmadin a few hours north of the Mulu Pass. "They won't stop," Elsa said, "neither can we," so we've pushed on through the hot morning air, shielded from the full force of the suns by the surrounding cliffs, keeping a steady pace. Slow and steady wins the race. We can't tire out the horses.

If they die, we die.

We're leading them on foot now, dwarfed by pointed spires and sheer rock walls. Deep fissures scar the sides of the road. Precariously balanced boulders loom over our heads. If it weren't for the wide strip of pale midmorning sky snaking between the clifftops, I'd swear we'd wandered back into the Manor and started down a corridor dotted with hazards and traps.

It almost feels like home.

Elsa doesn't want to talk about Yaku's betrayal. I asked how she was doing before we set off. Told her I'm here for her. She told me to shut up and ride. It stung, but I can't blame her. *I'm* still trying to wrap my head around it. Yaku's had plenty of chances to kill me. That night out on the flats, when Elsa had her nightmare. In our room at Orin-kin, before he took me Violet and me to the death pit. While I was *in* the death pit. Why didn't he? Too many witnesses? Or maybe he wanted to capture me alive and kicking, parade me in front of the rest of the Boboki first. The thought makes my skin crawl.

Elsa's up front now, leading Rex. Violet's been chatting with her for ages. The joy she felt from blowing up the wagon didn't last long. She's still annoyed I split last night. More than a little disappointed I refused to cause a quake on command. I apologized again. Tried to tell her everything Elsa told me in the watchtower, too, but Violet cut me off. Said she wanted to hear it from the woman herself, marched right on up to her and hasn't looked back once. I hate it. Can't help feeling there's a crack in the road between us, one that's getting wider by the second. I wish things could go back to the way they were, before Orin-kin, before Arakaan. Before we had any idea I was the third key.

On the other hand, Scab's once again his slow, useless, directionally challenged self, so at least some things are back to normal. "Anyone wanna swap horses?" I ask when he head-butts a wall.

Unsurprisingly, nobody says a word, except Aki.

Click-clack-click, he goes, which I choose to interpret as "What a bunch of jerks."

"I know, right?" I reply. "So rude."

Aki hopped off the silver horse to lighten its load soon after we left the Pass, and plopped Hickory in the saddle so he could sleep, slumped forward, drooling into the horse's mane. I thanked Aki for his help, told him the life debt's been repaid, waved goodbye and all. But he stayed with us, leading Hickory's horse on foot, keeping an eye out for danger all the while.

I'm glad he stayed, too. It's kinda nice having someone new to talk to. Sure, he can't understand anything I'm saying, but I don't let that stop me. I tell Aki about my dad, the Hollows' basement and our life on Bluehaven. I tell him how Winifred Robin smacked me in the head with her shotgun. How Atlas tried to sacrifice me on the Sacred Stairs. I tell him about the secret Manor gateway below the Museum of Otherworldly Antiquities, and how Hickory found me in the snow. I give him a blow-by-blow account of everything we've been through, and he listens to it all, towering beside me like a gray, smelly beanstalk, rattling his throat now and then, blinking his black, beady eyes.

I wonder how old he is, why he fled Roth's army, how he got his scars. Does he have a home? Will he go there once he figures the debt's been repaid? Does he have a family?

"Tell you what, Aki," I say, "I could murder a coconut right now. You ever tried a coconut before? They got coconuts in Arakaan?" He blinks at me again. "No? Well—"

A sniff behind us. A throaty goober-hock. The sound of spittle striking stone.

"Do you ever stop talking?" Hickory's awake, heavy-eyed and stooped, swaying in his saddle. The effects of the healers' oils have worn off at last. "Serious question."

"We're bonding," I say.

"Bond more quietly. My head's killing me." He squints around at the cliffs. "So we're on our way to this canyon city, huh? To get the second key."

"Yep."

"And I'm still here. I told you to leave me behind."

I shrug. "And I told you we need your help."

Hickory tugs at his loincloth. "You could've packed more clothes, at least."

"We didn't have time to pack," I say, and turn my attention back to Violet and Elsa. I feel like marching up there, butting into their conversation. *Hi there, lovely morning. DON'T YOU KNOW IT'S RUDE TO IGNORE PEOPLE?* "By the way, I talked to Elsa last night."

"Good for you," Hickory says.

I tug on Scab's reins. Amazingly enough, he obeys. Stops walking till Hickory's horse is plodding by our side. Aki watches us carefully. "She didn't mean to throw you in the pit. I mean, okay, she did, but only because she thought you were still working for Roth. There's this law here, see—"

"I don't care."

"—but I straightened it all out. The nomads won't hurt you again. We can trust her."

"There you go again. *We.*" Hickory nods at Elsa. "She doesn't know where it is, does she? The Cradle. The Manor shifted it."

142

I sigh. No point in lying. "We know the path ends right near some kind of spike pit, but I'm guessing they're as common as the creepy, self-lighting Manor candles. As for where the path to the Cradle starts, or how we're supposed to find it? We don't have a clue."

"Huh," Hickory says. "How unfortunate."

"Did you ever see any spike pits inside the Manor?"

Hickory nods. "Like you said, they're everywhere."

"But did you see any that looked suspicious?"

"They're spike pits, Jane. Looking suspicious is kinda their thing."

"But did you see—"

"One with a signpost saying *Cradle of All Worlds that-a-way* above it? No." He points down at me. "No more questions. I told you last night—"

"You're done. I remember." I slap his hand away. "But I still don't buy it."

"Why not?"

"Because you're you."

Hickory snickers at this. Brushes it off with a shake of his head.

We round a bend and pass under an impossibly huge spine and broken rib cage wedged between the upper reaches of the cliffs. The skeleton of some Arakaanian beast. The bones look like they've turned to stone. Violet and Elsa glance back at us. I figure they're about to ask me to join them, but they turn back to the road without so much as a blink.

"What's your plan, then?" Hickory asks me at last,

staring up at the skeleton. "Sneak into Roth's gateway, somehow bypass his troops without being seen, and start wandering through the Manor from spike pit to spike pit till you find the right one?"

"Something like that," I say. "We're still working out the details."

"He's gonna catch you."

"Roth has no idea we're out here—no idea we'll be sneaking in through the back door. Maybe he even sent his troops deep into the Manor to find us. The dune sea gateway could be unguarded, the corridors and chambers beyond it deserted. We don't know. Even if the gateway *is* guarded, we still have to try. The Manor binds the Otherworlds together—"

"Oh, here we go."

"They'd fall into chaos without it."

"So your dear ol' dad says." Hickory arches an eyebrow. "Wait, are you still calling him that?" I glare at him. He shrugs. "Just checking, given recent revelations. Point is, it's a lie. A bedtime story told by people to justify the Manor's existence and their own thirst for adventure. The Manor doesn't bind anything. You know what I reckon'll happen if it's destroyed? Nothing. The worlds'll keep on spinning, just like they always have. Difference is, nobody'll have to worry about Otherworldly armies anymore."

"We're not having this conversation, Hickory."

"Really? Sure sounds like we are."

"Keep your voice down." I glance at Elsa and Violet. "Look, even if you are right—which you're not—the

Manor's still important. There's this library on Bluehaven, filled with thousands of books written by people who've journeyed to the Otherworlds. All those stories, all those adventures . . . the townsfolk must've saved billions of lives over the years."

"So let heroes rise in the Otherworlds. Let 'em take care of their own backyards."

"And if you're wrong?" Again, I see all those Otherworlds decimated by the Cradle Sea. The townsfolk of Bluehaven screaming and dying. "If the Manor really does bind them all?"

"Then chaos'll reign, the worlds'll spin out of control, and life as we know it will cease to exist. But I'm not wrong. And if you'd seen half the things I've seen in there, you'd agree. The Manor isn't some hallowed space. It shouldn't be worshipped or saved. It's hell, and it should've been destroyed a long time ago." Hickory shrugs. "But, like I said, it's over. Roth's never gonna let that happen now. We've lost."

"We haven't lost. We're still here. We're still fighting."

"And you always will be, Jane, as long as the Manor's around."

"What do you mean?"

"I mean, there'll always be a Roth. Someone who wants to conquer and kill. You defeat him, someone else is gonna make a move on the Cradle. Maybe not today, maybe not tomorrow, but eventually, and they'll always come for *you*. The Manor's never gonna let you go. Never gonna let you walk away. You should tap out now, while you can."

"And do what? Crawl under a rock somewhere? Hide forever? I've lived in the shadows my whole life, Hickory. I can't go back to that. I won't. If someone else comes for me, I guess . . . well, I'll just have to fight them, too."

Hickory sighs. "You're a fool."

"Rather be a fool than a coward."

He snickers again. "I'm many things, Doe. Cowardly ain't one of 'em."

"Really?" I say. "Tell me, then, o brave one, who's Farrow?" The name works like a charm. Hickory clenches his jaw. Grips his reins white-knuckle tight. "She was your girlfriend back on Bluehaven, right? The Manor took you away from her."

"Don't you ever say that name again."

"Which name? Farrow?"

"I mean it, Doe."

"You were singing about her in the forest. That's the real reason you hate the Manor so much. Why you wanted to tear it down. You don't care about the Otherworlds. You just wanted revenge. Well, I'm sorry you lost her, but if she were still alive, she'd be ashamed." I poke Hickory's leg. "Actually, if she were here, I bet Farrow would—"

Hickory lashes out to grab me, but Aki snatches his arm, quick as a toad's tongue.

"—slap you," I finish. We all stop walking. Aki tightens his grip and snarls, nearly yanks Hickory out of his saddle. I stand my ground, lean in a little closer. "Guess you're not so brave after all, huh? Poor old Hickory, scared of a simple name."

"All good back there?" Elsa calls out. They've stopped walking, too. Violet's got her Boboki blade at the ready.

"Couldn't be better," I reply.

I nod at Aki. He lets go. Hickory sits up in his saddle, rubbing his arm. There's no snappy comeback, no death-glare. He looks genuinely hurt, and not from his wrist. This is a different kind of wound. Deep. Old. Invisible. But he isn't the only one with battle scars.

I give Scab's reins a gentle tug and walk on with Aki.

THE CANYON OF THE DEAD

The road narrows. The cliffs close in. A faint, hot breeze growls around us. Pebbles clatter, nudged by the darkling beetles as they scurry out of sight—pudgy, black, walnut-sized things. We ride in silence. Violet's back in the saddle behind me. Aki's the only one on foot, walking faithfully by our side.

Hickory's brooding behind us, deep in thought, and no wonder. How many years has it been since he heard someone say Farrow's name? The secret's out. He loved someone, once. Loved them so much he'd risk the ruin of all worlds to get revenge, just like Roth.

Must be a scary thing, knowing you have something in common with your enemy.

"We heard him say the Manor should be destroyed," Violet mutters after a while.

"He was just trying to get under my skin," I say, trying—and failing—to keep the heat from my voice. "Same old, same old." Ahead of us, Elsa pulls another bottle from her saddlebag, takes a swig and sneaks it under her cloak.

"Well, I think it threw Elsa, overhearing that," Violet says. "She went quiet for a bit. But I think she's okay now. She told me everything she told you last night. About Roth and the arrowhead."

"The Immortal War?"

"Yep."

"And Hali-gabera?"

"Jane—

"And Elsa's journey to Atol Na?"

"I said everything."

"Right," I say. "Sorry."

A brief pause. I don't want to ask this, but I have to. "Are we okay?"

Violet exhales. I feel her breath brush past my neck. "I'm sorry I overreacted when you got back. It's just . . . when I woke up and saw you weren't there, I thought the Boboki had thrown you from the balcony. I panicked. But I get it now. You had to do what you had to do, and it worked. You got Elsa to open up. Besides, it's good you weren't in the room when the Boboki attacked. Who knows what could've happened if you were?"

Aki scoops a bunch of darklings from the path and gobbles them down. Offers me a couple, too. "I'm good," I say, staring at a glob of beetle-gunk oozing down his chin.

"I'm sorry I tried to force you to cause a quake at the Pass, too" Violet says. "Elsa said I should go easy on you, and she's right. I just want to say, though: I know you're scared, but you can't hold back forever. You will have to use your powers again—soon, probably."

"Yeah," I sigh. "I know."

"But I won't force you. I promise. We all have our roles to play here. You're the hero. I'm the sidekick. It's my job to help and protect you. Nothing more, nothing less. That's what Winifred trained me to do, so that's what I'll do."

I hate hearing her talk like this. Laughable is what it is. There's no way I would've made it this far without her. If *she* were the third key, I bet we'd be kicking back on Blue-haven by now, sipping from a couple of coconuts. Side-kick? Uh-uh. She's more than that.

So much more.

"Violet—"

"Hard to imagine, isn't it?" she says, moving the conversation along. "Roth. With Neela. Living in peace. No mask, no army, no rotting stench. To be honest, I feel sorry for him. Not the Roth we know, but the man before the mask. The man who had to watch the woman he loves get shot through the heart. And those bone shards in his lungs . . ." She shudders.

I wish I could agree with her, but I don't. Roth took my dad. He doesn't deserve my pity.

"Mostly, I feel sorry for Neela," Violet continues. "She must've really loved Roth to take his place in the Cull. Imagine if she saw what he's become. If she knew what he's done."

"Yeah," I say, glancing back at Hickory, "imagine."

He's feigning disinterest, but I can tell he's listening in. Must be killing him, hearing snippets of Roth's past. I bet he's dying to ask us about him—he's known the guy longer than any of us, after all—but he's too proud.

"Don't suppose any of it matters now," Violet says. "Neela's long gone, and so is the man she loved. He died when the queen buried him. A monster rose from the tomb."

"And destroyed the only weapons that can stop him."

Violet shifts in the saddle. "I don't think we'd be here if that were true. A Dahaari weapon survived. I'm sure of it."

"But Elsa looked. For years. She didn't find anything."

"That doesn't mean there isn't one out there somewhere. I want to talk to this Masaru guy. I'm sure there's something they missed—something we're all missing."

I sigh. Violet isn't gonna give up. Not now, not ever. "Fine."

The path slopes downward, steeper and steeper, the cliffs so close we can touch them. I grip the saddle to stop myself from sliding onto Scab's neck. The warm breeze growls again.

"We're close," Elsa calls out. "Right on time."

"Time for what?" Violet asks.

"Noon. Only time we can cross the canyon. The suns clear the path."

"Clear the path of what?"

We round a super tight bend, the canyon walls open out, and we stop at the edge of a short drop-off, staring open-mouthed at the view before us.

"You've gotta be kidding me," Hickory mutters.

Elsa holds up her arms. "Welcome"—she hiccups—"to the Canyon of the Dead."

A thin path flanked by towering pillars of stone. Sheer cliffs riddled with thousands of holes, like honeycomb or holey cheese or the rotting gateways inside the Manor. But there are no gateways here. These are the ancient-beyond-ancient tombs, and they're deep and dark and *everywhere*, even way up near the clifftops. It's a stunning sight, but creepy, too. Almost as creepy as the—

"Scorpions?" Violet grabs my arm. "Nobody said anything about scorpions!"

They're scurrying over every inch of the path, crawling over every rock, flicking their black pincers at the hapless darkling beetles and feasting on them. A few are clustered nearby, fighting over the corpse of a bird. The whole canyon's overrun, the air alive with the constant *tick-tick-tick* of their legs and claws.

"Didn't I tell you?" Elsa says. "I'm sure I told you."

"Are they poisonous? Like, on a scale of one to ten—"

"Fifteen."

"*Fifteen?*"

"Maybe twenty."

"Oh no."

I can't believe what I'm hearing. "Violet, are you . . . scorpi-phobic?"

"That isn't even a word. And no, I'm not."

"You're shaking." I twist around in the saddle to look at her. "You can run along train-tops without blinking, but you're terrified of a few bugs?"

"They aren't *bugs*. I read all about them in one of Winifred's books. They're complex, deadly organisms, and in case you hadn't noticed there's a million of them."

"Not for long," Elsa says. "Watch."

The light slowly leaches down the southern clifftop as the suns near high noon. The scorpions up there scuttle back to the tombs like ants fleeing a storm. The darkling beetles remain, free to go about their buggy business till both suns pass overhead and the scorpions return to feast again.

"How long will we have once the path clears?" I ask.

"Two hours," Elsa says, "give or take. Plenty of time."

Minute by minute, the sunlight creeps down the cliff-face, slowly filling the canyon. We share our waterskins with the horses while we wait. Elsa passes around some flatbread and dried berries from her saddlebag. Violet nibbles on the berries one at a time, wide eyes fixed on the scorpions. Hickory plays with a sliver of flatbread. I wonder if he's eaten since we came to Arakaan. Elsa's watching him, too.

"Eat," she tells him. "You need your strength."

Hickory stares at her. Pops the bread into his mouth and chews. "Happy?"

Elsa smiles, but her eyes are still probing. She bites the head off a darkling beetle, spits it out, and—to Aki's apparent delight—tosses the rest into her gob, still-wriggling legs and all. "Ecstatic," she says, and swallows.

"Hey, hey, hey," Violet says. "Get ready . . ."

The first sun creeps into view, bathing us all in direct

light. We don our goggles to cut the glare as the sun clears the canyon path of scorpions. They scurry into every crack and tomb, but that *tick-tick-tick* remains, muted, as if a million angry clocks are hiding in the shadows.

"Let's go," I say.

Violet groans.

CHOSEN FAMILY

As if the canyon wasn't creepy enough, Elsa decides to hum a slow, eerie tune to pass the time. Aki plods along behind her, snatching up and gobbling down every darkling beetle he can. The canyon floor's littered with bones. Taw-taw carcasses, for the most part. I hope.

The first sun blasts us. Hickory throws a blanket over his bare head and shoulders to block out the sky. I scan the cliffs from tomb to tomb, both hoping for and dreading the sight of a coffin or a mummified corpse.

The scorpions *tick-tick-tick* in the dark.

"Do not fear death," Violet whispers behind me. I can feel her breath on my neck again, soft as a kitten's paw. "The dead have their secrets, but they're at peace."

I'm sure I've heard this somewhere before. After a moment I remember. The catacombs, back on Bluehaven. A certain scarred, red-cloaked adventurer.

"Winifred said that to me once."

"Not surprised," Violet says. "She said it so often it was like she was trying to convince herself."

"You reckon Winifred's afraid of the dead?"

"No. But maybe she's afraid of dying."

"Seems unlike her," I say. "She put herself in danger all the time, didn't she? Entered the Manor more times than anyone. I kinda figured she was fearless."

"Everyone's scared of something," Violet says.

Tick-tick-tick.

"You must miss her," I say, to take her mind off the scorpions. "You spent as much time living with Winifred in the Museum as you did at home with . . . you know—"

"My parents," she says. "You don't have to talk around them, Jane."

"I just wasn't sure if—I mean, I know things turned bad after I left."

"*Turned* bad?" Violet scoffs. "Things were always bad. They just got worse." She taps my shoulder. "Hey, what did you used to call them? The praying mantis and the—"

"Weasel," I say. "Sorry."

"Don't be. They deserved a lot worse for everything they did to you. Growing up in that house . . . I'm not saying I copped it as bad as you, but it wasn't exactly a loving environment."

"They were just trying to protect you."

"No," Violet says. "I think I scared them as much as you did sometimes."

"At least they're your actual parents, though, right?"

"*Pfft.*" There's her breath again, brushing past my neck. "You think that matters? There's more to family than blood, Jane. You have a stronger bond with John than I'll

156

ever have with my parents, and he's basically been a vegetable your entire life. No offense."

"None taken."

"You love him and he loves you, and that makes you family. Winifred and the others are my family—my chosen family. They gave you a hard time back in the day, sure, and maybe people like Atlas and Eric Junior and my parents haven't changed, but the ones on our side? They're good people."

A chosen family. I kinda like the sound of that.

"Truth is, I'm worried about them," Violet says. "You left the island six years ago, Bluehaven time, yet only a few days went by for you inside the Manor. Who knows how much time has passed back there since I left? Winifred's an old woman. Maybe she's already had to face her fear. Maybe they all had to. Food was scarce when I left. What if . . . what if—"

"They're alive, Violet," I say.

"But how do you *know*?"

"Because, I . . . I saw them. In a dream last night. Sure, they were all running for their lives because the Cradle Sea swept across the island, and they all died in the end, but they were very much alive to begin with. It felt so real. And Winifred was there. Stood her ground right to the end."

"Back up," Violet says. "You saw the Sea unleashed?"

I take a deep breath. It's time to come clean. "First, the Specters Gripped me. Because they know I'm gonna fail, and that makes me a threat. And then . . . I did fail.

In the nightmare, I was on the foundation stone and the power got away from me because I—I *felt* . . ." I can't say it. Can't tell her about the void in my chest. That I knew she was dead, along with Dad. "The Sea wiped out the Otherworlds, Violet. What if it was a vision of things to come?"

She rests a hand on my shoulder. Her head on the back of mine. For a split second, I'm sure—I *hope*—she's gonna hug me, and my fears are driven away by that warm, fuzzy-buzzy light. It's so overwhelming I wonder if the others can see it radiating through my pores.

Jane Doe, the third Arakaanian sun.

"We won't let it happen, Jane," she says. "Any of it."

Unfortunately, that's when Hickory yells, "Hey, are we almost there yet?" and Elsa shouts back, "We'll get there when we get there," and hiccups so loudly it echoes through the canyon.

Really kills the mood.

Violet lets go of my shoulder, leans back in the saddle. "Look."

The first sun disappears behind the southern cliffs—*tick-tick-tick*—but the second's already shining in the north. I adjust my goggles and scan the clifftops ahead. The canyon disappears around a distant bend. Elsa starts to sing drunkenly, veering her horse left and right across the path, verging way too close to the tombs.

I frown. "'By the way, did Elsa tell you about Betty?"

"Yep," Violet says. "I can't believe we get to fly in an actual plane."

"Hmm. You'll probably get to die in one, too."

"You don't reckon Elsa can do it?"

"I'm sure she could've, once upon a time. Now?" Down the path, Elsa burps, chuckles and tosses her empty bottle into a tomb. "I'm not so sure."

"She'll be fine. I bet flying a plane's like making a slow-burning fuse. Once you know how, you never forget." Violet twists in the saddle. "Think he'll join us?"

Aki's behind us now, still stuffing his face with darklings. I actually want him to stick around. He's strong. Fast. Like Elsa said, he'll blend in at the dune sea gateway. But surely the life debt can only stretch so far. I can't ask him to risk his life. Besides, we still have no idea why he fled Roth's army. He could have a bigger target on his back than mine. Doubtful, but you never know.

"I wonder if he has any idea who we are," Violet says. "What we're doing."

Aki offers a darkling to Hickory, who refuses with a blunt "Go away." Aki takes the hint, eats the beetle and grins at us, slimy crooked teeth and all. I can't help but smile back.

"I think he's just happy to be here," I say.

"Look!" Elsa cries out, pointing at the sky.

I picture the worst—Boboki raiders, a pack of Tawtaws watching us from the clifftops—but it's just a bright red bird flying through the canyon. Shielding our eyes against the sun, we watch it glide and soar, trilling a beautiful song. It swoops down, then flies higher and higher till it's just a red dot disappearing beyond the cliffs.

Elsa was right. There is beauty in this world. And it's worth saving.

But suddenly Aki rattles his throat, stops walking. Snarls as five more birds fly overhead. No, a dozen more—two dozen—a whole flock of them. And their singing doesn't seem peaceful anymore. They're panicked, fleeing something bad.

A hot gust of wind sweeps through the canyon. Dust swirls. The scorpions *tick-tick-tick* from the shadows. The darkling beetles scatter. Slowly, we look back the way we've come.

"No," I mutter. "Not now . . ."

A huge dirty cloud's blooming in the east, towering over the mountains, swallowing the jagged peaks.

Another sandstorm's on its way.

"Asmadin isn't far," Elsa shouts. "Ride. Now!"

THE SECOND STORM

Elsa leads the charge, cloak flapping wildly as she gallops down the path. The sandstorm's gaining on us, sweeping through the canyon, strangely silent beyond the thunder of the horses' hooves and the roar of the wind in my ears. Scab's gone into furry firecracker mode again. Violet's holding me tight. Hickory's riding beside us, his blanket gone, focused in a way I haven't seen since the Manor. Aki's in last place, pumping his long legs as fast as he can but falling way behind.

"He isn't gonna make it," I shout to Violet. "We can't leave him!"

"We don't have a choice," she screams back. "Look up!"

The upper reaches of the storm are arcing across the sky: a colossal wave breaking well ahead of the wall of sand. The suns'll be shrouded any second.

"Seriously, this world is the *worst*," I shout.

The canyon's plunged into shadow. The scorpions emerge from the tombs, tricked by the premature twilight. They crawl down the cliffs all around us, feasting on the darklings again. Scab tries to dodge the black clumps of stingers and claws, but the path's quickly overrun. He ploughs through them, kicking up his back legs, nearly bucking us off. Violet tightens her grip around my waist, buries her face in my neck, and screams. Hickory bellows behind us, swatting at the scorpions flung into the air. Aki's already vanished in the storm.

"Jane," Violet screams, "watch it!"

We duck under a low-hanging arch of rock just in time.

A gust of wind slams us. Dust-devils coil from the canyon floor. Before Elsa vanishes in the burnt-orange haze ahead, she points at a bend in the canyon. A path zigzagging up the northern cliffs. There's a tunnel in the middle, bigger than the tombs.

"Up there," I shout to Violet. "That must be the way to Asmadin!"

But it's too late.

The storm swallows us, belching sand and scree. Rocks whistle through the air. Scorpions fly into our faces, cling to our clothes. We cough and choke. Even with my goggles, I can barely see a thing. Scab veers right, galloping blind. We slam into Hickory. He swears at us and we swear back, racing next to each other up the cliffside path, which sure ain't wide enough for two. A chunk of the path breaks away. Scab leaps clear just in time. I pull on the reins and let Hickory draw ahead, and it's only now I realize Violet's got a new ride.

She's clinging to Hickory's back now—was thrown from horse to horse when we collided. They jack-knife to the right, a switchback in the path. Up we go, zig-by-zag, blasted by the winds. I'm covered in so many scorpions it's like they're sprouting from my skin. I can feel one crawling up my neck, taking shelter in my hair.

Through the driving sheets of sand, I see Elsa, Hickory, and Violet bolt inside the tunnel. Before I know it, Scab and I have made it, too. I rip off my goggles and dismount like the others, spitting sand and swiping the scorpions away. Hickory yanks one from his loincloth. Elsa flaps her cloak. Violet claws at her body, dancing up and down on the spot, near tears. I shake the scorpion from my hair and stomp every single one I can find. We clear the horses, too. Try to calm them down. Scab blinks sand from his big dopey eyes, nostrils flaring.

The tunnel's long and dim, the entrance capped by an open wooden door. Elsa and I both grab it.

"Not yet," I shout. "Aki's still out there!"

The storm rages on. Great swirls of sand blow through the door and down the tunnel, lashing the flames of the torches lining the walls, nearly blowing them out.

"Come on," I whisper.

Just when I think we've lost Aki for good, a tall, slender shadow appears in the haze, and he bursts inside. I help Elsa slam the door shut and slide a beam of wood in place to lock it. The storm howls. The door rattles. The torches in the tunnel burn a little brighter. There are alcoves spaced evenly down each wall, I realize now. A tall statue standing in each one.

Elsa leans against the door, head bowed, catching her breath. "We made it."

"Could I get some actual clothes now?" Hickory says. "Please?"

"Shut up, Hickory." I lean on the door, too, relief flushing through my veins. We did it. We're safe. Beyond this tunnel lies Asmadin, the Elders, Betty, and the second key. Everything we need to get back to the Manor. Everything we need to stop Roth and save the Otherworlds. Everything we need to save my dad. "You okay?" I ask Aki.

He looks me up and down. Rattles his throat, plucks a stray scorpion from my hair and pops it into his mouth. The Gorani must be immune to their stings. He's covered in them.

"Well, you're just full of surprises, huh?"

He grins at me, a scorpion leg wriggling between his teeth.

Elsa leans in close. She reeks of booze, but the sandstorm seems to have sobered her up. "It's just a short walk to the city. Stay sharp. We're not out of trouble yet."

Of course we're not.

"No guards," Elsa notes, staring down the tunnel. "There's usually three, at least."

"Um, Jane?" Violet's gaping at the statues in disbelief.

"What's wrong?" Hickory asks her. "You look like you've seen a ghost."

"That's Hali-gabera," Elsa says, striding back to Rex, yanking her crossbow from her saddle. "The founder of Asmadin. She's worshipped like a god around here."

The statues stand like sentries between each of the torches. I take a closer look at one—and freeze. It's ancient, but remarkably well preserved. The craftsmanship's incredible, the details unmistakable. The face. The scars. The flowing, stone-carved cloak.

"Impossible," I gasp.

We're surrounded by statues of Winifred Robin.

THIRD INTERLUDE

THE ONE THAT GOT AWAY

Have they reached the city yet? Have they claimed the second key? These are some of the questions Winifred asks herself as she sits in her study, staring at the painting of Asmadin hanging on the wall beside her cabinet. The canyon riddled with caves. How many years ago did she lead Jane down the stairwell behind this painting, to the catacombs and the secret second Manor gateway? Nine years? Ten? Yes, a whole decade, almost to the day, which means roughly four years have passed since she sent Violet into the Manor to help her. But only a few days will have passed for them. May the Makers protect them both.

Winifred pours herself a drink, sits back, and sighs. Outside, the sun will be setting, the farmers returning from their terraced fields with little food, the fisherfolk docking their boats, stacked with empty baskets yet again. Their world is dying, but they still have time.

A knock on the door. Mayor Atlas steps into the study. He is still a big man, square-jawed and strong, but he doesn't walk as tall as he once did. He has more wrinkles now, too: deep frown lines exaggerated by the lamplight.

"A word, if I may."

"Just one?" Winifred flashes him a crooked but kindly smile. Gestures to the seat across from her. "You may have as many words as you like, my friend."

Atlas prefers to stand. After all these years, he is still not comfortable around Winifred. She knows too much, has *seen* too much. He is certain there are secrets she has not shared.

"I'll get straight to the point," he says. "There's chatter among the townsfolk. Talk of abandoning the island, setting sail to the Dying Lands. The lands of our ancestors."

Winifred pours Atlas a drink. "They believe they'll be safe there?"

"They believe they'll have a chance."

"We cannot outrun this, Eric. No corner of this world or any other will be safe if Roth claims the Cradle. We must fulfil our duty and fight. Face the calamity head on." She nods at the second glass she's just filled. "Come. You've nothing to fear from me."

"It's not you I'm scared of," Atlas says. They both know this is not entirely true. Nevertheless, he takes a seat and downs the glass's contents in one gulp. "Tell me again."

"Eric—"

"I want to hear it. What is it about this man?"

"He is no man," Winifred says. "I have been tested many times on my adventures through the Manor, Eric, but never before have I faced someone so ruthless, so cruel. Most villains are driven by some twisted moral code, but Roth?" She shakes her head. Can still feel his hands around her neck, his rancid breath on her skin, his eyes probing hers, invading her every thought. She was lucky to survive that day on the cliffs of Kalanthoon. "He is driven by something much darker."

"Like what?" Atlas asks.

"Hunger," Winifred says. "Pain. Pure, malicious rage."

"You're afraid of him. Still."

"I'd be a fool not to fear Roth. Worse than that, though, I'm ashamed. Ashamed I survived when so many died. Ashamed I abandoned the very people I'd sworn to protect."

"Abandoned? If I remember the story correctly, you saved tens of thousands of lives. You left because you knew they would never be safe if you stayed."

"And that is my greatest shame of all. Roth learned that the legend of the Otherworlds was true through *me*. I fled to draw him away from Asmadin, yes, but in doing so, I led him to the Manor itself." Winifred stares into her glass. "This is all my fault."

Atlas scans the objects in Winifred's cabinet. Weapons. Vases. Books. Old, Otherworldly globes. At last, he understands. "That's what drove you back to the Manor so many times. You wanted to return to Arakaan. To face him again. Finish what you'd started."

Winifred nods. "Unfortunately, the Manor always led me somewhere new."

"So you saved more lives. Millions, by my reckoning."

Winifred smiles. "Who would've thought it? Eric Atlas consoling Winifred Robin."

"Desperate times." Atlas smiles, too, but only for a moment. "I have to tell the people something or we'll have a full-scale revolt on our hands. How long do we have?"

"Not long," Winifred says. "The die is cast."

"And your plan? Are you sure you want to go through with it?"

"I told you. Nabu-kai set us on this path. We cannot stray from it now."

Atlas grunts. "Are you sure the girls are up to the task?"

Winifred chuckles at this. "I assure you, Jane and Violet are more than capable." Her smile fades. "It's the boy I'm concerned about—if one can call him a boy. Technically, he's older than every ancient tome in the Great Library."

Here it is, then, Atlas thinks. *This is what Winifred has been hiding. A flaw in the plan.* "Hickory Dawes? *He* could be our undoing?"

Winifred swirls the liquid in her glass. "There was one moment when I touched Nabu-kai's symbol—one flash, one image—that was a little . . . blurred. Unstable. Perhaps it is nothing, but I've never been able to shake the feeling that this image, that particular moment, could change."

"Why? How?"

"Grief is a powerful force, Eric. You know that as well as I. Perhaps as powerful as love. After all, one cannot exist without the other."

Atlas frowns. "What are you saying?"

"I'm saying, Eric, that Hickory will have to make a choice, and if he makes the wrong one—if he falters when the time comes—then, well, let us say all bets are off."

"So what now, then?" Atlas asks. "The troops are ready and waiting."

Winifred downs the last of her drink. "Run the drill again. We march in three days."

PART
FIVE

THE PILLARS OF ASMADIN

Winifred Robin is Hali-gabera. Hali-gabera is Winifred Robin. She was here, in Arakaan, centuries ago, before Dad and Elsa stumbled through the dune sea gateway, before Roth invaded the Manor, before I was taken from the Cradle. *She* swiped away Roth's jaw. *She* led the mortals of Arakaan across the sands and founded Asmadin. *She* is the legend of old.

This changes everything.

"Why can't we tell them?" I whisper to Violet. "They have a right to know."

We're marching down the tunnel, keeping our distance from Elsa. Thankfully, she's too worried about the lack of guards to notice: eyes forward, crossbow at the ready. Aki's leading the three horses down back. Hickory's frowning at the statues. He knows something's up.

"They'll never believe us, Jane," Violet says. "We have no proof. And the Arakaanians worship her. They believe she died protecting them. What do you think they'll do if we tell them she's been living in an Otherworld?" She shakes her head. "We need to keep this to ourselves. For now. At least until we get the second key and figure out what all this means."

"It *means* she lied to us."

"She didn't lie. She withheld certain truths."

"That's called lying, Violet." The statues look so real. It's like Winifred's here, glaring at us, judging us. Younger than the Winifred we know, but still scarred and scowling. Brandishing swords and spears. Holding the arrowhead of Atol Na aloft, like a lightning rod. Offering it, like a gift. Swinging it, teeth bared. "How is this even possible?" I ask. "Hali-gabera's buried here in Asmadin. Elsa broke into the tomb. Cracked open her sarcophabus and everything."

"Sarcopha*gus*."

"Yeah, that. She said she saw bones in there."

"They must've faked her death. Winifred and her sidekick. Inigo. Wouldn't have been too difficult. Find some other dead body—maybe a corpse from the Canyon of the Dead—and wrap it up in secret. Inigo lugs it back to town, acts all sad and chucks it in the tomb. Done."

"Why, though?"

"She had to leave. Maybe she didn't want people to think she'd abandoned them. Maybe she was worried people would follow her and get themselves killed."

"And she had to leave because . . ."

"Elsa said Roth got into Hali—I mean, Winifred's—head, when she fought him down south." Violet clicks her fingers. "I bet he saw Bluehaven. That's why he pursued her all the way up here. He'd just had a taste of a different world and he wanted more. Winifred must've known he'd never give up trying to find her, so she fled north, across the dune sea."

I feel like smacking the head off every statue. "Winifred led Roth to the dune sea gateway. But she got away just in time. So he waited there. This is all her fault!"

"Jane—"

"And she didn't tell us. We're cleaning up *her* mess." I'm so angry I'd cause a quake if I weren't so shocked. "How come nobody knows about this? You've read all her books, right? All her entries in the Bluehaven Chronicles? Surely she wrote about this."

"She didn't." Violet shakes her head. "That's what I don't understand. She's been to desert worlds, but she's never mentioned Arakaan or Roth, I'm sure of it. She kept it a secret."

"Like I said. She lied."

"We're close," Elsa calls out. "Quickly now."

There's a spot of light up ahead, faint and hazy. The end of the tunnel.

Violet scans the statues again, nodding to herself. "This is why the Manor brought us all to Arakaan." She leans closer, lowers her voice. "Roth didn't kill Hali-gabera, which means he didn't destroy the arrowhead, either."

"You think it's here?" I look at the statues, too. Even I have to admit, Violet's theory makes sense. For the first time since who knows when, I feel a flicker of hope. "Where?"

"The dead keep their secrets," Violet whispers suddenly.

"You think it's in her tomb?"

"It *has* to be. Winifred worked so hard to save these

people—she wouldn't have wanted to leave them unprotected after she was gone."

"I just told you, Elsa already checked the sarcopha-whatsit."

"Maybe she missed it. Maybe it's hidden in a secret compartment. We won't know till we check it out. Until then, not a word."

"Not a word about what?" Hickory asks, falling in step beside us.

"None of your business," Violet says.

"It's her, isn't it?" Hickory nods at the statues, looks back at me. "The woman who smacked you in the head with a shotgun back on Bluehaven. The woman who had a creepy vision and sent you both into the Manor. Winifred Bobbin—no, Robin."

"How did you—"

'The scars. You told me she had a face full of 'em. Also, I heard most of what you said just now. Honestly, you two whisper so loud—"

"What do you care, anyway?" Violet asks him. "I thought you'd given up."

"I don't care," Hickory says. "And I have."

"Yeah, keep telling yourself that, pal," I say.

"Hey," Elsa whisper-shouts, "I said hurry up."

We gather round the exit: an archway in the side of a sheer cliff. The storm has moved on, but the air's still thick with dust. A wooden rope-bridge disappears into the haze. There isn't a breath of wind. No scorpion *tick-tick-tick*. The city's so quiet I can hear my heartbeat.

"We're going across that?" I frown at the bridge. "What about the horses?"

"They're used to it. But we'll leave 'em for now. Someone'll pick 'em up soon." She tucks the end of her crossbow into her shoulder. "I hope.'"

I take the reins from Aki's hand, tell him the horses have to stay. Violet pats Rex goodbye. I thank Scab for not killing me. True to form, he head-butts me, but it's softer this time, almost tender. "I hate you, too," I tell him, and smile.

The bridge creaks and sways as we cross it. The tunnel disappears behind us. It's like we're walking through a cloud. A network of interconnected ropes emerges from the dust all around us, strung up high and low. Small, tattered crimson flags are knotted along every one of them. Some kind of Arakaanian decoration. Some are decorated with bones—legs, arms and Gorani skulls—the rope tied around them, threaded through empty eye-sockets.

"Um," Hickory says, "is this . . . normal?"

Elsa ignores him, tightens her grip on her crossbow.

A gentle breeze makes the crimson flags shiver, the bones rattle and sway. Gigantic pillars of rock emerge from the haze—dozens of them—each connected by the web of rope. An eerie forest of stone bound in string. Some of the pillars soar above our heads, others poke from the gloom below the bridge like pointed teeth. They're adorned with carvings, too. Dark, empty holes, big and small. Columned alcoves. Decorative swirls. Weathered busts of Winifred Robin.

"Sheesh," I whisper. "She's everywhere."

"Stop," Elsa says, and we freeze. "Listen."

I can't hear a thing except the swaying creak of the bridge. Our own heavy breathing. I realize that's what's bothering Elsa.

"Maybe everyone's still hiding from the storm?"

"Maybe," Elsa says, "but unlikely."

We can see the end of the rope bridge now. It's fixed to another pillar—the biggest one yet. A thin path winds down the side of it, looping round and round, disappearing into the dust. Someone's waiting for us, dead ahead. A hunched figure bent over a walking stick.

Elsa quickly raises her crossbow, wobbling the bridge. "*Kala du napa!*"

A faint cackle. A rattle of beads. "*Nimbu tala,*" a croaky voice says. "Welcome."

Elsa doesn't move. "Masaru, where is everyone? The gate was unguarded."

"*Oda min,*" the old man coos. "Always so wary." He shuffles aside with another tiny cackle. "You are home, and all is well. Come, come. Let me see her."

"Oh, this guy isn't creepy at all,'" Hickory mutters.

Elsa lowers her crossbow. Looks wary, confused. Tries to hide it with a smile. "It's okay. We're okay." She holds out a hand. "Jane . . ."

Aki rattles his throat. Violet says, "Be careful."

I flash them a forced smile. "You heard her. I'll be fine."

Elsa leads me across the bridge. We step onto the pillar's stone landing, and I'm not exactly sure what I'm feeling, but it ain't a sense of calm.

Masaru's *ancient*: bald, wrinkly, and small. Bones dangle from his earlobes. The whites of his eyes are yellow. Pouches sag beneath them, big enough to smuggle baby birds, and his skin's so pale it's almost translucent. He's dressed in a cloak that might've been red once, just like Winifred's.

"Gods, am I glad to see you, *oda mun*," Elsa says with a short bow.

"And I you," the old man says, but his watery eyes are fixed on me. "Oh, yes . . ."

He hobbles over, shoulders bent, feet shuffling, circling me like a dog sniffing a tree. He sucks on his splintery teeth as he pokes my back, legs, and shoulders with his walking stick. When he reaches for my bandaged hand, I pull it away. Elsa shoots me a warning look.

Back on the rope-bridge, Violet pulls out her Boboki blade. Aki snarls. Hickory yawns.

"It's okay," I tell them, and hold out my hand.

Masaru prods the dirty bandage. Squeezes the wound, hard. I wince and yank it back, shocked. Masaru doesn't seem to care. Just stares at my eyes, *into* my eyes, and takes another step toward me, uncomfortably close. He smells sickly sweet, like honey.

"What is this?" Violet shouts. "Elsa, what's he doing?"

Elsa shushes her, though she looks a little bothered, too. She nods at me.

"Oh," I say, and take a step back. I figure she wants me to introduce everyone. "Masaru of Arakaan. I'm Jane Doe of . . . well, Bluehaven, I guess." I gesture at the others. "These are my friends, Violet Hollow, Hickory Dawes, and Aki, uh, Gorani? Don't worry, he's on our side." Masaru doesn't glance at them. Doesn't even blink. What is he waiting for? What else am I supposed to say? "Um, we come in peace!"

"Gods have mercy," Elsa mutters.

"Too much?"

"Just . . . stop." She shoves me aside, takes the Cradle key from around her neck. "We've got it, Masaru. All three Cradle keys are—"

"Show me," he says, holding out a bony hand.

Elsa blinks at him, startled, but hands it over. He inspects the key closely, muttering things under his breath. He has a fake key of his own, I notice, dangling from a thin chain around his neck, along with a dozen other necklaces bearing feathers, beads, and bird skulls. A plain clay medallion dangles from one of them. A palm-sized disc.

"It's the real deal," I tell him, nodding at the key. "I promise."

Masaru grins at me, another cackle quivering his bony chest.

"What's so funny?" I ask. "Elsa . . . ?"

"*Oda mun,*" Elsa says. Seems she doesn't get the joke either. "You're acting very strangely. We've come a long way, and I have so much to tell you. Yaku betrayed us. The Boboki attacked Orin-kin. We got away, but I fear they're not far behind us."

"Betrayal," Masaru croaks. He turns to Elsa at last. "I know a thing or two about that myself, *oda min.* Yes, yes, yes."

Elsa shifts on her feet. "I'm sorry, *oda mun*, I—I don't understand."

Masaru *tut-tuts* her. "*Té na casai*, Elsa. No more games."

The breeze blows again—stronger this time—swirling the cloud of dust till the suns peek through and the canyon city's revealed in all its dreadful glory. The towering, honeycombed cliffs. The long drop beneath us. All those dark, empty hidey-holes in the pillars, which aren't so empty after all. There are people crouched inside them, perched like birds of prey. A hundred-odd red-cloaked soldiers with rifles and machetes, bows and arrows, all of them drawn and pointed our way.

"Come, come,'" Masaru says. "The council is waiting."

THE SECOND KEY

The march to the canyon floor passes by in a daze. The sandy, spiraled path looping round the pillar. The swarm of red-cloaked soldiers following as we go, swinging from the ropes, climbing down, tracking our every step. The archers crouched on every ledge, arrows nocked and ready to fire. The sweat. The dread. Definitely not the welcome we were expecting.

No more games. What did Masaru mean?

Elsa ignored him. Played it cool when he instructed us to hand over our weapons. Violet objected, of course. Elsa told her to obey. Now she's gabbing at Masaru in Arakaanian, talking a million miles an hour, no doubt telling him the details Yaku's deception and the attack on Orin-kin. "The Boboki are coming for her, Masaru," she adds so we can understand. "We have no time to waste."

"*Dai dai, oda min,*" he says, clucking his tongue. "Always in a rush."

Elsa glances back at me, visibly shaken by his lackluster response. Tries to cover it with a smile. "Apologies, *oda mun,*" she says. "I'm just a little anxious."

"I am sure you are," Masaru says, playing the Cradle key through his fingers.

He should've given it back by now.

By the time we near the bottom, the suns are out in full force. The canyon walls are peppered with columns, caves, and curtained windows. Doors and perilous staircases. Undulating paths crisscross the canyon floor, weaving around the base of the pillars. A fair number of scorpions were blown over the mountain during the sandstorm. A bunch of club-wielding teenagers stand by, ready to squash them. Any ordinary day, I bet they'd make a game of it. Race each other. Right now, they're staring at us, clubs raised. Another classic Jane Doe greeting.

"No way," Violet whispers, gaping down the length of the canyon. "Jane, it's the painting. The one hanging in Winifred's study. Except for the creepy decorations."

"Glad you're enjoying the view, Violet, but I think we have more pressing concerns right now."

The red-cloaks swarm around the base of the pillar, flanking both sides of the path.

"This is all quite unnecessary," Elsa chuckles, but her eyes are a little too wide, too frantic. "We were heading to see the Elders anyway. We don't need this much protection."

"*Udun gór,*" Masaru says. "Perhaps it is not you we are protecting."

Through the procession of red-cloaks we go. Some stare at Aki. Others at me. Anyone'd think they've never seen an avatar of three ancient gods before.

None of this makes sense. These people have sheltered Elsa for decades. They're on our side. So why are they treating us like a bunch of crooks?

Across the canyon floor we go, into the shade of a large cave. More decorations hang from the walls. Knotted flags. Strings of teeth. Threaded skulls. Some of them, I notice now, are human.

"Perhaps a rest first," Elsa suggests, clearly trying to buy us time. "Before we see the council."

"No rest," Masaru says. "We go to the chamber now."

A staircase carved of stone. A sandy cliffside corridor. Open archways and balconies line one side. Intricate tapestries hang from the other: images of Winifred fighting Roth, holding the arrowhead up to the sky, leading people across the desert. I still can't believe she was *here*. In the last tapestry, she's standing on a mound of gray Gorani corpses. Aki snarls at it as we pass by, beady eyes narrowed.

A wooden door opens at the end of the corridor. Most of the red-cloaks stop and stand to attention. The rest march us inside the chamber. There are no balconies here. No windows or other exit, except for some kind of ornate circular seal in the middle of the floor, which could be another trapdoor, I suppose. I make a mental note not to stand on it.

The Elders are on their thrones, red-cloaked and wrinkle-skinned. Five women, five men. A single empty throne in the middle that no doubt belongs to Masaru. A false Cradle key dangles around each of the Elders' necks, but something isn't right. They don't look happy to see us. Don't look relieved. Their eyes are bulging, their foreheads beaded with sweat, and it's no wonder. Their hands have been lashed to the armrests of their thrones—a few of them have been gagged—and they're surrounded by a dozen red-cloaks wielding spears.

The council chamber's under siege.

"Elsa," I say as we're lined up before them, "what's going on?"

Her eyes are fixed on the circular seal. She looks just as frightened as the Elders.

Masaru shuffles over to his throne. The door slams shut behind us. The flaming torches lining the walls crackle and spark. Ten more red-cloaks have lined up behind us, preventing any chance of escape. I can tell Violet's mind is racing, sizing each of them up as she stares over her shoulder. Even Hickory looks mildly concerned. Aki rattles his throat by my side.

"*Kala tum dé nuun*," Masaru croaks with a clap of his hands.

"*Kala tum dé nuun*," the guards chant back.

Masaru gestures at me. "Third key, step forth."

I glance at Violet. She gives a subtle nod, but keeps her eyes fixed on Masaru.

"Go on, Jane," Elsa manages to say.

I step forward, unsure what to say, what to do. The ungagged Elders gasp. Some lean forward to get a better look, straining against the ropes around their wrists.

Masaru calls for order and starts croaking on about a bunch of stuff I can't understand. I mean, the old man could be listing his favorite fruits and vegetables for all I know. The other Elders stare at me with sorry expressions, breathing heavily into their gags. Masaru nods at us, points at us, and shakes his fist at the ceiling, rambling on and on.

"I can't take much more of this," Hickory mutters.

I know how he feels. "Hey," I shout over Masaru. "You about done?"

"Jane," Elsa almost-whispers, "what are you doing?"

"Speeding things along," I mutter, before I raise my voice so everyone can hear. "Listen, Masaru, I *was* gonna thank you for looking after Elsa's key all this time, but you're obviously up to some pretty dark shenanigans here. Don't get me wrong, I'm sure what you're saying is super fascinating and all, but we've had a really big day—a big week, actually—and we can't understand a word you're saying. Get to the point."

Clearly, he wants the keys for himself. I shouldn't be surprised. Should've known there'd be other players in this game, other parties desperate to claim the Cradle. But *why?* Does he want to control the Manor, like Roth, or tear it apart, like Hickory?

"The point?" Masaru says, glaring at me. "You dare command me—"

"I'm not commanding anything. I'm just saying the Manor's dying, a bunch of murderous raiders are headed our way and, quite frankly, I've gotta pee. Hurry up."

Masaru cocks his head at me, looks at the other Elders. I expect him to explode, but he cackles and shakes his head. "I like your spirit, my child," he croaks. "But you needn't worry, no, no. Elsa's plane is being fueled and the runway cleared of sand as we speak." Masaru rubs the clay medallion dangling from his neck. He grins at Elsa, baring his crooked, yellow teeth. "It is time, *oda min*. It took some—how should I put it—convincing? Yes, yes. But my fellow Elders and I have all entered our combinations. Yours is the only one left."

He claps twice. Two guards stomp over to the center of the chamber and stand to attention on either side of the stone seal. There are symbols carved around its edge, I notice now, almost like a clock. It's a giant combination lock: the vault Elsa mentioned in the watchtower.

She walks over, kneels, places both hands on the dial. Masaru watches her carefully, greedily. The two guards unsheathe their blades, and Elsa turns the dial two clicks to the right, pauses for a moment, turns the dial seven clicks to the left, then stops.

"Just so we're clear," she says, hands still fixed to the dial, "you need me, Masaru. Remember that. I'm the only one who can get us to the gateway."

"I am aware, *oda min*," he says. "Just as I am aware of your true intentions. You may have fooled the council, but I have known for many years." He nods at the dial. "Finish it."

Elsa looks up at him. "When did you figure it out?"

The old man sneers at her. "I saw the darkness in you the moment we met, *oda min*, but it was after your journey to Atol Na that I knew you had finally seen it, too. The desert changes people. Reveals many hidden truths. You cannot run from it. I have told you this."

What are they talking about? What intentions? What darkness?

"I shouldn't be surprised," Elsa says. "You are very wise, *old friend* . . ."

One more turn of the dial—*click*—and the chamber starts to rumble. Some kind of mechanism's turning underground. Masaru hops off his throne. Elsa steps back as the ancient seal rises from the floor, driven upward by a stone plinth. The dial on top's spinning slowly of its own accord, separating into a kaleidoscope of stone wedges that split apart and recede, unveiling a shallow stone basin. And in the middle of this basin lies a single brass key.

The second Cradle key, at long last.

The mechanism stops, the stone plinth waist-height. Silence falls upon the chamber. I go to grab the key, but Masaru nabs it first, and holds both Cradle keys up high for the guards to see. "*Yennatai*," he shouts. "*Nu sarro ta bonté luun!*"

"*Yennatai*," the guards chant back. "*Nu sarro ta bonté luun!*"

"What does that mean?" I shout. The guards beat their weapons against their chests and cheer. The Elders shake their heads in defeat. "Hey! What did you just say? Elsa—?"

She's out of it. Staring vacantly at the empty plinth. The spark inside her has been snuffed out.

"*Yennatai* means *victory*," Masaru croaks. "I said the Manor is ours at last."

Theirs? But—

"A new age is about to begin, my child. Hail Roth, conqueror of worlds!"

BETRAYAL

If I had a rupee for every time I've been held at knife-, machete-, and/or gunpoint over the past week I'd be able to buy a whole coconut grove. The crap's really hit the cartwheel now. Elsa's frozen. The red-cloaks have drawn their weapons. Violet and Hickory have been gagged and forced to their knees, their hands tied behind their backs. Some chump tried to nab Aki, too, but Aki threw him into the wall, grabbed the guy's machete and leapt beside me. Now he's snarling at them while I aim the machete at Masaru's shriveled, ugly mug.

We've got ourselves a stand-off.

"Now, now," the old man says. "Let us not make this difficult."

"You're the one making things difficult. *Hail Roth?* Seriously? The guy's evil! He started the Immortal War. He destroyed this world. Hell, he killed most of your ancestors."

"Do not presume to lecture me on the history of my own people, my child. Tell your Gorani to stand down and we can talk like civilized people, yes?"

"Are you gonna let my friends go?"

"I am afraid I cannot do that."

"Then I'm afraid I can't be civil. Tell me. Why are you doing this?"

"Why?" Masaru beams at me, a maniacal gleam in his eyes. "Jane, Roth *saved* our people. He freed us from the tyranny of the Dahaari. They were not benevolent rulers. They used us, exploited us, kept the riches of Arakaan for themselves."

"I thought the mortals worshipped the Dahaari. I thought they lived in peace."

"*Bah!*" Masaru screws up his face. "A lie we've been fed for generations. Our people were little more than slaves! They worshipped the Dahaari out of fear. Even as a child, I understood. We should have sided with Roth and his Gorani in the Immortal War." He steps toward me. Aki snarls again, stands his ground. "Our ancestors were going to surrender to Roth, until that blasted Hali-gabera ruined everything." Violet and I glance at each other. "If it weren't for her, we wouldn't have had to live in the shadows all these years, scratching around in the dirt. We could have been the new gods of this world. We could have lived in peace."

Violet was right. Definitely best we don't tell him Hali-gabera's our friend. Well, Violet's friend. I'm not so sure where I stand on that front.

"So you've been lying to everyone all this time?" I ask. "Using Elsa as bait?"

Masaru turns to her. "What is that phrase you taught

me, *oda min?* Good things come to those who wait?" Elsa says nothing. The old man cackles. "Yes, yes. I like this phrase."

He nods at the guards around me and Aki. They step closer, machetes at the ready. Aki rattles his throat and clenches his fists. I grab his arm, tell him to wait.

"You need a hobby, old man." I'm stalling. Trying to figure a way out of this mess. "I mean, *forty-seven years?*"

"A small price to pay for salvation."

"Salvation?" I shift my stance. Hold the machete a little tighter. "You're a fool, Masaru."

"I am a *visionary*, my child. The only one brave enough to do what is right for our people. I was the one who convinced these fools"—he waves at the other Elders— "to take Elsa in. I saved her life. Told her everything she wanted to hear. Yes, we would keep her key safe. Yes, we would give her shelter until you or that—that *man* you call a father came to find her. For forty-seven years, I've put up with her foolish antics, drunken outbursts and lies."

"If you hate her so much, why didn't you take her to Roth right away?"

"You are the one he wants, Jane. The one he needs. I had to be patient."

I glance at Violet and Hickory, still gagged and bound. Elsa's standing beside them, but I'm not gonna get any help from her. Something's snapped inside her. It's like she's had a run-in with a Specter, been Gripped. We're outnumbered. Surrounded. Trapped.

"Look," I say, "if you hand me and the keys to Roth,

194

everyone in this world's gonna die. He'll unleash the Cradle Sea. I know it. I've *seen* it. Trust me, you don't want that. Help us. Please. We can't let Roth anywhere near the Cradle. We can't let him win."

"He already *has* won, Jane. His power is too great. You know this. Why fight it?"

"What makes you so sure Roth isn't gonna kill you, first chance he gets?"

"Because you and the keys are not the only gifts I will present to him, Jane.'" Masaru gazes at the ceiling, clutching the medallion dangling from his neck like it's his own heart. "Roth will gaze into my soul and see only faith, reverence, and sacrifice. The people of Arakaan will be spared, the dune sea gateway sealed, and I?" Cue that maniacal gleam again. "I will stand by his side in the timeless space of the Cradle, guiding him, serving him, shaping the futures of all worlds forevermore. It is my right—my *destiny*."

Ugh, I really hate this guy.

"He'll gaze into your soul and see a bunch of lost marbles, Masaru. The Makers left me behind to protect the Manor, and that's exactly what I'm gonna do. Tell your goons to give me the keys and let us go, or I'll . . . I'll . . ."

"What?" Masaru says. "Hmm? Cause a quake? Bring down the mountain? Elsa just told me how you froze at the Mulu Pass. Fear is holding you back. Good for us, I think. Not so good for you." He sighs. "You should be thanking me. I am offering you safe passage back to the Manor. An armed escort. I am offering you immortal life!"

"Trapped inside the Cradle with Roth in my head? That isn't a life." I raise the machete a little higher, nod at Violet and Hickory. My hand starts to shake. "Let them go. Let us all go."

"Easy, my child," Masaru says. "Your companions are quite safe. For now." Masaru strolls over to Hickory. "Especially this one. Elsa told me you served Roth for many years, my son."

Hickory looks at me, at Violet, at Elsa.

Masaru runs a hand down Hickory's cheek and plucks the gag from his mouth. "You knelt before him. He deemed you worthy." A shadow passes over Masaru's face. His lip quivers. "And now you travel with these . . . these heretics! You betrayed him. How could you?"

Hickory grits his teeth. "Back off, old man. You don't know me."

"Oh, but I do, my son," Masaru says, resting a hand on Hickory's shorn head. "Or at least, I know your type. You are scared. Weak. I am guessing you wanted to claim the Cradle for yourself and tear the Manor apart. Just like our old friend Elsa here."

"Hold on," I butt in, "what was that?'"

"Jane, Jane, Jane." Masaru straightens up and smiles. "Don't you understand? Can you not see? The Boboki may be ruthless, but they were not trying to kill you at Orinkin, my child. They were trying to take you from us." Masaru nods at Elsa. "And save you from her."

"Save us?" I say. "From . . . no, they *attacked* us."

"Are you sure?"

They didn't use their weapons, Violet said in our room.

I see the tattooed Boboki girl reaching out to me in the stables. I see the look on Yaku's face when we fled. Hear him screaming Elsa's name.

"Elsa?" My voice cracks. "What's he talking about?"

Hickory stares at her, confused. Violet yells into her gag, struggles against the rope around her wrists. Because Elsa isn't even trying to prove Masaru wrong. She's just standing there, utterly still, head bowed as if caught mid-prayer. And it hits me. Sits heavy in my gut.

Masaru's telling the truth.

I step back. My knees buckle. Aki stops me from falling.

"Elsa genuinely believed the Boboki were coming to kill you, Jane," Masaru says, "but it was not so much your life she was worried about—rather, the downfall of her own nefarious plan. She has been lying to you from the beginning. I do not blame you for believing her." He gestures at the Elders lashed to their thrones. "They believed her for years. *We must help her,* she would tell them. *We must help the one with amber eyes.* And they wanted to, Jane. Why, up until this morning, they thought they were." He chuckles to himself. "I knew, though. I heard her whispers in the night. You think Roth is evil? No, no, no. This"— he wags a crooked finger at Elsa—"is evil. She is no friend to you."

I wish the old man was just messing with my head, but Elsa isn't denying a thing.

I clench my fists. Feel that familiar jolt of pain up my left arm. "Elsa, why?"

"I've already told you,'" she says at last. "Together, we can make things right." And she turns to me, looks me dead in the eye. Cold. Detached. *I saw the darkness in you the moment we met,* Masaru said. I think I can finally see it, too. "I'm sorry, Jane. It's the only way to make him pay for everything he's done. The only way to stop him, once and for all.'"

Aki snarls. I'm sure Violet's holding her breath, just like me.

"What are you saying?" I ask, although I have a bad feeling I already know.

"In your blood lies the power of the gods, Jane," Masaru says. "The power to heal the Manor . . . or destroy it." He slips both Cradle keys into his pocket. "Elsa's plan has always been to take you into the Cradle and spill your life upon the foundation stone. Her plan is for you to die."

THE DUNGEON

"So let's get this straight," Violet says. "Roth wants to possess you, claim the Cradle, conquer the Manor, and cover every Otherworld in infinite darkness."

"Mm-hm.'"

"The Elders were going to help you stop him."

"Apparently."

"But Masaru took them hostage and plans to hand you over to Roth because he *actually* thinks they'll become best buddies or something."

"Pretty much."

"And Elsa wants to—"

"Sacrifice me inside the Cradle, unleash the Sea and tear the Manor apart, obliterating Roth and his army, killing my dad and every other prisoner still stuck in there, plunging the Otherworlds into absolute chaos and quite possibly ending life as we know it."

"So . . . not the best scenario."

"No," I say. "Not quite."

We're in separate cells, somewhere underground. It's stuffy and dark, smells like stale pee. We're the only ones down here, except for a couple of guards out in the tunnel who keep telling us to shut up. Aki was shot with a sedative dart as soon as the council meeting ended. Maybe they've already taken him to the plane. Hickory was marched off somewhere with Masaru. We have no idea where Elsa is. To be honest, I don't care.

My cell's tiny, covered in sheets of rusted metal from floor to ceiling to make sure I have no contact with stone. Even the door's made of metal. There's a little barred window near the top, but my shackles are bolted to the floor. I can barely kneel, let alone stand. A bit over-cautious on Masaru's part, but you can't blame him. He was expecting a grown woman, after all. A true avatar of the Makers. Aris reborn.

"I'm sorry, Jane," Violet says from her cell. "I still can't believe it."

Unfortunately, I can.

I have no doubt you'll shine when the time comes.

Their power lies within you, and it will awaken.

I'll be right beside you. I won't stop fighting, not until we're standing atop the foundation stone. We'll make Roth pay for what he's done. We'll make everything right, once and for all.

Elsa was talking about my sacrifice all along. I clasp my hands in my lap. They haven't stopped shaking since the council chamber. I feel like I'm gonna throw up.

"She said it herself," I tell Violet, "out on the flats: she isn't the woman she used to be."

"What about the Boboki?" Violet rattles her chains for the hundredth time, trying to break free. "Do you think they're still coming for us? Coming to help us?"

"I guess we'll find out soon enough."

"Shh!" one of the guards says.

"Shush yourself," Violet snaps at him. "Well, they'd better hurry." She grunts and strains against her chains. "Ugh!" I hear her plonk herself down. "I feel bad we beat them up. The Boboki, I mean. Gods, Aki kicked one of them off the balcony. Hickory stabbed one with a spoon. And the wagon! I hope we didn't blow any of them up. Yaku will understand, though, right? They came in the middle of the night. One of them put his hand over my mouth, and—"

"*Shh!*" the guard says again, thumping his fist on her door. "*Kalanthai!*"

"How about you come in here and say that to my face?" Violet yells.

"Cut it out," Elsa says.

She's marching down the tunnel with two guards, by the sound of it. I can hear their boots. Weapons clanking around their belts. They mutter something, our guards mutter back, and they all march off.

"Are you both all right?" Elsa asks once we're alone.

"Like you care," Violet says.

"I care very much, actually." Elsa seems more with it than she was in the council chamber. I guess the shock of Masaru's deception has worn off. "I need you alive."

"So you can kill me later?" I say. "Thanks."

Shuffled footsteps. A jangle of chain outside my door. "We don't have time to argue. Turns out Masaru's been brainwashing the guards of Asmadin for years, convincing them to swear allegiance to Roth. Most have been turned, but not all. I managed to convince mine to take a quick detour on our way to the airstrip. They want to help us. Well, I should say, they want to help me."

"You came here just to tell us that?"

"No." Another step closer. Another jangle of chain. Elsa peers through the barred window of my cell, backlit by the torches in the tunnel. "I wanted to see you before I start prepping for takeoff. I don't blame you for being angry, Jane. I know you'll never forgive me, but I assure you, the Boboki *are* coming. When Yaku attacks Asmadin—and he *will* attack—you can't try to escape with him. You hate me? Fine. But you need me. I meant what I said at the council. I'm the only one who can fly us safely across the dune sea."

"Cool," I say sharply. "That it?"

"Not quite," Elsa says. "I want you to know why."

"Why you want to kill me? Save your breath. I know. You want revenge."

"He killed my boy! Roth pinned Charlie to the wall and watched as—as my baby . . ." She can't say it.

I close my eyes and see Elsa in the shipwreck, etching her baby boy on the wall. I see her crying, wailing, screaming at the suns, moon, and stars.

But all I feel is anger.

"I'm sorry that happened to you, Elsa," Violet says. "I'm not even going to pretend I understand how terrible it was. But John does. Charlie. Jane's *dad*. He lost a son, too, and you don't see him trying to—"

"Charlie *left* me," Elsa says. "We made it out of the Cradle. Got away from the two Guardians that escaped and led Roth far from the entrance so he'd never know where it was. He almost caught us again. Came so close to grabbing you, Jane. But *I* saved us. *I* found the trap that let us get away. And after all that—everything we'd been through—Charlie abandoned me." She grips the bars of my window with her shackled hands. "For you.'"

"He didn't abandon you, Elsa, he—"

"You got out, Jane. You were free, but I was trapped inside that hell-scape for *fifty-odd years*. Half a century of running and hiding from Roth's army and the Cradle Guardian."

"Specter," Violet says.

"What?"

"We call them Specters."

"Well, I call 'em Guardians, and I saw 'em first."

"Okay, okay," Violet mutters. "Tetchy."

"As I was saying," Elsa continues, "it was hell. I forgot the taste of food, the sound of laughter. I wasn't Roth's prisoner anymore, I was the Manor's." She unfurls her hands between the bars of the window, catching invisible rain. "Then, one day, I heard water . . ."

"The river," I whisper. The hall of waterfalls.

Elsa nods. "I crawled out of my hiding space. Hadn't felt or tasted water in so long. It was . . . beautiful." Elsa's voice trembles. "That was when the Guardian found me. It filled the hall with that bright white light. Caught me. Took me to the nightmare realm."

"We call that the Grip," Violet says.

Elsa clenches her fists but keeps staring down at me. "You know what it does, then. What it shows you. Can you guess what I saw in there? Which moment I was forced to relive?" I nod. "That's right. I was back in that cell, choking on Roth's stench, watching my sweet baby boy die over and over again. I can still see it, feel it, feel *him*, Jane, whenever I close my eyes.'

I remember Hickory saying the same thing.

The Grip never really lets you go.

"The Specters are connected through the Grip," I say, barely managing to keep my voice steady. "You saw Dad in there, too. He said you were together for a while."

"A very short while, but yes. I told him about the waterfalls. Charlie held me. Said he'd come for me. Promised he'd find a way." She shakes her head, as if disgusted by the idea. "Then I woke up."

She vanished from the Grip, Dad told me on the train, *before we could say goodbye.* The Specter spared her, just as it spared Hickory. Just as it spared me.

"It hovered over me for a moment," Elsa says, "then floated along a corridor, through a door I'd never been able to open before. It led me to a gateway. I'd found others in my time—none of them let me out, obviously, but this one did." Elsa shakes her head. "I actually *thanked* the Guardian as it disappeared back down the corridor. I thought the Manor was taking pity on me at last, leading me to safety, leading me *home*. But no. I stepped onto the salt with shaking legs, and by the time my eyes adjusted to the glare, the gateway had shut. I was trapped, here in Arakaan, right back where I started. That was the moment that truly broke me. The final twist of the knife." She wipes a tear from her cheek. "Roth ruined my life, Jane—because of the Manor, because of the Makers, because of you. I don't want revenge. I want justice."

"Justice?" Violet says. "You're talking about killing a *child*, Elsa."

"Not a child," she says, looking down her nose at me. "A vessel. Believe me, I wish there was another way, Jane. You know I tried to find one. I nearly died searching for the Dahaari weapons. But it was thanks to that struggle, that failure, that I finally understood."

The desert showed me, she said in the watchtower. *The desert made me see.*

The woman with glowing amber eyes and footsteps like thunder.

"The Makers didn't just pour their life force into the foundation stone," Elsa says, "they poured it into you. *You* are the weapon I need. I was the one who took you from the Cradle in the first place. Feels only right that I should be the one to take you back."

I pluck at the bandage around my hand. I can feel it now, despite the fear and doubt still clawing away at my insides. In my palm, an itch. In my gut, the first ebb of the furious tide.

"Believe it or not," I say, "someone's already tried to sacrifice me to the Manor this week. Didn't turn out too well for the other guy."

The edges of Elsa's face crease with a smile. "Violet told me, your first night here. The mayor of Bluehaven, yes? I must admit, I was relieved when I heard you nearly leveled the island. Tell me, was it really fear for Charlie's life that drove the destruction, or fear for your own?" She doesn't wait for an answer. "I guess we'll see. Charlie won't be joining us in the Cradle, of course, but"—she nods at Violet's cell—"I'm sure I'll find a suitable substitute."

That does it. Anger flushes through my veins, swirling the furious tide. I spring to my knees, straining against the chains.

"Atta girl," Elsa says, delighted. "My, my, imagine the damage you'll cause on the foundation stone when your powers are amplified a hundredfold. And don't worry. Unlike the mayor, I *will* finish the job."

"Mighty confident for a woman with shackles around her wrists," Violet says.

"Masaru's betrayal is unfortunate, yes," Elsa says. "I was so busy playing everyone, I never stopped to wonder if anyone was playing me. He's been ahead of me every step of the way, this is true, but the tables are about to turn. All this?" She glances around at the dungeon, jangles the chain binding her wrists. "'It's a complication, nothing more."

"Well, I hate to complicate things further," Violet says, "but Masaru isn't the only one who fooled you. Hali-gabera isn't buried in that tomb, Elsa. The body you saw was a decoy, just like the dummy keys. Hali wasn't born of the sands. She came from *across* the sands, from Bluehaven. Her real name's Winifred Robin, and she's very much alive."

I guess we're not keeping it a secret anymore.

"Don't be ridiculous," Elsa scoffs. "Hali-gabera died over a thousand years ago."

"Time does strange things in the Manor," Violet replies. "Roth didn't kill her. Didn't destroy the arrow-head. Winifred fled back to the Manor to draw him away from Asmadin, and she gave it to Inigo before she left, to keep it safe. It's hidden in her tomb, I'm sure of it."

"Nonsense. I checked every inch of the tomb."

"Check it again. You say killing Jane in the Cradle is the only way to defeat Roth. I'm telling you it isn't. This is why the Manor brought you back here, Elsa. This is why *we're* here, too. It's all because of the arrowhead. If you just—"

"Enough!" Elsa cries. "We have to unleash the Sea. There is no other way."

"But—"

"Let it go, Violet," I say through gritted teeth. "She's never gonna help us. She's no better than Roth."

"Excuse me?" Elsa says.

"You said it yourself, back at Orin-kin. All this mess started because he lost someone he loved—because he was so consumed by grief and hatred he didn't care who he hurt."

"I'm nothing like Roth."

"Oh, really? What about the Otherworlds, Elsa? If you unleash the Sea, they'll—"

"What? Be destroyed? Descend into chaos? You shouldn't put so much faith in legend, my dear. What did Hickory call them in the canyon today? Lies and bedtime stories?"

My breath catches. My stomach sinks.

"To think, I nearly had him killed. Thank you for saving him, Jane. Really. He'll make a valuable ally once we return to the Manor. He and I have so much in common, after all . . ."

"You want to *recruit* Hickory?" Violet says. "He'll never side with you."

"I think we all know that isn't true. After all, he's betrayed you before." A door opens somewhere down the tunnel. The guards have returned. "Time's up," Elsa says with a sigh.

"What about all the innocent people still trapped in the Manor?" I ask, yanking on my chains again. "My dad and Roth's other prisoners? You gonna sacrifice them, too?"

"Kill several hundred to save several billion? Sounds like a fair trade to me."

"You'll die, too," Violet says. "You know that, right?"

"Silly girl," Elsa says. "I died when Roth murdered my son." She steps away from my door. "I'll see you both soon. Don't be late. Wouldn't want to miss your flight . . ."

PRECIOUS CARGO

Night has fallen. A chill has crept through the dungeon tunnels, this labyrinth of rank odors and dark, empty spaces. We're being marched who knows where by a host of red-cloaked guards. I have no idea if they're on Masaru's side or Elsa's. Either way, they're not on ours. Violet's been muttering escape plans for the past hour or so.

"We just have to delay takeoff," she whispers to me now. "Give the Boboki a chance to catch up. As soon as we're free, we nab the keys from Masaru, head to the tomb and find the arrowhead. Then we find Aki, get Hickory—if you really insist—and split. Make our own way across the dunes. Elsa and the old man can rot out here together, far as I'm concerned."

Thing is, I don't wanna run. My mind's been racing since Elsa left. I can't believe I'm about to say this, but—

"We have to go with them, Violet."

"What? No, Jane. Yaku—"

"Doesn't have a plane. Elsa may be our enemy, but she's right: we need her. Every day we waste out here is another day my dad and the rest of the prisoners suffer—another day the Manor continues to crumble and Roth closes in on the Cradle."

Violet glances at the guards and scratches her head, rattling the shackles around her wrists. "So we should . . . let Masaru take us? Just like that?"

"Just like that."

"And when we get back to the Manor? What then?"

I pull at a loose thread of the bandage around my hand. My palm pangs again. I can still feel it: the gentle ebb and flow of the not-quite-furious tide swirling deep in my gut. Sure, I'm still scared. I can still see that crumbling Manor corridor and all those Otherworlds lying in ruin, but my anger at Elsa and Masaru is clouding it all. Comes down to this: I've come too far and gone through too much to be handed over to Roth or slaughtered on the stone.

"Then we give 'em hell."

Violet arches her eyebrows. "Child of the Makers indeed. Don't get me wrong, love your attitude, but what about the arrowhead? We can't leave Arakaan without it."

"Don't worry." I've been thinking about this, too. "I know exactly where it is. You were right. The dead do keep their secrets, but somebody beat Elsa to it."

It was Elsa's comment about Masaru that sparked it. A fleeting remark that sank its teeth into my gray matter the moment she left.

He's been ahead of me every step of the way.

"Masaru knew Elsa was searching for a Dahaari weapon," I say. "He must've known she'd check the tomb. Elsa told me the remains in there were a mess.

They're ancient, sure. Makes sense. But what if they were really damaged because Masaru had already rifled through them?"

Violet goes quiet for a bit, then nods. "That's good thinking, Jane. Really good."

"Don't sound *too* surprised."

"But why would Masaru keep it a secret all this time?"

"Because—"

"Shh!" The guard behind me jabs my shoulder. "*Kalanthai!*"

I shoot a glare at him over my shoulder so fast I give myself whiplash. "Because he had to make sure Elsa stuck around. He *needed* her to think sacrificing me in the Cradle was the only way to defeat Roth, to lure us in—so he could get his hands on all three keys."

"But then he could've just destroyed the arrowhead for Roth. Chucked it into a volcano."

"Nah. Roth used to wear it around his neck, right? To keep it close, in case one of the Dahaari slipped through his fingers. Probably wore it as a medal of honor, too. A messed-up little trophy." Now for the kicker. "Just like Masaru's wearing it now."

Violet stops in her tracks, till Captain Shooshie jabs her in the back. "The medallion . . ."

"Hidden in plain sight," I say. "In the Elders' chamber, Masaru said we weren't the only gifts he'd be presenting to Roth. At the time, I thought he was talking about his loyal service or whatever, but he was clutching that thing. I bet the arrowhead's inside it."

"Jane, I could kiss y—" Violet begins, but she cuts herself off and splutters a string of half-words. Her eyes bulge. I swear her cheeks flush a deep shade of reddish-brown. "I mean, well done."

She's mortified, but me? All I can think is, *I think she likes me too, I think she likes me too, I think she likes me too.*

In short, I'm thrilled.

That is, until we're marched out of the tunnel and into the canyon.

"Oh, crap."

The people of Asmadin are standing in the cold, red-cloaked like the guards. Women, men, children: the whole city's gathered to see us off. Torches line the paths and flicker from the windows and caves dotted all the way up the cliffs and pillars. It looks as if a million fireflies have filled the canyon, twinkling like the strip of stars above. Masaru's hunched before us, resting a hand on an open metal crate. Two wooden beams have been lashed to either side. It looks big enough to carry a person, if said person was roughly my height and crouched in a trembling little ball, which—unfortunately—seems to be the idea.

"Welcome, my children." Masaru claps. The guards stand to attention. Most people in the crowd bow their heads. Something tells me they're not here by choice. "It is time."

The true Cradle keys dangle around Masaru's neck, glinting in the torchlight. The clay medallion's there, too. Violet glares at him—at *it.*

"Don't," I whisper through frozen lips. "Not yet."

"Time for what?" she asks Masaru instead, nodding at the open metal crate. "We're not squeezing into that thing, if that's what you're thinking."

"Not you," Masaru says. "Just Jane. It is a rather crude mode of transportation, yes, but we have a bit of a walk to the next canyon. We will not be taking any chances."

Hickory's behind Masaru, flanked by a couple of guards, his gag and shackles removed. He's free, but he isn't fighting. Isn't trying to flee. He's just standing there with his head bowed, dressed in a red cloak of his own. I bet Masaru's been trying to recruit him, too. Surely Hickory wouldn't fall for it, but if he hasn't, why is he acting so strange?

"Get in, Jane," he mutters. "You have to."

"You will be quite safe," Masaru says. "You have my word."

"It's okay," I tell Violet. "Stay close, if you can."

"Always." She gives my hand a quick squeeze. "See you on the plane."

The look on her face almost kills me.

I continue down the rocky path alone. The crowd shuffles back as I pass. The other Elders are here, too, bound, gagged, and trembling behind Masaru.

"No cushions?" I ask when I step up to the crate.

The old man cackles and cranes his neck up at the stars. "Take a good look, my child. This is the last time you and I will stand under an open sky."

"'Call me *child* one more time, and it'll be the last time you stand, period," I say.

And that's when an explosion rocks the canyon.

A flash of fire. A barrage of yelling. A volley of arrows zipping through the air, clattering against the cliffs, while swift shadows dart down the pillars and swing from the decorated ropes.

"Boboki!" the guard behind me screams, and the crowd scatters.

They've come to save us at last, whether we want them to or not.

"No, no, no," I shout, "we're okay! We've got everything under control!" Which is funny because, as soon as I say it, a guard leaps forward, shoves me into the crate, slams the lid over my head and bolts it shut, plunging me into darkness. "Hey! You son of a—"

The crate lurches and sways and I'm tossed to and fro, slammed up and down as the red-cloaks lug me along the path as fast as they can. There must be four of them, the beams resting on their shoulders. I can hear them grunting. It's a mad dash for the airstrip.

Another explosion rocks the world, much closer than before. The red-cloaks stumble, the crate lurches, and all I can do is try not to crack my head open as I'm bounced around in the dark. That, and try to calm the furious tide swirling stronger and stronger in my gut.

I don't want to sound ungrateful, but if the Boboki destroy Betty we're screwed. I can hear them now, dozens of raiders chanting, storming and shooting their way through the canyon. Machetes clang, rifles blast, arrows *thwat-thwat-thwat*, and I can't see a—

Wait. There. A tiny, rusted-out hole to my right. I smoosh my face up to it and see black-cloaks fighting red-cloaks. Rifles flashing and torches whipping by. Violet joining the fray, ducking, rolling and weaving.

"Hey!" I smack my hand on the crate. "Violet, I'm in here!"

"I *know*, Jane!" she shouts back. "Everybody knows! Shut up and let me"—she leaps out of view, a red-cloak goes flying by—"concentrate! Yaku's here. They've already"—there she is again, leaping onto someone's shoulders—"captured Elsa and taken the plane!"

"That's fantastic!" We're finally getting the upper hand. Sure, I'm trapped in a box, but still. One step at a time. "Where's Masaru? We need—"

"The arrowhead," Violet says. "I'm on it!" She smacks the guy in the head, flips him around, and lands on her feet. "Sit tight." She disappears into the battle once again.

"Like I have a choice," I mutter.

At least I'm kinda safe in here.

A volley of rifle-fire splits my eardrums. The guards cry out, my stomach jumps into my throat, the crate hits the ground, and I bounce and hit my head.

"Gah!"

Now the crate's spinning and sliding down a steep slope, gathering speed. "*Somebody-y-y-y-y,*" I cry, my voice juddering with every bump. The crate hits something, flips through the air, and crashes down hard. My whole body's aching. I think the gash in my palm has opened again, because it's burning with pain, and I can feel the canyon trembling through the crate. I'm causing a quake. Perfect timing, as always.

"Not now!" I scrunch myself into a ball, roll back, and kick at the crate lid. The bolt rattles, but the stupid thing won't budge. "Hey! Violet! Anybody!"

Footsteps. A whole bunch of them bustling around the crate. Murmured chatter and a harried, "Steady now—one, two, three," as the crate's heaved again.

"*Hickory?*"

"Nice and comfy in there?" he asks, huffing and puffing on my left. He's helping the red-cloaks. He's *actually* helping the red-cloaks.

"What the—whose side are you on?" I shout.

"'Right now?" he says. "Undecided."

"Do not worry," a familiar voice grunts on my right.

Wait—not the red-cloaks. The Boboki. "Yaku? Is that you?"

"You're a hard girl to catch, Jane Doe."

"I'm so sorry about Orin-kin," I say, steadying myself against the jolt and sway of the crate. "We didn't mean to hurt your people. I mean, let's be honest, you could've said something . . ."

"You really need to—shut up, Jane," Hickory grunts between breaths. "And calm down. If you bring—down the mountain now—we're done for."

"Get me out of here, then!"

"Not yet," Yaku says. "We're nearly there."

I can hear the rumble of the quake now, lurking beneath the sounds of the battle like a brewing storm. I can feel the trembling cliffs and pillars. The path cracking below the crate. I clench my bandaged hand shut and hold it to my chest. Think about Dad's big brown eyes, Violet's smile, Aki offering me a darkling beetle—but nothing works. I can't shut it out, can't stop it. Being stuck in a box sure isn't helping.

I can barely breathe.

Another sound now. One I've never heard before. An electric whine. A loud *putt-putt-putt* and frenzied whir that's getting louder and louder by the second.

Betty.

I almost cheer. Figure we must be home free. I'm about to ask if anyone's seen Violet or Masaru when a Boboki raider to my left cries out in pain, and the crate tilts to the side. Hickory, Yaku, and the other guy skid to a halt. Footsteps thud around us. Weapons clatter. I mash my face up to the tiny hole again. Looks like the red-cloaks have us surrounded.

A woman with a booming voice yells an order. Swords are unsheathed around us. But then I catch a different, blessedly familiar sound. A throaty *click-clack-click*. Aki's woken up. And he isn't happy. He snarls, the red-cloaks scream, and I hear terrible things. Crunching sounds. People shouting as they're thrown far and wide. Cries of pain cut short. Hickory saying, "Whoa, it's me," and, "Not them, either. They're with us. Get her on the plane!"

"Aki," I shout, pounding my good hand on the crate. "I'm okay. I just—whoa!"

The crate lurches up higher and faster than before. Aki grunts. He's lifting it all by himself, marching me up some kind of ramp onto Betty.

The whirring and *putt-putt*ing's deafening now. The crate tilts dangerously as Aki sets it down. There's a great wrenching sound—metal bending metal—and at last the lid pops off, flooding me with grimy electric light. "Thanks, buddy," I gasp, popping my head out. Aki pats me like I'm a dog.

Betty's a hunk of junk. The small circular windows are cracked and filthy. The hull's all patchwork metal, just big enough for Aki to stand up straight and not smack his head. Rusty benches are bolted along each wall, but other than that, the plane's empty.

"*This* is your marvelous machine?" I shout at Elsa.

She's up in the cockpit, flicking switches and tapping dials. The tattooed Boboki girl from the stables of Orinkin is watching over her, a curved blade at the ready. Two red-cloaks are gagged and grumbling beside her, hands tied around a bench-leg. Elsa's guards.

"Jane," Elsa says, "glad you could join us. Sit down and shut up."

"You do not give orders anymore," Yaku tells her, stomping up the ramp with Hickory.

The other Boboki men are staying behind to hold off the red-cloaks, drawing their weapons, standing their ground. The tattooed girl runs to join them, pausing before Yaku as she goes. They lock eyes. Touch their foreheads together and mutter something I can't hear. The girl glances at me, nods once, and leaps down the ramp to help the men.

"Take off," Yaku shouts at Elsa. "Now!"

"Wait," I say. "We can't—"

Elsa releases a lever. Betty shudders and roars, starts crawling forward.

"Stop!" I scramble out of the crate. "We're not leaving without Violet!"

The ramp's still down, dragging along the airstrip. Aki grabs my arm and stops me from leaping down it. I can't hear it over Betty's roar, but I can tell the canyon's still quaking. The airstrip's cracking. The cliffs are crumbling. A tumbling boulder wipes out a few red-cloaks bolting our way. The others fire their rifles, and we duck for cover. An arrow flies through the cabin and lodges into the back of Elsa's chair. Our Boboki defenders are quickly overrun. Yaku's about to pull a big lever down the back when I shout, "Not yet—look!"

Violet's here at last, blasting her way through the red-cloaks on horseback with a longbow slung round her shoulders and a sack slumped over the saddle in front of her. No, not a sack. A person.

Masaru.

"Get that ramp up and strap in," Elsa shouts. "We're running out of runway!"

"Wait," I shout back. 'Slow down!"

"We've only got one shot at this, Jane, especially if you tear the canyon apart!"

Elsa flicks another switch. Betty picks up speed. The

whole cabin shakes and rattles. Elsa veers left, throwing everybody off balance and clipping the wingtip on the canyon wall. She swears, course-corrects, and shouts something about a newly formed crevice in the runway.

"Jane," Hickory shouts, "calm down!"

"You calm down!" I stumble back toward Yaku and the ramp. "Hurry, Violet!"

She's clear of the red-cloaks, getting closer and closer. Riding Scab, I realize. Makes sense. No other horse in all the worlds would be wild enough to chase a plane.

"Come on," I scream, reaching out a hand. "Go, boy, go!"

The red-cloaks take aim and fire. Yaku shoves me aside just in time. Bullets ricochet around the cabin, sparks fly. Violet and Scab weave, dodge and pull alongside the ramp. Aki leaps forward, reaches out and plucks Masaru from the saddle. The old man's unconscious, his shriveled limbs flopping around. Violet springs from the saddle a second later, and Aki catches her in his other arm, safe and sound.

"Get out of here, Scab," I shout. "Go!"

He peels off to the side with a whinny and vanishes from sight. Aki ducks back inside, dumps Masaru on a bench, and sets Violet carefully on her feet.

"Whoa," she gasps, swaying slightly, her dark hair wind-blown and wild. "That was intense."

Yaku leaps for the lever, yanks it down hard. The ramp rises a foot or so and stalls. He tries again, but it's jammed. Hickory runs to help him. They squabble and work together at a different lever, cranking the ramp manually instead, but it isn't fast enough, because something else is coming our way now: two big, round, yellow glowing eyes parting the crowd and lighting up the crumbling runway, gaining on us with incredible speed.

It's a car—no, a truck—just like the ones I've seen in books.

"Where'd they get a *truck*?"

"Another project of mine," Elsa shouts, glancing over her shoulder. "Didn't I tell you? Runs quite well, actually. Clutch is a bit stiff, but—"

"Shut up and fly," Violet and I shout together.

I catch a glimpse of the runway through the grimy windshield. Betty's headlights keep flickering on and off, but the moonlight's bright enough to see. Elsa was right: we're running out of road. There's no mountain blocking our way. We're about to go over a clifftop.

"The crate," Hickory shouts, jabbing a finger at my casket. "Toss it!"

Aki hurls it out the back. The crate bounces along the runway, but the truck swerves at the last second and continues speeding toward the slowly rising ramp. It's too high for the red-cloak behind the wheel to drive aboard, but he could still ram us, and then what?

We need another weapon. We need *me*.

I wrench the bandage from my palm, dig my fingers into the wound, jump onto the ramp before anyone can stop me, and hold out my bleeding hand. I think about Elsa's betrayal, Masaru's madcap plan, and Roth, Roth, Roth. I let the furious tide overflow, my blood catch in the wind. I can feel each drop as it hits the rock and sand. I can feel every jarring crack, every yawning fissure, every boulder breaking free from the canyon walls. The pain's excruciating, but I embrace it. I clench my hand into a bloodied fist. The rock shatters like glass. I shove my fist into the air, and a pillar explodes upward right beneath the truck, sending it flying and flipping through the air just as it's about to hit us.

"Jane," someone shouts, "stop!"

But I can't. The power's too much.

I send my fury way back toward the red-cloaks and their guns, splitting the runway in two. I can feel the vibrations of their footsteps from here. They're panicking, fleeing back to Asmadin, but there's no escape. I could squash them all right now if I wanted.

It'd be so easy.

"Jane!"

Somebody grabs my ankle and yanks me backward into the cabin. Betty pitches sharply, the runway disappears, and we soar over the cliff, into darkness. In the blinking electric light of the cabin, I catch a glimpse of Hickory and Yaku dangling over the black void of the open ramp, racked by the wind. Of Masaru, awake at last, hugging a bench-leg. Of Violet clinging to my ankle, and Aki clinging to hers. Of Elsa up in the cockpit, and the two captured, red-cloaked guards dangling behind her. I'm freaked out. Beyond terrified. Betty's leveling out, but it's still so noisy and windy, and my limbs have turned to stone.

The furious tide's wiped me out.

"It's okay," Violet shouts, pulling me close. "Look at my eyes. Breathe."

I look at her eyes. I breathe. And pass out.

HICKORY'S CHOICE

I slip in and out of consciousness, the soft cocoon of a
dreamless sleep slowly spinning me in, holding me tight,
then unraveling, over and over again. Darkness comes
and goes. Spared from my usual nightmares, now it's the
glimpses of the waking world that scare me. I see Elsa leaping out of the cockpit while everyone else fusses over me.
I see her freeing the red-cloaked guards behind them, pulling weapons from a hidden cache. I try to warn everyone,
but the cocoon smothers me again. I hear raised voices,
threats being made. I see a stand-off. It's Elsa and her red-
cloaks against Violet, Aki and Yaku. Three versus three.

I see Hickory in the middle, and Elsa throwing him
a gun.

"You really want to destroy the Manor?" she says.
"You're with us."

More threats. More shouting.

"We can end this. Wipe the slate clean, once and
for all."

"Hickory, no!"

"The Manor ruined your life."

"Don't listen to her!"

"You lost someone, yes? You can be with them again."

"Drop it right now!"

I hear Masaru cackling. See Hickory frown at the gun in his hands.

"Hickory," I manage to say, "please . . ."

He points the gun at Elsa, then aims it down at me.

"I'm sorry, Jane," he says. "I told you. You really don't know me at all."

And the cocoon spins me through the dark once more.

YAKU'S TALE

I wake up to Betty's low, rumbling growl. Head pounding. Drool trailing down my chin. My hand's been rebandaged, but it still hurts. I've been given a blanket, but I'm shivering. It's so cold in here the trembling floor feels like a sheet of ice. I don't even want to think about the darkness yawning beneath it. The long, deadly drop to the rolling dunes below. It's enough to make a girl feel sick. We're flying. We're *actually* flying.

It might be exciting if it didn't feel so unnatural.

The cabin lights are off. Beams of silver moonlight seep through the windows. Masaru's tied up across from me, watching me. Violet's passed out by my side. Maybe she was knocked out during the stand-off with Elsa and . . .

Hickory.

The traitorous slimeball's leaning over Violet now, probably about to strangle her in her sleep. I flex my fingers, wriggle my toes. All my limbs are working, ready to fire. The fool didn't even tie me up.

Big mistake.

Before Hickory can say, "Holy crap, Jane's awake," I crash-tackle the jerk to the ground and start laying into him as hard as I can. I don't care if the red-cloaks grab me. Let them come. I tell Hickory I hate him. That he's no different from Elsa or Masaru or Roth, and he can join them in hell for all I care. "I should've left you in the death pit," I scream.

"Get off me!" he shouts. "Jane, stop! I'm on—ouch—your side!"

The cabin lights flicker on. I'm pulled off Hickory so easily it's almost embarrassing. Not by Elsa or her red-cloaks, though. By Yaku. And Violet's here, too, stepping in front of me, gripping my shoulders. She wasn't knocked out, she was sleeping.

"Jane, it's okay," she says. "We're all okay. Look at me. We're safe."

"No, I—I caught him," I say, confused. "He was about to strangle you!"

"I was fixing her blanket so she wouldn't get cold!" Hickory sits up, grimacing. "I fixed yours too, you little brat."

"You . . . *what*? Did I wake up on a different plane?"

"He's on our side, Jane," Violet says.

I stare at them all in turn. "But I saw him side with Elsa—"

"I was pretending," Hickory says.

"He knocked her out the moment she turned her back on him." Violet points down the back of the plane. Elsa and the two red-cloaks are bound together with rope near the closed ramp, out cold. "See?"

I rub my head. "Ugh. Is it too much to ask for a bit of honesty around here? Masaru's on our side, then he isn't. The Boboki aren't, then they are. You"—I jab a finger at Hickory—"you're all over the place, and don't even get me started on Elsa. She's—" I freeze, too afraid to look. "Wait, if she's down there, who's flying the plane?"

Violet nods at the cockpit. "Like you said, he's full of surprises."

Aki's squeezed into the pilot's chair, knees bent up around his head.

"So . . . we're okay, then," I say.

Hickory slumps down on a bench, rubbing his cheek, clicking his jaw. "We *were.*"

"We're better than okay." Violet holds out her hand. Masaru's golden chain is coiled in her palm, along with the two Cradle keys. "Go ahead. Take them. They're yours."

I hold out my right hand. Violet lets the golden chain slip through her fingers, and the two keys drop a second later. Part of me expects something to happen—a pang in my palm, maybe a vision of the Cradle or some kind of message from the Makers—but there's nothing. I can't even tell which key's which; they look and feel the same. So small. So plain. Strange, to think the future of every Otherworld depends on two such ordinary things.

"Huh," I say. "I guess that's that, then."

Clearly, the others were expecting something more, too. Yaku shifts on his feet. Hickory frowns. Violet chews on her tongue for a bit, then closes my fingers over the keys with a smile.

"The three Cradle keys," she says, "reunited at last."

I slip the chain over my head. "And the arrowhead?"

The medallion isn't dangling from Masaru's neck anymore. Violet's already done the honors. She tosses me a feathered arrow—the one that was wedged into the back of Elsa's chair—beaming as bright as the Arakaanian suns.

She's replaced the regular arrowhead with the one from Atol Na. It's super light, sharp and pale, the color of a dirty tooth, still flecked with tiny spots of red baked clay, and it's no longer than my middle finger. Awful tiny for a legendary weapon. I can't believe Winifred used *this* to take out Roth's jaw. I can't believe *this* is all we have to work with.

"Well," I say, handing the arrow back, "better than nothing, I suppose."

Violet slips it into her belt and picks up a longbow from the bench. "I nabbed this on my way to the plane. I'll only get one shot, but that's all I'll need."

"Yeah, I—wait, what? Why you?"

"I'm a crack shot, remember? All those years Winifred had me training instead of burning things? She was preparing me. I'm the one who's supposed to kill Roth. I'm sure of it." She stares at me—*glares* at me—daring me to defy her. "I can do this, Jane."

"Okay" I say. I don't like the idea of Violet going anywhere near Roth, but I can tell she isn't gonna back down from this. Unless I can come up with a better plan. I turn to Masaru. He's staring at us. "Did he tell you how he found the arrowhead?"

"We questioned him," Violet says, setting her longbow

down. "Turns out he broke into Hali's tomb when he was a kid, years before the Manor brought Elsa back to Arakaan."

"He said he wanted to *spit on the traitor who defied our rightful king*," Yaku says.

Violet nods. "He found the arrowhead in the sarcophagus. Figured Roth *gave* it to Inigo after he killed Hali-gabera as a sign of his compassion, in hopes that they'd one day *see the light*."

"He thinks it's his destiny to return it to Roth." Yaku spits at Masaru's feet. "*Ladaal.*"

Masaru narrows his eyes, crusty old nostrils flaring over the gag in his gob.

"Did you tell him about Winifred?" I ask.

Violet nods. "Didn't believe me. Big surprise."

I turn to Yaku. "What about you?"

He shuffles uncomfortably. "It's difficult to get my head around. But you have no reason to lie. If you say Hali-gabera lives, then . . . Hali-gabera lives."

"Oh, she lives, all right. Lives, lies, smacks people in the head with shotguns."

Yaku frowns at me, confused.

"Long story," I add. "So we've got the keys, the arrowhead. What now?"

"We rest," Yaku says. "Gather our strength." He sits on the rusty bench across from Masaru, casting a wary eye over Betty's rattling hull. "Elsa charted a rough course for Roth's gateway, but it was mainly guesswork. Your Gorani friend seems to know where to go. I would guess he's been to the gateway before, or close enough to it. Can we trust him?"

"We can." I'm so thankful Aki's here, I could hug him. Maybe I will. First, I take a seat beside Yaku. "Thank you for coming for us. But I don't understand. Elsa told us the Boboki were murderers."

"They were, once," Yaku says. He sighs. "My parents died when I was young. A hunting accident. I was raised by Elsa and her group, out on the flats. I grew up hearing stories about the amber-eyed woman who would one day come to Arakaan. The woman who could move mountains. Elsa told us the story many times herself." He smiles sadly. "You were my hero, Jane. I used to sneak out to the salt-flat gateway at night. I wanted to be the first to greet you when you arrived." His smile fades. He frowns at Elsa, still out cold. "Everything changed when she returned from Atol Na. She was . . . different. One night, I fell asleep by the gateway. I awoke when I heard Elsa staggering over the salt. I scrambled out of sight. She was drunk. Ranting about a vision she'd had in the desert—a vision of you, Jane, here in Arakaan. Before she passed out, she swore she was going to kill you in the Cradle. Unleash the Sea, wipe out Roth and tear the Manor apart. I was terrified. I had no idea what to do."

"Why didn't you send word to the Elders?"

"I was sure they were in on it—Masaru, especially. He and Elsa were always close. Even if they weren't, I had no proof. It would be my word against hers. I knew I needed help."

"The Boboki didn't kidnap you, did they?" I say. "You sought them out."

Yaku nods. "Rena Boboki had been banished by Masaru and the Elders for trying to kill Elsa. I knew she would side with me. So I ran away. Found them, deep in the mountains."

Violet crosses her legs on the floor. "Brave kid."

"Desperate kid," Yaku says. "But the Boboki were not evil bandits—nothing like the stories we had been told. They took me in. Gave me water, food and shelter. Rena was very old. Fierce, but kind. I told her everything. She believed me. Believed in Elsa's vision, too. Said the spirit of the desert was showing us the way. That one day you would come, Jane, no matter what. It was our duty to help you—to help Arakaan. The decision was made. We would keep Elsa alive, but watch her closely. I would pretend I had been kidnapped. Make her believe she had saved my life. Make her believe I *owed* her. I would stay close, earn her trust, and report back to Rena when I could."

I lean against the rattling hull. "I don't know what to say, Yaku. All that waiting and watching. You must've been disappointed when I showed up looking so . . ."

"Young?" Yaku smiles. "Shocked, more like it. And worried. I was furious when you jumped into the pit to save Hickory—such a risk—but when you stood up to the Gorani? I was impressed. Still, I had to pretend I was on Elsa's side."

"Why didn't you say something?" I ask. "Out on the salt flats?"

"Again, I had no proof. I knew you would take Elsa's word over mine, because of her connection to your father.

I was the one who tied you up when you first arrived, after all." Yaku turns to Hickory. "I'm sorry I hurt you that night." He nods at Violet. "I'm sorry you were scared. I had to obey Elsa's instructions."

"And at Orin-kin?" I ask.

"We couldn't risk smuggling you to safety out in the open. A nighttime raid seemed the best option. You were all supposed to be sleeping in your room. When we saw your guard returning from the watchtower, Jane, we rushed. Made mistakes. Sadly, some of my brothers and sisters lost their lives, but they knew the stakes when they volunteered to help."

"Were many people injured at the Pass?" Violet asks. "When the wagon exploded?"

Yaku shakes his head. "We got away. Set off for the northern road at once."

Violet breathes a sigh of relief. "We owe you a great debt, Yaku."

"You owe me nothing," he says. "I'm doing this for my people—for Arakaan—not for you. I will help you get to the Manor, but I will not step inside. I will not leave my home."

I scratch my head and cringe. "Speaking of, I'm sorry I kind of . . . broke Asmadin."

Yaku smiles. "What is broken can be rebuilt. You are not the only one who can shape stone, Jane Doe." He shrugs. "It will just take us a little longer."

FARROW

Aki can barely fit into the cockpit, but he looks right at home. I'm sitting in the janky chair beside him, afraid to move. There's a panel packed with switches and dials in front of us. A couple of control-stick thingies Yaku called yokes. I'm worried Betty'll drop out of the sky if I so much as touch them. In the cracked windscreen, I can see our reflection. Human girl and Gorani. Beyond that, the black night sky. It's like we've set off into space, or the space between spaces, like Po traveling to the Otherworlds before she met Aris and Nabu-kai. Before the Manor was made.

I've got a small stack of old parchment in my lap: Elsa's maps and calculations. There's a sketch of the dune sea gateway, too. A giant open door in the base of a cliff, like the entrance to a massive cave. Dad told me Roth built a metal frame inside it when he entered the Manor, to keep the gateway from closing. Couldn't have his supply route cut off. The gateway looks as big as a house, and it's flanked on either side by two zigzagging, cliffside roads. Both roads lead to a ramshackle stronghold on the clifftop: the camp Dad and Elsa were taken to when they were first caught.

Not exactly a pleasant destination.

"So . . . you've been here, right?" I say to Aki, tapping the drawing of the open gateway, pointing at him and then back at the drawing. "You know where it is? You've been inside?"

He blinks at me, rattles his throat and nods.

I explain what we're trying to do. Show him the Cradle keys, describe the foundation stone, tell him how we have to save the Manor and stop Roth before it's too late.

Aki just cocks his head.

"Hang on . . ." I flip through the pages till I find a blank space. Grab a chip of charcoal from the little compartment next to my chair and do a sketch. "Roth. You know him, right?"

I've drawn his face, half-mask and all. It kinda looks like it was done by a three-year-old, but Aki gets the picture. He snarls at the drawing and spits between our seats.

"I hear you, buddy," I say, and draw a big X over Roth's face. "That's why I need to stop him." I hold up the two keys again. "'I have to get to the Cradle before Roth ruins everything."

Aki presses a button, releases the yoke in front of him, grabs the parchment and charcoal and sketches a picture of his own. I glance out the window, scared we'll hit a mountain or something, but Betty flies true. When he's finished, Aki takes control of the plane again.

He's drawn four stick-figures—four Gorani—standing side by side.

"Are these your friends?" I hold a hand to my chest. "Your family?" Aki does the same, and nods. "Are they . . . alive? Um. Are they . . ." I thump my hand lightly, like the beating of a heart. Aki rattles his throat softly, shakes his head. "Oh. I'm sorry. Did Roth . . ." I tap the crossed-out face. "He killed them, didn't he? That's why you escaped. Why you broke the bond. Roth betrayed you."

Aki blinks at me.

"You never owed him anything," I add. "You don't owe me anything, either. You don't have to come with us. You're free."

How can I make him understand? I pretend my wrists are bound together, then yank them apart, snapping invisible chains. I flap my hands like two birds heading for the horizon. I'm about to give up, when Aki reaches over, gently takes my hand, and places it over his heart. I can feel it beating, just like mine. *Ba-dump, ba-dump, ba-dump.* He nods at me. Holds his other hand over my heart, and smiles. Nearly makes me cry. "Okay," I say. "Together."

I want to say we'll make Roth pay for everything he's done, but that's exactly what Elsa told me. I give Aki a thumbs-up instead. He gives me one, too, then takes the parchment back to gaze at his family. I decide to give him some privacy. "Rattle if you need anything."

I go check on the others. Violet's asleep, snuggled up with her longbow on the bench. So cute. Yaku's farther down, keeping an eye on Masaru, Elsa, and the two red-cloaked guards.

Hickory stirs when I pass him. "Can't sleep either, huh?"

"Nah." I sit next to him on the bench. Tap my hands in the awkward silence. "So—"

"Hey—"

"Sorry—"

"No," Hickory says. "You go. Please."

"Well, I just wanted to say, you know . . . sorry. For hitting you. And saying you were no different from Roth and Elsa. I was out of line."

"No," Hickory says with a sigh, "you weren't."

I frown at him. "What do you mean?"

"This afternoon, Masaru told me what Roth did to this world, and why. I got the fanatical version, of course, but he spared no detail. It scared me—more than anything's ever scared me before." He pauses, struggling to find the right words. "I used to believe there was nothing more terrifying than a monster I couldn't understand. Now, I think the opposite's true."

I scratch my ear, trying to make sense of what he's said. "You're saying . . . you understand Roth? Killing all those people, starting a war, all because Neela was killed?"

Hickory nods. "Pain. Isolation. Grief." He stares at Elsa, still slumped over down the back of the plane. "These things can tear even the strongest people apart."

"Speaking from personal experience?"

Hickory takes a deep breath, clasps his hands. "I told you, back in the Manor. I was alone for so long in there I began to forget everything. Bluehaven. My family. I was truly, utterly alone." He sniffs, wipes his nose. "Then the

Manor started changing. That acrid smell drifted through the corridors. I didn't know what it was, but I knew something was . . . off." He nods at Aki, up in the cockpit. "I remember the first time I saw the Leatherheads. Thought my mind was playing tricks. I avoided them for ages, but they found me in the end."

"They shot you," I say. "Carted you off to Roth's lair. You told us that, too."

"But I didn't tell you what happened next. Roth was delighted when he saw me." Hickory taps the side of his head. "I've seen more of the Manor than anyone, after all. He trawled through my memories, but I'd been in the Manor so long, what he found was a scattered mess. He grew frustrated, was about to kill me, but realized I was worth more alive. He knew I was desperate to get out of the Manor, so he showed me what he was looking for."

"The Cradle," I say. "The keys."

"One key, remember? He didn't show me *you*, or your dad or Elsa. Didn't want me to know the whole story. Didn't want me beating him to the prize. He just told me to bring him one key and whoever was carrying it. Promised he'd release me from the Manor at last."

"He told you to catch any other people you came across, too, right?"

Hickory nods slowly. "Gave me one of his masks to show the Leatherheads I was under his protection. Made me the first bounty hunter. Then he let me go. I fled as far as I could. Told myself I'd never help Roth. But then—must've been a year or so later—" He pauses. "You once asked how many people I turned in. How many I led to their deaths."

Part of me doesn't want to know anymore, but I still find myself asking, "Are we talking, like, ten? Twenty?"

"One," Hickory says, but he might as well have said one hundred, judging by the look of shame on his face. "A man, unremarkable in every way. I don't know which world he came from or how he found his way into the Manor. We couldn't understand each other, but I knew he was afraid. I comforted him. Told him to follow me. Before I realized what I was doing, we were halfway to Roth's lair." A tear rolls down his cheek. "I got in and out as quickly as I could. But I heard the man's screams as I fled into the Manor again."

"Why did you do it?" I ask. "If you were so scared—"

"I did it *because* I was scared—of Roth, of his army, of spending another thousand years trapped inside the Manor." He wipes his cheek. "Everything changed when I met her."

"You mean Farrow," I say. "You met her *inside* the Manor?"

"Yes."

"She wasn't from Bluehaven?"

"No. She came from Barjuun. A peaceful world of green, rolling mountains."

Farrow, Hickory tells me, was a shepherd. She loved it, too, tending her flock of goats, camping out under the stars. But one night, a storm swept over the mountains and her flock scattered—some of them into a deep, dark cave. It was there that Farrow found a door.

A Manor gateway.

She touched the stone, the cave shook, the door rumbled open, and candles flickered to life in the corridor beyond. She stepped inside. The gateway closed behind her.

"Bet she really hated goats after that, huh?" I say. Hickory frowns. "Sorry, I just meant, if it weren't for the—she wouldn't have—anyway, carry on."

Apparently, a goat or three ran into the Manor, too—right into a booby trap. That was when Farrow knew she was really in trouble. The gateway wouldn't open again, so she wandered deep into the Manor, got lost. Wasn't long before she found Hickory.

"I was building my hideout in the middle of the maze," he says, "hammering together a couple of Manor doors. I looked up and . . . there she was."

She was beautiful. Black hair. Dark eyes. Hands calloused from years of wielding her shepherd's crook. Farrow was wary of him, kept her distance, but Hickory comforted her. Again, he didn't want to offer Roth a new prisoner. Again, he started to anyway.

It was a long journey to the fortress. Hickory and Farrow understood each other. Spoke the same language, in more ways than one. Hickory had found a friend at last. When they were a day's march from the fortress, he realized he couldn't turn her in. He broke down and told her everything—about Roth, about the half-mask, and the man he'd led to his death.

"And she forgave you?" I ask. "Just like that?"

He shakes his head. "She left me. Fled into the Manor. I don't know how much time passed before I saw her again. I'd gone back to my hideout. I was in a bad place. Very bad. I used to step outside my shack, stand at the edge of that dark abyss and"—Hickory clears his throat—"never mind. I'd been there before, of course, in the bad place, but something always held me back. Fear. Hope." He shrugs. "But one day I couldn't feel it anymore. Couldn't feel . . . anything. I was so tired. That was when she found me again. She pulled me back from the edge."

"Why did she come back?"

"I asked her the same thing. She just told me we had work to do. It took time, but we became friends again. Eventually something more. We finished the shack in the center of the maze. Plotted and planned, dreamed and laughed. We lived together for . . . must've been fifty years, or thereabouts. For the first time in as long as I could remember, I felt truly free." Hickory smiles. "She was my world, and I was hers. I suppose we were lucky, in a way. Most people never know that kind of love."

"Now I *really* feel bad we blew up your shack."

"Don't sweat it." Hickory's smile fades. "Didn't feel the same after she was gone."

"Can I ask . . . what happened to her?"

Hickory steels himself. Takes a deep breath. "We worked tirelessly to beat Roth at his own game. Started scouring the Manor for the Cradle key—for any clues at all. Laid plenty of traps for the Leatherheads and Tin-skins, too. We swore we'd claim the Cradle and tear down the Manor to ensure nobody would share the same fate as ours."

It all ended while they were out searching for the key. Some Leatherheads found them. Farrow and Hickory fled but were caught in a booby trap. Stone-slab trigger. A single spear. A simple but deadly device.

"It was my fault," Hickory says. "I should've seen it coming. It should've been me." He stares down at his hands. "Farrow died in my arms. I made her a promise first, though: I'd finish what we started. So I kept searching. Kept fighting. And one day"—he looks at me—"I found a girl in the snow."

Once again, I don't know what to say. I finally know the full truth about Hickory, and it's more tragic than I ever imagined.

"The point is," Hickory says, "I lost my mind in the Manor. But when I knew I'd lost Farrow forever? That was when I truly went mad. Buried alive for a thousand years . . . who's to say I wouldn't turn out like Roth?" He looks straight at me. "Who's to say you wouldn't, too, Jane, if you lost what matters most?"

My nightmare. The pain I felt on the foundation stone when I knew—I just *knew*—Dad and Violet had been killed. The emptiness. The void. How do I know that sadness wouldn't turn to rage? Maybe I'm more like Roth and Elsa than I thought. Maybe we all are.

"But I'm done letting grief rule my life," Hickory says. "I want to help you."

"Save the Manor," I say. "Stop Roth. No tricks."

"No tricks."

"You're not just saying that so you can turn around when we're all standing on the foundation stone and take a big steaming dump on us, are you?"

"What? No. Don't be disgusting."

"You can't blame me for having trust issues."

"I'm on your side, Jane. I still think the Manor's dangerous, and you're gonna have to think long and hard about what you do with it when all this is over, but—well—it's simple. Farrow wouldn't want more innocent people to die. I can't promise I'll stick around after Roth's gone, but until then . . . I'll do whatever it takes to stop him."

I smile at Hickory. "Told you. Push comes to shove."

He smiles back. "Push comes to shove."

"I mean, fixing our blankets while we sleep? That's devotion."

"Ugh, I knew I shouldn't've done that."

"You love us. It's okay. Perfectly natural."

"Shut up and let me sleep." Hickory wraps his cloak tight around his shoulders, leans back against the hull. I'm about to head back to the cockpit when he says, "Thanks, Jane. I've never told anyone about Farrow before. I just . . . miss her. So much."

"She'd be proud of you, Hickory," I say. "I am, too."

THE CRADLE PATH

Dawn comes quickly up here in the sky. The suns rise in a burst of reddish-gold, illuminating the dune sea: an undulating, dappled expanse of rolling mounds, shadowy troughs, and towering sandcastles shaped by the winds. It's a desolate place. Barren but beautiful. I think I finally understand the appeal of flying.

"Can you believe this?" I ask Violet, fogging up my window with my breath.

"Uh-uh," she says, glued to a window of her own.

We can see Betty's wings too, dangling a couple of big engines and propellers apiece, spinning so fast they're a blur.

"Elsa charted these regions using ancient records in the Elders' library." Yaku's kneeling on the floor behind us, Elsa's papers spread out before him. He hands a map to Hickory. "Assuming she got this right, we're not far from the gateway."

The bundle of nerves in my gut knots a little tighter. "Let's get back to it, then."

We've been going over the charts for ages, trying to work out how to get into the Manor and past Roth's lair. Yaku has sketched a rough map of his own. "Elsa's plan is still our best bet," he says. "We circle far around the gateway"—he draws a long, curved line—"so we will not be spotted or heard, and land a safe distance on the plateau behind."

I glance back at Elsa. She's glaring at us with bloodshot eyes. The two red-cloaks are awake as well, all bound together in one merry parcel. Masaru hasn't slept a wink. He's just sitting there, calmly watching us all. Disturbing is what it is.

"Apparently, there's a supply route up there." Hickory taps another sheet of parchment. "A road heading north, from the top of the plateau to some sort of ancient city. One of Roth's old stomping grounds. We wait till nightfall, sneak up to the road and hijack one of Roth's supply vehicles. Aki suits up and takes the wheel. We hide in the back and hope for the best."

"I'll come with you to the top of the cliff," Yaku says, drawing another line on his map. "Then I'll jump out here and hide—provide cover or make a distraction if you need it." He marks a cross on the map, at the base of the gateway. "There will most likely be a checkpoint here."

"The Leatherheads have no idea we're out here," Violet says. "I doubt they'll give the vehicles a second glance. Of course, getting inside the Manor's just the start." She turns to Hickory. "How far is it from the gateway to Roth's fortress?"

"According to Elsa's notes," he says, "about a day's hike on foot, maybe more. In a truck, considerably less. Wish I could tell you more, but I never got close to it myself."

"Never got close to the gateway?" I ask.

Hickory shakes his head. "There are Leatherhead checkpoints at every intersection surrounding the fortress. Spotlights, barbed wire, the works. Soon as I saw them, I knew I'd never have a chance. And don't get me started on the lava. Nasty stuff."

"Wait," I say, "What's lava doing around Roth's lair?"

"It's streaming through a weakened gateway," Hickory says. "Corridors are full of the stuff now. Spewing down stairwells, over balconies—you think those waterfalls in the Manor were impressive, wait till you see a lavafall."

"I can imagine," Violet says, breathless and wide-eyed.

"Focus," I tell her, nodding at Elsa's notes. "Does she say anything about the corridor beyond the gateway?"

"Just that Roth turned it into a road."

"Okay, so we break away from the convoy as soon as we're inside. Find a hallway or a door, and hope the Manor shifts us far away from Roth and his fortress and . . ."

And everyone in it.

I stare at the charts, heart rattling my rib cage. It kills me that Dad's in that place. That we're gonna be so close and yet so far. That we can't rescue him and the rest of Roth's prisoners before we find the Cradle.

We just can't risk it.

Get to the Cradle, he told me on the train. *I love you.*

Violet gives my shoulder a gentle squeeze. "We'll head back and get him, Jane."

"As soon as we can," Hickory adds. He nods at Masaru, Elsa, and the red-cloaks. "What about them? We leaving them behind on the plateau?"

"Masaru, definitely," Yaku says. "He *wants* to be captured. He'll alert the Gorani to our presence the first chance he gets. Elsa can't be trusted either, but this is not my decision."

Elsa isn't glaring at us anymore. If she wasn't gagged, she'd be smiling. She knows we need her alive.

"I know she betrayed you, Jane," Hickory says quietly, "but the mission comes first. We can't just wander aimlessly *and hope* the Manor sets us on the right track. The place is falling apart. Even if it wanted to help us, it might not be able to. What do we know about this path to the Cradle she mentioned, apart from the spike pit near the end of it?"

"Basically nothing," I say.

Violet cracks her knuckles. "Let's remedy that, then."

With a nod at Aki to show him everything's okay, I head to the back of the plane with the others. Masaru hums into his gag when we pass him. Yaku plucks Elsa's from her mouth.

She spits at our feet. "That Gorani better not break my plane. Betty needs a soft touch."

"No more stalling," I say. "Tell us how you found the Cradle."

She sniffs. Stretches out her neck and rolls her shoulders. "Untie me first."

"Tell us, or we'll throw you off this hunk of junk."

"*Junk?* Wash your mouth out. And we both know you wouldn't dare, Jane. What would Daddy say if you killed the woman he loves?"

"If he knew what you'd become? Not much, I'd guess."

"Come, *oda min*," Yaku says. "You still have a chance to make things right."

"You wanna talk about making things right, *old friend?*" Elsa scowls. "After everything I've done for you—everything I've taught you—*this* is how you repay me?"

"Hey!" I shout. "Tell us how you found the Cradle, right now. How did you and Dad escape from Roth? He started taking you both out into the Manor, right? Figured you'd have better luck finding it than him because you're not evil. At least, you *weren't* evil, back then."

"And he was right, wasn't he?" Violet says. "You were making progress."

Elsa glowers at us. I wouldn't be surprised if steam started hissing from her ears.

"Fine," she says at last. "After Roth killed my son—after he'd deemed me fit enough to help Charlie continue the search—he marched us out into the Manor constantly. We went deeper and deeper, deciphering clues, dodging traps, following the path of Cradle symbols."

"Cradle symbols carved into the stone," Hickory says, deep in thought.

Elsa nods. "But the path only ever took us so far. The Manor was working against us. We knew it'd never let Roth near the Cradle. He knew it, too. One day—night—whatever it was—a guard forgot to lock our cell.

We sneaked out. The place was deserted. We ran. Found ourselves back on the Cradle trail. I wanted to pick a different path, get away, but Charlie wanted to *save the worlds*. What he really wanted was revenge . . .

"This time, the path kept going. Very long. Very dangerous. Eventually, we came to a grand hall." She stares into space, like she's right back there, taking it all in. "It was big. At least twenty stories high. Hundreds of balconies, archways and doors. It seemed safe, so Charlie stepped inside and, as soon as he did, the stone fell away beneath his feet. I grabbed him just in time. The floor was false. I'm sure you can guess what lay below."

"The spike pit," I say.

"We were about to turn back when we heard a Taw-taw bark far behind us, and we knew." Elsa's voice trembles with rage. "Roth had *let* us escape. We scanned the walls for a sign that we were still on the right path. That's when Charlie saw it: a Cradle symbol etched onto the floor of the hall, near the portion that had fallen away. And beyond that, another."

"You had to pick your way across."

"Quickly, too," Elsa says. "Even the stones with the Cradle symbols on them were only safe for a moment. They crumbled as soon as we jumped to the next. We were about halfway across when the whole thing started to collapse. We ran, leaping from stone to stone. By the time we made it to the other side, the entire floor lay in ruin between the spikes below."

"Then where did you go?" Violet asks.

"Through a door. Down a hallway. The keys were on a pedestal at the entrance to the Cradle."

"Which door?" I ask. "Tell us exactly—"

"So you can ditch me when we land?" Elsa *tut-tuts*. "I don't think so, sweetheart."

Violet grabs her by the collar. "You pathetic, twisted—"

"There are hundreds of doors in that hall, and if Roth's army's on our tail—let's face it, a highly likely scenario—you won't have time to check them one by one. Then you have to actually *open* the Cradle. No small task if you don't know the secret."

Violet releases her grip. "What are you talking about?"

"We all know the Makers are cruel," Elsa says, "their methods unique. The door to the Cradle itself is a puzzle. Another trap. Deadly one, too. Simple but effective. Charlie and I figured it out, of course, but only just in time. Take me, and you'll pass through in a breeze." Elsa grins at me, ever so sweetly. "I told you I'd be right beside you till the end, Jane. I meant it."

I grit my teeth and clench my fists. I'm about to say "Fine" when Hickory turns to us, wide-eyed.

"Jane. Violet. A word, please?"

Leaving Yaku to watch over Elsa and the red-cloaks, we huddle a safe distance away.

"I know where it is," Hickory whispers. "The path to the Cradle."

"What?" Violet says. "You've *seen* the Cradle symbols somewhere?"

"Technically, no." Hickory nods at me. "But she has."

"*Me?*" I whisper, racking my brain. "What are you—I haven't—"

"In the booby trap," he says. I can barely hear him over the rumble of Betty's engines. "The one we tripped when we were being chased by the Tin-skin, soon after we met."

"No way . . ."

Hickory's right. All those stone-plate symbols and crushing columns. The diving and ducking, scrambling and screaming. We were there. Right there.

How could I be so stupid?

"Elsa." I dash back down the plane. "When you and Dad were on the path to the Cradle, did you pass through a room covered in square stone plates? Plates with symbols on them?"

She blinks at me, taken aback. "Yes."

This is huge. This is it.

"And when you hit the Cradle symbol, the door sealed you inside, a whole bunch of columns shot across the room, and a trapdoor opened in the ceiling so you could get out?"

Elsa shakes her head. "No . . . there were *two* Cradle symbols. Charlie and I pressed them at the same time and a trapdoor opened in the *floor.*" She gazes up at me in wonderment. "You were there. You were on the path, but you went the wrong way."

"Not my fault," Hickory pipes up behind me. "For the record."

"We were trapped in there with a Tin-skin," I say. "I saved us. Kind of."

"Never mind who did what," Yaku says, "where is it?"

251

"Far away from Roth's fortress," I say. "Way back near the—"

I freeze. Images from my nightmare flash through my mind. Roth. The Specters. That grand, frozen hall—the very first hall the Manor took me to. I saw myself in there. *Wait*, I shouted at her, *you're going the wrong way!* I set off through the snow to stop her. The snow that had to be at least six feet deep. The snow that was hiding a very pointy secret.

Return, the voice said.

Not just to the Manor. Not just to the Cradle.

To the beginning.

My legs get all wobbly. I've gotta sit down. "I've been there. To the hall with the spike pit. I just didn't know it." Everyone's watching me. Violet, Hickory, Elsa, Yaku and Masaru. Even the red-cloaks are craning their necks my way, and I don't think they can understand a word I'm saying. "I know where the Cradle is." I grip the two keys tight. "It's—"

"Don't," Violet jumps in, glancing at Masaru. "If things go south inside the Manor—if Roth gets into our heads—he'll know it, too. Don't tell any of us."

"What if something happens to me?" I ask. "If I die, the secret's lost."

"If you die," she says, "we're all goners anyway."

That's when Aki rattles his throat, alarmed. Betty suddenly banks to the left, and we're all thrown off our feet. We scramble back to the cockpit.

"Aki, what the—"

He slams his fist on the window to his right and rattles his throat, spraying the grimy glass with slobber. I dash to a side window with Violet and Hickory to get a better look, but can't see what he's fussing about. Rolling dunes. The sky. A tiny black cloud and trail of—

"Smoke!" I shout. "Down there. See it?"

But it's already slipped out of sight.

"What's going on up there?" Elsa shouts.

"It was a flare," I say, sick to the stomach. "A black flare, I'm sure of it."

"An outpost?" Yaku says. "Out here?"

Aki snarls again. Another flare's been fired. It streaks up into the sky ahead and explodes with a silent puff. Seconds later, a third flare's fired, much farther along the dunes, and a fourth, way out near the horizon. A tiny black squiggle. An inverted exclamation mark.

"A network of them," Hickory says, "probably leading to the gateway."

The Leatherheads know we're coming.

"Aki, change course," Violet says, darting from window to window.

"Swing west," Hickory says, checking Elsa's charts. "Jane, tell him to—"

"No," I say. Everyone freezes and stares at me. I'd be staring, too. I can't believe I'm about to say this. "We have to follow the flares. Head straight to the gateway."

"What?" Hickory ditches the charts. "No, Jane—"

"We've lost the element of surprise. Any moment now, the entire camp above the gateway's gonna be called to arms. There's no way we'll be able to sneak inside, which means we'll have to fight our way in, and the longer we wait, the longer they'll have to prepare. We need to strike now and get inside the Manor before word reaches Roth."

"How?" Violet asks. "How can we take on that many Leatherheads?"

I shrug. "We'll figure that out after we land."

Masaru cackles into his gag, shaking his head and rattling his beads. Can't believe his good fortune. Elsa narrows her eyes at me. She actually looks impressed.

The others may not like it, but they know I'm right.

Our plans have been shattered.

We're flying into battle.

CRASH LANDING

Turns out this bucket of bolts can fly *fast*. Before we know it, we're soaring high over the dune sea's tiny camps with their clusters of ant-sized tents and Leatherhead specks. Some open fire at us. Others are already on the move, leaping from dune to dune on these big lizard-looking creatures, headed back to the gateway.

"Reinforcements," Hickory grunts. "Well, this keeps getting better and better."

The edge of the dune sea emerges from the morning haze far ahead, lapping at the base of a sprawling plateau. The winding cliff cuts through the desert from east to west. Way off to our right, I spot a dark smudge along the clifftop: the main Leatherhead camp. And below it, big and wide and dark: the open Manor gateway.

Click-clack-click. Aki points at something in the sky.

"What's wrong?" I ask, but then I see them. "Oh, crap."

Three small planes are rocketing towards us.

Aki tilts the yoke hard—we veer sharply to the left—and a volley of bullets peppers Betty's side with a *rat-a-tat-tat*, blasting right through her rusted hull. We duck for cover, shielding our ears against the noise. The planes roar past, so close the wind thumps us as they go, like a slap from the sky itself. Masaru's near tears, he's loving this so much.

"What do we do now?" Violet shouts.

"Keep flying," Yaku says. "Try to lose them over the plateau."

"How?" I scream. "There's nothing out there!"

Aki pulls back on the yoke. Betty climbs, veering to the right this time.

"Jane, Violet, Hickory, check those windows," Elsa shouts from the back of the plane. "We need eyes on those birds. Yaku, get back here and untie me."

"No way," I shout.

"You want to make it to the plateau in one piece?" She barks an order at the red-cloaks bound to her back. They stop wriggling around at once. "Untie me right now! No time to argue!"

Yaku looks at me. I turn to Violet and Hickory.

"She built the thing," Hickory says. "Let her fly it."

I nod at Yaku. "Just her, though. And if she tries anything funny—"

"She wouldn't dare," he growls, and hurries to set Elsa free.

We scramble back to the windows, scanning the sky for the three planes.

"They've split up," Hickory shouts. "Two went left—"

"The other's up there to the right," Violet shouts. "They're coming back around!"

"Yes, yes, yes!" Masaru cackles. He's managed to slip free of his gag. "No escape this time, little ones! Roth will wrench the keys from your filthy, charred re—"

BAM. Yaku knocks him out cold.

"Finally," Elsa says, rubbing her wrists and storming past them both. She jumps into the copilot's chair, flicks a few switches, and starts shouting orders at Aki like "Level off," and "Speed up to two-fifty knots," and "Quit snarling," miming each point to drive it home.

"Please tell me you have a plan," I say. We're soaring east now, in line with the cliffs.

"Working on it," Elsa grunts. She digs around in a compartment beside her, tosses me a pair of old binoculars. "The encampment. In the distance. Tell me what you see."

I adjust the focus on the binoculars. The view's shaky, but I can see that the zigzagging cliffside roads are packed with trucks and troops, heading to the ramshackle encampment above. Twenty-odd tanks are trundling into position around it, too, cannons aimed skyward.

"Leatherheads," I say. "Hundreds of them. Tanks and trucks, too. They'll be on us like flies the moment we land."

"Heads up!" Violet shouts from the back of the plane.

Thwat, thwat, rat-a-tat, another round of bullets tears through the cabin. Everybody hits the deck. Two planes shriek by, and one of the red-cloaks cries out. The other's slumped forward, unmoving, a puddle spreading around him as red as his cloak.

"Third plane's coming," Hickory shouts at Elsa. "Do something!"

"Aki, follow my lead," she cries. "Everybody hold on! Three, two—"

They slam their yokes forward. Yaku and I grip the backs of their chairs just in time as Betty nosedives toward the dunes. My stomach jumps into my throat. My legs leave the ground. I feel like I'm floating. I glance beyond my flailing legs and catch a glimpse of the red-cloaks squished against the back ramp, Violet and Hickory clinging to a bench, and Masaru dangling unconscious beside them. And ahead, through the grimy windshield, the dunes rocketing toward us, way too fast. All I can see is sand.

We're gonna crash.

"Elllsssaaaaaa!"

"Now, Aki!" They pull back, straining and screaming with the effort. "That's it, that's iiiiiiit!" Betty pulls up just in time. We clip the peak of a towering dune, skim the surface of the sandy sea, and soar up, up, up again, the view through the windshield nothing but sky.

It worked. The third plane missed us.

"Power levers back," Elsa says, leveling Betty out. "Don't wanna cook the engines. Fuel?" She checks a dial. Taps it frantically with her finger. *Fuel?*

"No, no, no," I say. "Don't tell me . . ."

"Check the wings," she says. "Hurry."

I dash to a window halfway down the cabin and swear under my breath. The underside of the wing is leaking all over. Our fuel's being stolen by the wind.

"How bad is it? Jane, what do you see?"

"Um, picture a giant sieve."

"This side is no good, either," Yaku says behind me.

Elsa swears. "We're not gonna be able to shake these guys. I hate to say it, but our best bet is to surrender. Put her down on the plateau, and—"

"Don't you dare," I shout. "We can't give up!"

Aki rattles his throat and veers Betty to the right as—*BOOM, BOOM, BOOM*—three massive explosions nearly blast us out of the sky. The tanks have opened fire. We're soaring over the camp now, headed for the flat open wasteland of the plateau. I turn to Violet, Hickory, and Yaku. They shrug at me, out of ideas.

Think, think, think.

Betty's riddled with holes. We're losing fuel. There's no way we'll be able to fight our way through that many Leatherheads once we land. We won't make it anywhere near the—

"Oh!" I say, struck by a very bad idea that just might work. "Oh, oh, oh!"

"What?" Violet asks, but I'm already dashing back to the cockpit.

"The gateway. Elsa, how big is the corridor on the other side?"

"What?"

"The corridor. Inside the Manor. You said Roth turned it into a road. How big is it?"

"Very," she says, slowly cottoning on. "But—"

"Can you do it? Is it long enough?"

Rat-a-tat-tat, ka-boom! The planes shriek past again, taking out an engine this time. The propeller on the far right smokes, shudders, and dies, shot to pieces.

Still, Betty soldiers on.

"You said it yourself, Elsa, we've only got one shot at this. The Leatherheads are gathering at the top of the cliff. The gateway's pretty much unguarded." I put a hand on Aki's shoulder. He looks back at me. *Click-clack-click.* "Can you do it or not?"

"We'll lose the wings upon entry," Elsa says.

"So what?" I say. "Do we need those on the ground?"

"Valid point."

"Hey!" Hickory says. "What's going on?"

Elsa buckles in, starts swinging Betty in a wide arc. "Brace yourselves! We're going in!"

Hickory gawks at us both. "Into the *Manor*? Right *now*?"

"Yes," Violet says, hungry-eyed, like all her birthdays have come at once.

I turn to Yaku. "I'm sorry. I know you don't want to leave Arakaan, but—"

"We have no choice." He stares out at the desert. "I know. I will help you to the end, Jane. Then I will find my way home."

"We're all gonna die," Hickory says.

"Shut up!" Elsa shouts. "We can do this."

While she tells Aki the plan—miming, pointing, shouting—the rest of us prepare for landing. Violet and I find a bundle of rope and lash it around the bench behind

Elsa, so we can strap in. Yaku frees the red-cloak from the dead-cloak and ties him to the bench beside Masaru. The old man's coming to. He'll be thrilled when he wakes up inside the Manor.

If we don't crash and burn, of course.

The Leatherheads are in a frenzy, sprinting from their dwellings and leaping into their vehicles as we soar over the cliffs again, back to the dune sea. Elsa and Aki take us out wide, preparing to line us up with the gateway. I can see it through a back window. It's propped open by rusty beams and buttresses, big enough for us to shoot on through. Sheer terror aside, I wonder how Elsa feels, being back here. This is where she was first captured by Roth all those years ago.

This is where her nightmare started.

The tanks and planes open fire again. Rockets streak past us, trailing white smoke. More bullets tear through the cabin, shattering windows, blowing another engine to bits. Elsa and Aki swoop us down and swing Betty round, not so nice and steady. The dunes whip past the windows. The gateway's in our sights now, dead ahead, looming closer by the second.

Elsa glares at us over her shoulder. "Sit down!"

The four of us clamber to the bench and strap in.

"After we land, stay close to me," Violet shouts. "Still got the keys?"

I nod. "Still got the arrowhead?"

She smiles and holds my hand. "We've got this, Jane. We're nearly there."

Hickory grabs my other hand. "I'm really starting to regret my decision to help you two."

Yaku closes his eyes, muttering some kind of prayer.

Aki *click-clacks* his throat. Elsa shouts, "Here we go—easy now—hold on!"

I clench my eyes shut. Squeeze Violet's and Hickory's hands as tight as I can, and—

SMASH.

We hit the ground and explode through the gateway. Betty's wings are ripped from her sides. We scream, clinging to the bench and each other. My eyes flick open as the back of the plane snaps off in a shower of sparks, and still we careen through the corridor, crashing through who knows what. The lights cut out. Betty bounces, scrapes the ceiling, lands again. The wheels snap off and she lurches, jarring my neck and knees. We skid and spark, grind to a halt.

And, just like that, it's over. We're alive. Back in the Manor at last.

Now for the hard part.

HOMECOMING

My ears are ringing. My head's hammering. The rope binding us to the bench comes undone, and I collapse onto the floor in a daze, coughing and gasping. I can't see a thing. Someone tugs my arm. Says my name. Helps me to my feet and holds me. We stagger through the smoke to the back of the plane. Gunshots fire somewhere. Somebody screams.

"Violet," I gasp. "Hickory?" The person holding me grips me tighter. "Slow down . . ."

"Here," they shout. A man. "Over here! I've got her! I'm on your side!"

A jangle of beads. A bony arm digging into my side.

Masaru's dragging me from the plane.

"Get off me!" I shove the old man, slip out of his grip, trip down the broken ramp and land in a heap on the floor. Manor candles dance and spin. Sparks burst from Betty's crumpled hull, lighting up the corridor like miniature fireworks. A stampede of boots echoes around me. Leatherheads *click* and *clack.* A Tin-skin barks furiously. Chains rattle.

"Here," Masaru cackles, clawing at my clothes, my hair, my neck. "Praise be to Roth!"

The old man waves his arms and jumps up and down like an excitable dog, until—*wham*—Hickory shoves him aside and helps me up.

"Time to go."

"Violet," I say. "Where's—"

The Leatherheads open fire. Bullets ricochet around us, sparking off the wreck, blasting the corridor to pieces. We duck into a nearby hallway, leaping over debris. Elsa's red-cloaked guard's already here, wide-eyed, panicking, babbling things under his breath.

"Jane," Violet cries out from inside the wreck. "Run!"

I try to help her, but Hickory grabs me and pulls me back into the hallway as another volley of rifle-fire tears the corridor apart. "Let—me—go! We have to save her!"

"Get out of here," Violet screams. "Hickory, if you've got her, go!"

"You can't save her if you're dead," Hickory says, pulling me farther down the hallway. "Run now, fight later. We'll get her back, Jane. I promise."

Hickory's right. The Leatherheads are swarming around the crash site.

We dash down the hallway, following the frantic red-cloak. My knees ache. My back, too. My body's still recovering from the crash, but I can't stop. Judging by the racket behind us, a Tin-skin's caught our scent.

We take a right, a left, leap down a stone staircase,

and come to an archway boarded up with long, rotted planks covered in faded red crosses.

"Not a good sign," Hickory says.

But we can't turn back. The Tin-skin's almost here.

We pry a plank away. I'm about to squeeze through when the red-cloak shoves me aside and scrambles into the darkness first.

"Hey," I shout, "slow down—you don't know what this place is like!"

Chandeliers flicker to life, illuminating a long, downward-sloping corridor and the red-cloak bolting down it. Me and Hickory squeeze through after him, warning him to be careful. We scan the walls and floor for traps and triggers, but our pal's already found one.

A stone-slab switch in the floor.

The corridor rumbles. We turn around as a panel above the archway slides to the side, revealing a gigantic, perfectly round boulder. A boulder that's already rolling forward.

"You've gotta be kidding me," I mutter.

"Run!" Hickory shouts.

The Tin-skin bursts through the planks. The boulder squashes it at once, crashing into the corridor and bowling toward us, scraping the walls, knocking the chandeliers. There's no way we can get around it, no way we can jump it. Forward is the only way, and fast.

We run. The corridor gets steeper—the boulder picks up speed—but the end's in sight. I'd like to think we're in with a shot, but the red-cloak's skidding to a halt up ahead, and for good reason.

A trapdoor's opened at his feet. A gap in the floor several yards long.

"Don't stop," Hickory yells. "Jump, jump, jump!"

I step up the pace. Focus on the glowing chamber beyond the trapdoor. The red-cloak backs up, takes a run-up and jumps just as we reach the edge. The three of us leap over the gap and land together safely on the other side. I spin around just in time to see the boulder fall into the seemingly bottomless pit, scraping down the sides.

Hickory sits up and grunts. "So nice to be back."

I collapse onto my back. "At least we got away from the Tin-skin."

Thrilled by our escape, the red-cloak leaps to his feet and cheers. But the party ain't over yet. We've landed in a small torch-lit chamber full of statues armed with serrated swords. And as the boulder hits the bottom of the pit with an almighty crash, the final mechanism of this infernal device is triggered.

A huge stone tablet rolls into place over the chamber's archway, sealing our retreat. I shout, "Duck!" pull Hickory to the floor, and clench my eyes shut as the statues swing their blades. One of them slices so close I feel the air brush past my cheek. I hear the red-cloak hit the deck a second later, and after that—nothing.

I refuse to look. "Um, Hickory? Is he . . ."

"Yep."

We lie in silence for a bit, catching our breath. I don't know what to say. Technically, he was one of the bad guys, after all. One of Elsa's goons. It's a bit awkward, really.

I mean, we've gotta get moving. Gotta get back to the others. "We should probably—"

"Go," Hickory says. "Yeah. There's another door across the way. Just watch your step. He's . . . all over the place."

TAKEN

"Maybe they got away," I say. "Violet can take care of herself. She has Aki. And Yaku. I bet they're waiting for us near the plane. Hiding."

"Maybe," Hickory says, but I can tell he doesn't believe it. "This way. I think."

We climb a winding stairwell, a bunch of Manor candles lighting the way. It feels so strange being back here, knowing everything I know now. I clutch the two keys dangling around my neck as we walk. Run the fingers of my free hand along the stone wall.

I'm part of this place. This place is part of me.

All those years I hated it—all those years I was afraid of it—the Manor was waiting for me, haunting my dreams, calling me back. Now I'm here at last, armed with the truth. Question is, how far will I have to go to save it? The Makers poured their life force into the foundation stone. Am I supposed to do the same?

What if I'm walking to my death?

"So," Hickory says, "the Cradle entrance. It's in the snow, right?"

"How did you—I mean, maybe? No. I'm not supposed to say."

"I know." Hickory pauses at the top of the stairs, makes sure the coast is clear, and waves me forward. "But Elsa said the booby trap with the crushing columns was near the end of the Cradle path. And you said you've been to the hall with the spike pit floor before. *You*. Not *we*." He shrugs. "The snow's the only place you were alone for a while."

Ugh.

"Don't worry, I'm not asking for specifics. Violet was right when she said not to tell anyone. I can help you get back to the snow, but it'll be a long journey. Too long. Too risky. You're gonna need to speed things up when the time comes."

"What do you mean, speed things up?"

"You're the third key. The Manor can shift rooms. Stands to reason you can, too."

I stop walking. "How?"

"No idea. You're the child of the Makers—you work it out. But once we rescue the others, we may not have a lot of time, so I'd get thinking good and hard."

"Oh, sure," I grunt, "I'll get right on that." Cause quakes. Shift rooms. Heal the Manor. I wish I came with an instruction manual.

"You'll figure it out." Hickory holds up a hand—*stop*. Waves it—*go*. "You've got both keys, and you have way more control of your powers than you did a few days ago."

"I don't know about that," I say. "I mean, yeah, I stopped that truck from hitting the plane, but once the power takes hold, it's . . ." I want to say brutal and terrible and actually kinda wonderful, but I don't. I can't. "Dangerous," I settle on instead.

"So take it easy. Whenever you've caused quakes in the past, you've been a little . . . worked up, right?"

"That's putting it lightly."

"You've been scared. Angry. If those feelings cause you to tear stone apart, maybe"—he shrugs—"maybe the opposite ones might mend it."

I blink at him. "Think happy thoughts? Really? That's your big theory?"

"I'm just saying, take a step back," he says. "Relax. Try to cause a quake when you're in control of your emotions and see what happens. Focus on something good."

Something good. Easier said than done when you're being hunted by an army.

"First things first," I say. "We've gotta get back to Betty and—"

The sound of trucks, rumbling in the distance.

We pause, share a look, creep quietly down a corridor to our left, and duck behind a balcony balustrade overlooking a vast, smoky hall. Roth's road cuts right through it. There are Leatherheads everywhere; marching, hauling crates, standing guard around a line of cloth-topped trucks. Tin-skins bark and gnash their teeth. Torches and fire-drums throw nightmarish shadows upon the walls.

"Get your stinking hands off me!" Violet's being forced toward one of the trucks, hands tied behind her back. I wanna save her. Right now.

Hickory grabs my arm. "Don't even think about it," he whispers. "Wait. Watch."

Yaku's right behind Violet, swollen-eyed and bloody-lipped, but walking with his head held high. Elsa's being marched to the trucks, too: resigned, silent. Masaru's last in line, pleading with the Leatherheads, pulling frantically on his chains. Aki's nowhere in sight.

"What's the plan?" I whisper to Hickory. "Create a distraction? Sneak down and set 'em free? I don't know if I'll be able to cause another quake just yet, but I can give it a shot."

Hickory frowns, goes to say something, thinks twice.

"What is it?" I ask. "What's wrong?"

"It's just . . ." He looks out over the hall again. "We have both keys. You know where the Cradle is. You could claim it right now. Shouldn't we just—

"Leave them? Uh-uh. No way."

"We can beat him, Jane. We can beat Roth."

"And then what? Roth has my dad. I'm not letting him get Violet, too. Besides, *she* has the arrowhead—unless the Leatherheads have taken it off her. Roth gets his hands on it, he'll chuck it in the lava and truly be invincible. We have to save her. You promised, Hickory."

"And if they catch you too?" he says. "If Roth gets his hands on—"

"The keys!" Masaru cries out, down in the hall. "I have the keys! Look, look, look!"

I turn back to the balustrade so fast I smack my head on the stone.

Masaru's nodding down at his cloak. "*Naika de kaya.* The hem. The hem! I fooled them. *De kaya.* There. Look, look!"

A Leatherhead looks Masaru up and down. Grabs the hem of his cloak, feels around for something inside, and slices it open with his blade.

"No, no, no," Hickory mutters.

The Leatherhead holds something up to the light. Two small, thin, metallic things that catch the firelight and gleam.

The Cradle keys.

I grab the keys around my neck. "Fakes. That son of a . . ." I feel sick. Like I'm sinking into the stone. He must've swapped them in secret, after the council meeting. Always one step ahead, just like Elsa said.

The Leatherheads *click* and *clack* and fire their rifles into the air in celebration. Violet screams. Yaku scowls. Elsa tries to kick Masaru as he's marched past them to a truck farther up the line. They're taking him to Roth right now, along with the keys. That settles it, then.

"Hickory—"

"I know," he says through gritted teeth. "We don't have a choice. Follow me."

We back away from the balcony, stand and turn around together—

And come face to face with a Leatherhead.

"Oh," I say. *Crap.* "Um. Hi."

Its rifle's pointing right at me. I can see myself reflected in its glassy gas mask eyes.

Click-clack-click, it goes, about to raise the alarm, when—*THWUNK!*

Another Leatherhead cracks it over the skull from behind with a crowbar. Our assailant gurgles, sways, drops its gun, and collapses. We raise our hands in surrender, just in case, till Captain Crowbar snickers, rattles his throat and pulls the gas mask from his head.

Praise the Makers, it's Aki.

And he's got the bow and arrow, too.

THE GODS OF CHAOS

We've come up with a plan. Good one, too, as far as last-minute plans go. Step one—commandeer a truck—has already gone off without a hitch, thanks to Aki. Soon as we sneaked downstairs, he strolled up to the last truck in line, hopped inside, and unleashed hell. The truck shook. A window cracked. Ten seconds later, the door flew open and both Leatherheads came flying toward us, almost dead.

"So glad he stuck around," Hickory said as we dragged the bodies clear.

Now we're sitting in the back—shielded by the cloth-top, surrounded by crates of weapons, no less—rumbling along with the rest of the convoy toward the fortress.

Toward Roth.

Leatherheads stomp around the truck at every check-point. We hold our breath and grip our weapons tight but pass through each of them undiscovered.

I should be trembling, but a strange sensation's come over me. A feeling that this is how it was always supposed to be. We're gonna save everyone. Not just Violet, Yaku, and Elsa, but the rest of Roth's prisoners, too. I'm gonna find Dad, hug him, free him at long last.

Every passing second brings us closer together.

I snap the chain around my neck and ditch Masaru's useless fake keys. Grip the arrow tight and run a finger over the tip. It's so sharp I nearly draw blood. Far as we could work out from Aki's rattles and hand gestures, Violet threw it to him while she was being captured. Told him to find me. Everything depends on this. We're only gonna get one shot.

"Let's run through the plan," I say.

Hickory's stocking up on weapons. Knives, guns, grenades, you name it. "Again?"

"Again."

He sits back against the cloth-top and sighs. "Once we're through the main gate, Aki'll follow the rest of the trucks to the garage, beneath the main keep. Violet and the others will be marched to Roth's throne room, on the upper level of the fortress."

"Ugh, trust Roth to make himself a throne room."

"We," Hickory continues, "will head to the cell block. It's on the upper level, too."

I nod. "We free as many prisoners as we can. Arm the strongest and storm the throne room. I'll distract Roth, make sure his eyes are fixed on me." I hand Hickory the arrow. "You fire this, but only if you have a clear shot at his heart. Sure you can handle that?"

Hickory tucks the arrow into his belt and pats Violet's bow, rattling on the floor of the truck by his side.

"I'm two thousand years old. Pretty sure I can fire one measly arrow."

"I'm, like, two *gazillion* years old, and I'm sure I couldn't." I glance at Aki. "Anyway, if we're seen by any Leatherheads on the way to the cell block—"

"We pretend to be Aki's prisoners and let him lead the way. Relax, Jane. We'll be fine. We take Roth down, grab the Cradle keys, free everyone and flee into the Manor. The Leatherheads'll be too distraught to follow. In fact, I bet a lot of them'll be glad Roth's gone."

I huff out a deep breath and feel that sense of certainty again, a flicker of a thrill. "You're right. We've got this." Roth's gonna rue the day he decided to mess with the Manor.

We drive for an hour, maybe two, following the convoy down winding corridors and across pillared halls, through archways and holes blown into walls. I imagine Violet, Yaku, and Elsa bound up together in another truck. I picture Masaru, bouncing along farther up the line, shedding happy tears. Old fool has no idea what he's gotten himself into.

After a while, I tug at my tunic, fan myself down. "It's baking in here."

Hickory shuffles over to a slit in the canopy. "Understandable. Take a look."

The corridor's a blur, glowing fiery red. Aki slows the truck to a crawl, and we rumble with the rest of the convoy onto a rusty chain-link bridge strung up through the middle of an enormous hall. There's a lake of bubbling lava way down below the bridge. Little archways, balconies, and staircases dot the far walls, all of them glowing garishly in the lava-light.

And we thought Arakaan was hot.

Most incredible of all are the statues. The hall's full of them. Colossal, demonic things rising from the lava all around us, their beastly legs and pointed horns wider than wagons. Some of them soar so high we can't even see their heads. One snarls up at us from below, its fanged mouth wide enough to swallow a truck whole. Another's muscular arms stretch across the hall from one side to the other, as if it's holding up the walls.

"Have you ever seen—"

"Uh-uh."

"Can you believe –"

"Nope."

The convoy caterpillar crawls. The bridge sways gently, strung up by a network of huge chains bolted to the surrounding walls. Before Roth came, this hall must've been a marvel of the Manor. Now it's in decay, smoke-stained, and many of the statues are metal-plated, which only makes them scarier.

"Aris must've carved them," Hickory says, "in the Beginning. Maybe it's some kind of tribute to the fallen gods."

"The Gods of Chaos," I whisper.

The gods that Po, Aris, and Nabu-kai tricked into the Manor, whose combined energies clashed and swirled inside the Cradle, creating the hazardous Sea. Whose absence from the Otherworlds enabled life to flourish and thrive. If this is what they looked like, I'm glad the Makers did away with them. I just wish their essence hadn't remained. The most destructive force imaginable, hidden at the center of all things—our ultimate destination. Lucky us.

We rumble off the bridge and down a new corridor. The air's so terrible here I can taste it. Burning rubber, coal, and rancid meat. The stench of Roth, lingering like the stench of death.

We're getting close.

The truck slows. Hickory and I peek over Aki's shoulders. All we can see is the back of the truck in front of us and the Manor walls on either side, every inch covered in a rough patchwork of metal plates. Roth-proof, like the statues. A gate rattles up ahead. The convoy crawls through.

Aki twitches his head at us. *Get down.*

The brakes squeal. The truck lurches to a halt. Leatherheads stomp around the truck and Tin-skins bark, competing with the constant clanging of metal on metal, the hiss of steam and the *clunk-clunk-clunk* of turning cogs. The crack of a whip. A scream.

"No turning back now," Hickory says. "We're here."

THE KEEP

Masaru and the others are marched out of the garage. We can hear Violet giving them hell, kicking and swearing. A siren blows, and the rest of the Leatherheads clear out quickly, boots like rolling thunder. Once the coast is clear, Aki hops out of the truck, opens the back flap, and hands Hickory and me a pair of shackles each. We slip them around our wrists, clasped but not bolted—in front of us, not behind our backs.

"Ready?" I ask Hickory.

"Ready," he replies, and we duck outside.

The garage is big, filled with trucks and supplies. There's even a rusty old tank. Every bit of stone's covered in that patchwork of rusted steel, as if an Otherworld of metal has crept through a weakened gateway and taken over, like the lava and the snow.

It's eerily quiet.

"We're beneath the main keep," Hickory whispers, handing Aki the bow and shotgun.

"Keep your gas mask on, buddy," I say, gesturing to make sure Aki gets the point. "Stay close behind us. If we're spotted, act like you're turning us in. When we see

Roth, hand Hickory the bow—he'll take the shot. Hickory, you still got the arrow?"

"No, I threw it into the lava—of course I still have the arrow."

"Just checking." I take a deep breath, scan the area. "All right. Let's go."

We head through an archway and sneak up a narrow metal-plated stairwell. It's a long climb. That rancid stink gets worse the higher we go. We pause at every new flight, every archway, but there are no Leatherheads in sight. Makes me even more nervous.

"Quick question," Hickory mutters. "What if I miss?"

"What do you mean?" I whisper-shout. "You said you wouldn't."

"Yeah, but . . . what if I do?"

"Then I'll kill you myself."

He plucks the arrow from his belt and grunts. "Fair enough."

We reach the top of the stairwell and creep down a dark corridor. When we pass an open balcony, we're granted a view over the central keep. A dirty old hall ten stories high, dotted with archways and galleries, topped by a crumbling dome held together by disjointed metal beams. Machines and barrels of coal litter the floor down below—inactive conveyor belts and drums of newly crafted weapons—all circling a clearing in the center.

The place is deserted.

"Over there," Hickory whispers, pointing to the right of the hall with his shackled hands.

A crooked structure of rusted steel has been built against the far wall. Stationary platforms and pulleys scale the wall beside it. There's a line of tiny, barred windows at the top.

"The cell block."

Down the corridor we go. Up another flight of stairs. Still no Leatherheads, no Tin-skins. Nothing but empty chambers and a deep, discomforting silence.

"Something's wrong," Hickory mutters. "This is too easy."

"No turning back now, remember?" I say.

Aki lifts his mask. He looks scared, too. I give him a reassuring nod.

We sneak up an enclosed ramp into the cell block. The structure creaks and groans beneath our feet. It's dark. Reeks of something other than Roth. Stale pee, sweat, and fear. We stop, let our eyes adjust. See two rows of single-celled cages slapped together on either side of a narrow walkway. They're all empty. Chains dangling, doors ajar.

"I'm telling you, Jane, this isn't right," Hickory says.

"Throne room." The wound in my palm throbs. "Now."

Hickory scans the empty cages again, grips the arrow tightly. "Aki, stay close."

We move through some kind of guards' quarters and sneak back into a metal-plated Manor corridor. There's an open door ahead. I peek in.

The throne room's empty, too.

We step inside, blasted by a wall of heat. The whole metal-clad chamber's bathed in lava-light. Roth's throne is ugly: a hulking black metal thing. I spit at it when we pass by. The air's so thick with his stench I can hardly breathe. We must've just missed him.

The balcony across the room overlooks a pillared hall filled with broiling lava. There's a lavafall way off to the left. Looks like a giant, glowing tongue lapping at the lake. I wipe the sweat from my forehead, turn around.

"Where the hell is everyone?" I ask.

That's when we hear it—*BOOM, BOOM, BOOM*— a menacing beat echoing through the fortress. A metallic clanking and stomping, back toward the keep.

Me and Hickory ditch our shackles. Aki *click-clacks* at us—tries to stop us—but we're already running towards the sound, out of the throne room and down the corridor, past the cell block to an open gallery of metal-plated archways overlooking the keep.

I can't believe my itching, watery eyes.

Leatherheads are marching through every archway of the lower level, every door, beating their weapons as they gather around the barrels and machines. And there, standing in the middle of them all, staring up at us with those cold, cold eyes, is Roth.

The furious tide stirs in my gut. My palm prickles. Five people are kneeling before him, gagged and bound. Masaru, Yaku, Violet, Elsa, and—

"Dad." He's hurt. Slumped forward, swaying slightly. His shirt's sweat-stained and splattered with dried blood. His shaggy, graying hair's flowing down over his face.

Roth signals to his troops. They stop clanking and

stomping, and more Leatherheads appear in the gallery around us, barging through doors and clambering over the edge of the keep, rifles raised and ready to fire. One grabs Hickory and throws him to the floor. The same Leatherhead grabs my right arm, pulls it firmly behind my back, pins me against a nearby column, and starts patting me down.

I'm about to fight back, when the Leatherhead slips something up my sleeve.

Something long and thin, with a very pointy end.

The arrow.

"*Aki?*" I whisper, flushed with relief.

He rattles his throat ever so softly in my ear, then snarls for show. Spins me around, grabs my hands and shackles them, not behind my back, but in front again. I imagine him winking a black beady eye at me behind his gas mask. Because he hasn't bolted them properly.

I can still do this. Aki ditched the bow to blend in, sure, but there's another way. Elsa told me how, back in the watchtower of Orin-kin.

When we're shoved onto one of the wooden platforms, it isn't despair I feel. It isn't fear. It's something else. Something powerful and real.

It's hope.

EENY, MEENY, MINY, MOE

All eyes are on Hickory and me as we're lowered down to the keep. Especially Roth's. The platform sinks slowly—*squeak, creak, squeak, creak*—and with every passing second, the fug gets worse. That bitter, eye-watering stench. The itch on my skin. Everybody's suffering. Violet. Yaku. Elsa. Dad's barely conscious. Masaru looks like he's having second thoughts about his devotion to Roth already. Serves him right, the fool.

The platform hits the floor. We set off across the keep with Aki and two Leatherheads. The closer I get to Dad, the more I want to tear this place apart. Deep shadows well beneath his eyes. His nose and ears are crusty with dried blood. It's killing me, being so close and not being able to go to him, not being able to hug him. Elsa keeps glancing at him—trembling with fear and rage, struggling to breathe—but I don't think Dad has seen her. Will he recognize her when he does? I'm sure Elsa's wondering the same thing.

Roth's having a grand ol' time. Watching the reunion with glee. He grabs Dad by the hair and lifts his head a little. Soon as Dad sees me, he sits up straighter, utters my name into his gag and makes a desperate, whimpering sound. The furious tide stirs in my gut again, but I rein it in. As much as it pains me, I can't let it go now. Gotta play it cool. Stay sharp.

Like Hali-gabera. Like Winifred Robin.

Roth holds up a hand, telling us to stop. One of the Leatherheads grabs my arm. Aki snarls at it, shoves it aside, and grabs me instead. Nice of him, but not the smartest move. Roth's creepy eyes narrow a fraction. Hickory must notice it, too, because he quickly wheezes, "Where are the other prisoners, Roth?"

Roth takes a long death-rattle breath and flicks his hand. The Leatherheads behind him stand aside. The prisoners are all there, bound and gagged, lined up against the wall. There are dozens of them, wide-eyed and filthy. Some could've been here for decades. I recognize some of them from the train. I wish I could free them all right now and take them to their homes. I will. I swear it.

"So, how are we gonna do this?" I ask Roth. "I assume you have the two keys."

He pulls down the collar of his cloak. Masaru's thin, golden chain is sitting pretty around his neck, the two Cradle keys resting on his pasty, mottled chest.

"Suits you," I say, stifling a cough. "But I'm gonna have to take them now."

Violet shouts something, words muffled by her gag. Hickory squirms in the grip of his hulking Leatherhead guard. I notice he hasn't been shackled. Perfect.

Roth just stares at me, a sick kind of glee in those cold, creepy eyes. I figure he's about to come over and try to take a gander inside my head, but instead he turns on his heels, starts wandering back and forth behind the others—slowly, deliberately—watching me, but pausing now and then behind Masaru, behind Yaku, behind Violet and Elsa, like he's picking out the ripest fruit at a market. He's wondering who to choose, who to read. Treating it like a game.

"Stop it," I tell him.

Masaru whimpers. I don't pity him, but I don't want Roth to read his mind, either. If he does, he'll learn about the arrowhead, and my plan will be shot.

"I'll tell you everything," I say. "I know where the Cradle is. I haven't told any of them. Let everyone go, and I'll take you there. We can go right now. Just you and me."

Violet objects again. Dad does, too. He even tries to stand, but only manages to get to one knee before he collapses. It kills me. Roth loves it, though. Chuckles into his half-mask.

"Take *me*!" I shout. "I'm the one you want."

But the more I plead, the more he toys with me, walking, pausing, walking again—Violet, Yaku, Elsa, Dad—running a hand over their heads. My eyes flick to Elsa, and I can't help thinking, *Pick her. If you have to pick someone, please, let it be her*, because she's the only one who doesn't know about the arrowhead. The only one who can't ruin my plan.

Roth stops. Turns back to Elsa with a satisfied sigh. He saw where I was looking. Thinks I care about her the most.

Before I can say another word, Roth lifts her up, turns her around, and slips the gag from her mouth. She spits at him, right between the eyes.

"Wanted to do that for years," she gasps. "You really are one ugly son of a—"

Roth growls. His heat-shimmer breath burns her skin. Elsa struggles in his arms, but it's pointless. His eyes are locked onto hers. He's already trawling through her mind, making her body convulse and her legs jitter. It's horrible to watch. I may hate Elsa for what she was gonna do to me in the Cradle, but I wish things hadn't come to this.

Before I try to stop Roth, though, I wriggle my fingers till I know I've got Violet's attention, then twist my semi-shackled wrist around just enough to show her the tip of the arrowhead poking from under my right-hand sleeve.

Her eyes bulge. She gives her head a subtle shake. *Don't you dare.*

I shoot her a sad smile back. *I have no choice.*

"Hey, garbage guts," I shout, shaking Aki from my arm. "You win. If you kill her, you kill our only chance at getting inside the Cradle. Let her go. Now."

Roth blinks. Breaks the connection. Takes a slow, trembling breath and sets Elsa down. He kneels over her while she shivers in a sweaty mess, and clenches his fists. I know what he's thinking. He just learned the second key's been in Arakaan all this time.

"Sucks, huh?" I say. "I'd be angry, too. You've been searching for it all these years, and there it was, right back where you started. She told us all your secrets, too."

Roth stands tall. Steps over Elsa, one step closer to me. "That's right," I wheeze. "I know everything about you, ya chump. I've been to Arakaan." He takes another step closer. "I know about the Dahaari Cull and the Immortal War." And now for the kicker. "I know about Neela."

Roth growls through his mask.

"Poor woman," I say. "Imagine what she'd say if she saw you now—if she *smelled* you now. Hell, I bet she'd be glad she was shot through the heart and thrown into a volcano."

"Um, Jane?" Hickory mutters behind me. "Bit much, don't you think?"

Roth growls again. This time, I take a step toward him.

"Come on, then," I say. Aki rattles his throat. Hickory mutters my name again, but I don't stop, don't turn back. I keep my eyes fixed on Roth's. No matter how much it hurts, no matter how sick it makes me feel, I can't let him look away. "Have a read. I promise I won't stop you this time." I tap my head with my left, bandaged, arrow-free hand. "It's all here. Everything you wanna know. The secrets of the Manor. The key to conquering the Otherworlds. All you have to do"—one more step, we're unbearably close—"is look."

Roth's rancid breath prickles my skin and blasts my throat dry. He stares into my eyes, and I stare into his: that cold, burning blue. I can feel him probing and prodding around, trying to get inside my mind, just like he tried to on the train. I know I can stop him without breaking a sweat, but I keep my word. This time, I want to draw him in, keep him focused, distracted.

I picture the Hollows' basement door and open it. Roth's on the other side. I let him in. Let him look down at my raggedy mattress on the floor, and Dad's alcove near the corner. I can feel Roth pushing, trying to leave the room and see something else, but I keep him here. Show him the rats and the spiders, and the bluebird on the windowsill. I even sing him a song.

> Bluebird on the windowsill,
> You're so small, you can't sit still.
> Bobbing up and down, so fine,
> Your voice is just as good as mine . . .

I can feel Roth's hands around my neck, my feet leaving the floor. I can feel my breath catching, but that's okay. Because I can also feel the arrow, slipping into my right hand.

> Bluebird, bluebird, sing me a song,
> Of distant shores, come along
> Across the seas, away from here,
> I long to fly, to disappear . . .

Roth growls and pulls me closer. My legs jitter, hot tears stream down my cheeks, but I don't mind, because the arrowhead's slicing through the bandage around my left hand now, reopening the gash in my palm, and the furious tide's ready to go. It's time.

Bluebird, bluebird, don't delay,
It's getting late, we cannot stay.
Hey Roth, we found the arrowhead,
Say goodbye, you'll soon be—

"Stabbed right through the heart, you prick," I wheeze.

Roth's eyes widen, his mind reels back, but I'm already gripping the arrow with both hands, already plunging it up into his chest as hard as I can. His flesh tears. He shrieks, drops me, and staggers back. I hit the floor hard, slam my hand onto the stone, and let go.

"Now, Hickory! Get the keys!"

Everything happens at once. Hickory breaks free of his guard and tackles Roth. The ground cracks. The prisoners scatter. Violet and Yaku scream into their gags and Aki leaps beside me, shielding me from the Leatherheads, who are already coming to get us, already opening fire. But they're too late.

The floor's tearing apart, crumbling, falling.

And we're all going down with it.

VIOLET'S FIRST TEST-DRIVE

A quick drop. A shower of stone. Aki and I bounce once on the back of a soft-topped truck and fall through a second later as the cloth's torn by bricks and boulders. We hit the tray between crates of supplies, coughing, winded, wiping dust from our eyes. Not the smoothest exit, sure, but it worked.

We're out of the keep. Almost free.

"The others," I gasp, slipping from my shackles. "We've gotta make sure they're okay."

The hole in the ceiling's big. They must've fallen down somewhere nearby. A few Leatherheads, too. In a few seconds, Roth's entire army's gonna jump down to join the party.

We scramble out of the truck, squinting through the cloud of dust.

"Find Violet," I tell Aki. "*Violet.* Go!"

Aki nods and darts off between the trucks. I spin around, searching for—

"Jane," Hickory gasps.

He and Roth have landed right beside the truck. Roth's still alive. Got his hands around Hickory's neck.

The arrow's protruding from his chest.

I missed his damn heart.

"Get off him!" I hurl a rock at Roth's head, and it explodes upon impact, doesn't leave a mark. Gets the jerk's attention, though. He drops Hickory. Uh-oh.

I turn and run, stumbling and tripping over rocks. Slide under a truck and scramble to my feet on the other side. Roth's right behind me, death-rattle breaths like scraping stone. I catch a glimpse of him grabbing the end of the arrow as we run, trying to pull it out. Shadows drop through the ceiling all around us: Leatherheads with rifles and Tin-skins ready to hunt.

Violet shouts my name. I turn to find her, trip, fall, and scrape my hands and knees.

Roth's on me in a flash, picking me up, spinning me around, pinning me to the wall. My eyes burn and water, but I can still see clearly enough to grab the arrow. I twist it, angle it toward his heart and try to shove it deeper before he chokes the life out of me. Roth shrieks. A gurgled, guttural cry. I can see the shock in his eyes, the outrage, but there's something else too, something I never thought I'd see.

Fear.

Roth grabs my hand, grips it tight around the arrow, and yanks it from his chest. Doesn't make a sound this time, just tosses it to the floor, grabs my neck, and squeezes so hard stars burst before my eyes, and then—

Click-clack-click.

A darting shadow. A swinging metal beam.

Aki sends Roth flying across the room.

"Thanks," I gasp, rubbing my neck.

Roth's okay, of course. Already getting up, his half-mask chipped and cracked. He clenches his fists and shrieks at us, ready to charge again, when—

BAM!

—a truck slams him into the wall.

Violet's behind the wheel. "Get in," she shouts, backing up, swinging the truck around.

Yaku throws open the back flap. "Come on!"

I grab the arrow off the floor and we chase the truck as Violet floors it, headed for the exit. Aki throws me on board the second we're close enough and leaps up behind me. Hickory's already inside, catching his breath. Elsa's trembling in the corner. She's still recovering from Roth's intrusion, but can't stop staring at the arrow in my hand. Praise the Makers, Dad's here, too. Alive, but only just. Who knows where Masaru's gotten to? Right now, I really don't care.

"Go, go, go!" Yaku shouts.

Roth's peeling himself from the wall.

"Wait," I shout. "What about the keys?"

"No worries there," Hickory coughs, rubbing his throat. I could hug him. Both keys—the *real* keys—are dangling from his hand. He tosses them to me. "*Now* you're reunited at last."

I slip the chain over my head and hold them to my chest. "About time."

We crash through a metal gate, burst into the corridor and speed back down the road, bowling through a troop of Leatherheads. Violet takes a hard right and sideswipes a wall.

"Where the hell did you learn to drive?" Hickory shouts.

"Winifred taught me," she replies.

"In theory," I shout, stumbling over to check on Dad. "She taught you in theory!"

Violet changes gear. The truck grinds and roars.

"Better hang on, then."

I tuck myself down next to Dad. Hug him, check his wounds, push his hair from his face. He's out of it. Mumbling. Can barely open his bruised, swollen eyes.

"I'm sorry," he says. "I'm so, so sorry. I wanted to tell you the truth, but—"

"It doesn't matter, Dad," I say. "I understand. And it's okay. I know everything. I know I'm the third key, and I know you're still my dad, and I know where the Cradle is at last. We found—"

"Elsa?" Dad mutters. He blinks, trying to focus. Sweeps over Elsa without recognizing her. She stares back at him, tears welling in her eyes. "Where is she?"

I don't know what to say. "Dad, she's . . ."

"Dead," Elsa says. "She died a long time ago."

"Oh." Dad closes his eyes. "I was sure she . . . I'd hoped . . ." He reaches out a hand. I hold it tight. "I'm sorry, Jane." His voice cracks, trails away. "I wish . . . you could've met her. She really was amazing . . ." And with that, he falls silent, head lolling to one side.

"Dad," I say, shaking his shoulder, panic rising. "*Dad?*"

Elsa wipes a tear from her cheek, turns away.

"He's unconscious," Yaku says, kneeling by Dad's side, checking his pulse. "That's all." He hands me a rag. "For your hand. Don't want you tearing apart the road while we're on it."

"Actually, that might not be a bad idea," Hickory says from the back.

We've got company. Another truck's roaring down the corridor behind us with Leatherheads leaning out the windows, clinging to the sides, wielding blades and big sticks with hooks.

"Faster, Violet, faster!"

She floors it, the wind blowing through her open window whipping her hair. "Find a way to lose them!"

Our truck's all but empty. There are no weapons. Just a gas mask or three and some shackles. And I can't cause another quake, not so soon. Even if I could, it'd be way too risky. There could be lava flowing beyond these walls. "We have to outrun them!" I yell.

We speed past a deep, molten corridor; cross another chain-link bridge. Violet screams, "Hold on!" and soars over a short staircase into a wide, sprawling hall, and still, we can't get away. We dodge bullets and duck for cover. I hold on to Dad for dear life. The pursuing truck speeds alongside and slams us. A bunch of Leatherheads jump on board. Hickory, Aki, and Yaku kick and punch them clear. One of the Leatherheads tries to grab the wheel through the driver's-side window. Violet kicks open the door and sidewipes a pillar, knocking the Leatherhead—and the door—clean off. Another slashes the side of the canvas cloth-top open and catches me around the neck with one of those hooked sticks, but Elsa leaps forward, yanks the stick down hard and sends the chump tumbling under our wheels.

"Thanks," I gasp.

She snaps the stick in two over her knee. Goes to say something, thinks twice.

"Somebody help me out!" Violet shouts. "I don't know where I'm going!"

"Aki," I shout, pointing at Dad, "watch over him, please." I scramble into the seat beside Violet and scan the hall. "There! Ten o'clock! Turn—now!"

Violet yanks on the steering wheel. We skid and slide but make the turn in time and speed into a new corridor. Unfortunately, the other truck makes it, too.

"Check that compartment," Violet says, pointing in front of me.

I rustle around inside. "Bingo." A pistol. I toss it back to Hickory.

He catches it, clicks the flicky-bit, takes aim and fires, just as the truck's about to ram us again. Their windshield shatters. The Leatherhead driver slumps against the steering wheel and the truck veers left, side-swiping the wall, shooting sparks. We cheer—

Until another truck explodes past it a second later, gaining speed. This time, Roth's behind the wheel.

Are you kidding me?" Hickory raises the pistol.

"What are you doing?" Violet shouts, glancing in the rearview mirror. "Don't bother shooting at him—aim for the tires!" Hickory aims again and fires—*bam, bam, bam*—but Roth weaves the truck, dodging every bullet. Violet turns to me. "Still got the arrow?"

I pat my forearm. "Got it. Unfortunately, we don't have a bow."

"It wouldn't work anyway," Yaku shouts, pointing back at Roth. "Look! His chest!"

We look over our shoulders and through Roth's windshield. He's wearing a metal vest, a chest-plate shielding his heart. "Damn it!"

"Hey, watch the road," Hickory screams. We're about to run into a wall.

Violet cries out, takes a hard left and scrapes along another wall. Hickory loses his footing and drops the pistol. It slides along the bed of the truck toward us—

Only to be stopped by Elsa's foot.

She leans over Dad and whispers something into his ear. She kisses his forehead, and his eyes open for a moment as she gazes at him. A flicker of recognition on his face. Confusion.

Elsa nods at him, just once, and picks up the pistol.

Roth's smashing through his windshield, clambering to the front of his truck. Must've wedged down the pedal, because the truck's still surging ahead.

And he's gaining on us.

"He's gonna jump!" I scream. "Elsa, shoot the wheels!"

"Not yet!" she replies, getting to her feet, checking the gun. "Two bullets left."

"Do it *now!* Violet, go, go, go!"

But there's bad news up ahead—a dead end. A stone balustrade with nothing but chasm beyond. A fierce red glow. A giant stone hand reaching out in the distance.

We've doubled back to the hall of gods.

"Wait—no—stop, stop, stop!"

"Don't you dare," Elsa screams. She hands half of the Leatherhead staff to Violet. "Wedge it between the pedal and the seat. Everyone jump on my command!"

"*Jump?*" I say, scrambling into the back again. "From a speeding vehicle?"

"You've survived worse." She nods at my forearm. "Masaru had the arrowhead all along, didn't he?" I nod. Elsa clenches her jaw, closes her eyes for a moment, then stares down at Dad. "Seems I've been wrong about many things. Well . . ." She grabs a pair of shackles from the floor. "I may not be able to kill Roth for you, but I can help you get away."

"You're coming with us, Elsa."

"You have your father now. You don't need me."

"Here he comes!" Yaku screams.

Roth's clinging to the front of his truck, getting ready to jump, the wind whipping his cloak.

Everyone packs into and around the two front seats. Aki grabs Dad and holds him tight. Ahead, the cavern looms closer.

"Come on!" Elsa screams at Roth. She raises the pistol and fires. His front wheel explodes. Roth jumps. His truck crashes into the wall, flips and rolls, but Roth's already landed safely in the back of ours.

"Now!" Elsa shouts.

Hickory, Violet, and Yaku throw themselves into the corridor. Aki leaps out with Dad. I go to grab Elsa's arm to make sure she comes. She snatches my wrist instead and pulls me close.

"I told you, Jane. Life is a series of sacrifices."

She tries to push me from the truck, but she's too late. Roth's already on us. He grabs my arm, shoves Elsa's aside, and pins me to the back of the seat.

"Get off me," I shout, "or we're all gonna die!"

Roth looks out the windshield. The fiery light of the hall glows in his eyes. He's about to drag me from the truck, when—*click*—Elsa shackles his wrist to hers, holds the pistol right up to his mask with her other hand, and squeezes the trigger. *BAM!*

The mask explodes. Roth shrieks. I catch a glimpse of the horror beneath, but only for a fraction of a second, because Roth's turning away. Because Elsa's shoving me out of the truck. Because I'm hitting the ground hard, and screaming, rolling, scraping my skin, spinning around and around. Everything seems to slow down. I look up just in time to see Roth fighting Elsa, trying to shake her off. But she isn't budging.

The truck crashes through the balcony and soars over the edge, like it's learned to fly. Then it vanishes.

"No!" I leap to my feet and stagger to the edge just in time to see the truck hit the lava way down between the statues. There's a burst of flame—a bubble-broth of churning, spitting fire. The truck sinks in seconds, taking Roth and Elsa with it.

She's gone. She's really gone.

Violet staggers to my side, grazed and bruised, nursing her elbow. She holds my uninjured hand. We stare down into the cauldron, the updraft of heat blowing our hair. Hickory joins us, too, rubbing his head, swearing under his breath.

"Why did she do that?" Violet asks. She sounds angry.

"So we could get away," Hickory says. "She bought us time, but that's all. It won't take Roth long to claw his way back to the surface. He'll never stop chasing you, Jane."

He's right—I know he is—but I feel so numb, so empty.

Yaku and Aki limp up to us. Dad's unconscious, cradled in Aki's arms. He was lucky. We all were. I hold his hand, fighting back tears. He recognized Elsa back there in the truck. I'm sure he did. What am I supposed to do when he wakes up? What do I say?

"We need to leave." Yaku's staring down at the lava, the red glow glinting in his eyes. I can't imagine what he's feeling. He knew Elsa the longest, after all. Longer than anyone, really, even Dad. "They're coming."

A rumble of trucks, back the way we came.

I turn to Violet. "The other truck back there. Reckon you can get it going?"

"If it wasn't too badly damaged in the crash," she says, "yeah. Can you take us to the Cradle?"

I glance at Hickory. *The Manor can shift rooms*, he said. *Stands to reason you can, too.*

"Get us somewhere safe," I say. "Somewhere quiet. All I need is a door."

FOURTH INTERLUDE

LIKE FIRE

It is a strange sensation, swimming through lava. It is thick. Glutinous. When Roth's hand breaks the surface and he hauls himself onto the foot of a statue, the lava clings to him. A radiant second skin. It has fused the metal plate to his chest and burned away his clothes. The remnants of his shattered mask will have melted now, along with the truck—and Elsa.

Roth feels only the pain in his chest where the arrow pierced his flesh. The wound will never heal, but he will live. From the lava itself, he feels barely a breath of warmth. He wipes it from his eyes, surveys the lofty wall he has to climb, shakes his head.

He should have known Elsa would try something like this. Should have sensed it when he read her mind. After all these years, it should be a comfort to know he can still be surprised. It will not happen again. He will hunt down the girl. He will take what is his at long last.

But first, the climb. Roth clambers up the statue. Leaps over to the wall at its knee. He jumps from columns to archways, from balconies to broken stairs.

The girl and her friends had better be running fast.

When he bounds onto the chain-link bridge, Roth realizes he is not alone. An old man is gaping at him nearby, trembling. The old man who flew into the Manor with the third key. What did Elsa call him? Masaru. Yes, that was it.

Roth approaches him, spots of lava sizzling on the rusted steel with every step.

"My lord," the old man stammers in his mother tongue. He kneels in the middle of the bridge. "Praise be. I was searching for you. I feared you had been slain." He is clutching one of Roth's masks. Two of his curved sickle blades. "I—I was not stealing these." Masaru carefully places them on the bridge. "I found them, back at the . . . after they . . . I—I was looking for you. I thought you might want them." He bows. "I am your most humble servant."

Curious, Roth thinks, *for a servant to look so afraid.*

"What did they tell you?" Masaru says, almost hysterical now. "What did the girl show you? Did she—no, no, no." He licks his lips, holds a bony hand to his chest. "Yes. It was me. I saved the arrowhead for you. I was going to present it to you as a gift!'"

It was a mistake to admit this. Roth towers over the pitiful man. He will not read him. Will not subject himself to mundane thoughts and empty promises. He remembers men like this from long ago. They are all the same. Sycophants. Cowards. Fools.

"I beg you," Masaru stammers. "Do not kill me. All I have ever wanted was to serve you."

And you will, Roth thinks.

He will throw Masaru from the bridge in a moment.

First, he needs the old man's clothes.

PART
SIX

THE DOOR TO NOWHERE

Our new ride putters down the corridor, belching black smoke. Violet and Yaku got her going while Hickory dragged the dead Leatherhead clear. Aki kicked out the shot-up windshield and helped me tuck Dad safely aboard. We left before the rest of Roth's army showed up, but we know the score: unless I can work my magic, they'll find us soon enough.

One door. One measly door. Easier said than done.

Seems all the doors in this maze of twisting corridors were either smashed by Leatherheads, burned by lava or rotted away by Roth long ago. No doors, no shifting rooms. No shifting rooms, no escape.

Everyone's on the lookout, peering through the gaps Yaku sliced in the cloth-top. Violet's leaning over the steering wheel as far as she can. She can only just reach the pedals, I realize now. The thing was built for Leatherheads, after all. "See anything back there?" she asks, gunning the truck over another bridge. The molten river below blasts us with heat. There are lavafalls everywhere, flowing from balconies, oozing down stairs. "Hickory?"

"It's not like I'm gonna keep it to myself if I do," he says. "Just drive."

I wanna help them look, but I have a task of my own. "Dad." I squeeze his hand. "Hey, I know you're in a lot of pain, but we need your help. I need you to wake up.'"

He moans a little. Squeezes my hand back.

"That's it," I say. "We did it, Dad." I hold up the two Cradle keys, give them a jangle. "See? We got the keys. Everything goes according to plan, we'll be at the spike pit soon, but El—" I can't even say her name. She's gone, and Dad never got to say goodbye. "There are hundreds of doors around the pit, right? We need to know which one leads to the Cradle, and what we're gonna find at the entrance." I dab the sweat from his brow. Wipe the dried blood from under his nose. "We were told there's some kind of final test. A booby trap. Dad? Hey . . ." I tap his cheek, but he's already slipped away again, gone back to sleep. We're gonna have to figure it out ourselves—assuming I can get us there in the first place.

Violet swings us around another bend and slams on the brakes. Hickory swears.

I scramble to my feet. "What's—oh."

The end of the corridor. The end of the road. The end of Roth's domain. We're parked in front of a thin archway with nothing but darkness beyond. The truck's too big to fit through.

"We walk from here," Violet says.

"I say we run," Yaku says. "Listen."

There's that distant rumble of trucks again, getting louder by the second.

"Aki." I point at Dad. "Can you carry him, please?"

Candles and torches flicker to life the moment we step through the archway, illuminating a vast—thankfully lava-free—pillared hall. The walls are bare. No doors. No passageways. The chamber's so wide, we can't see either end.

"Which way?" Violet asks.

"Let's just get to the other side," I say.

We jog, keeping a steady pace, and the archway shrinks behind us, lost in the forest of pillars. No one utters a word. We huff and puff, look this way and that. Violet tries to give me an encouraging nod, but I know she's scared. If we don't find a door soon—

"Jane," Yaku shouts, "there!"

On the far wall dead ahead, emerging from the gloom like a gift from the gods: a small dark rectangle. A regular, run-of-the-mill Manor door.

"About time," I say, and bolt for it.

I try the handle. "Locked." Fumble the chain from around my neck, shove one of the keys into the lock and turn it. It clicks, and I yank the door open, only to be blasted by a wall of heat.

There's no floor on the other side. No bridge or balcony. The stone has crumbled away. There's just a short drop to another molten river oozing down a deep corridor. We're trapped.

I slam the door shut. "Damn it."

"Focus, Jane," Hickory says, stepping up to my side. "You can do this."

"Okay." I grip the handle and close my eyes. "The snow. I'll focus on the snow."

Violet gasps. "The Cradle entrance is in the snow?"

"What is snow?" Yaku asks.

"Fluffy frozen water," Hickory says. "Far away from here. It's where me and Jane first met, actually. I shoved a bag over her head. Saved her life, though. She was about to freeze to—"

"Could you shush, please?" I snap. Everyone zips it. "Thank you."

I grip the door handle—picture that grand, frozen hall—and open the door as quickly as I can with a triumphant, "This time!" But no. Nothing but lava.

I slam the door again, and that's when we hear a metallic squeal, back the way we came. A deep, rolling rumble, and—just like in Roth's fortress—the sound of a thousand stomping boots.

The Leatherheads have found us.

"Keep trying, Jane," Violet says, backing off to the right. "I'll check down here. Try to find another door. Yaku, you take the other side. Hickory, Aki, stay and guard Jane."

Violet and Yaku turn and bolt. Aki tightens his grip on Dad, stands guard at my back.

"The Manor's all messed up, Jane," Hickory says. "It can't help you—not in the way you want. *You* have to control it. Command it. Just take a breath. Relax. And reach out."

The Leatherheads are chanting, their *click-clack-click*s echoing closer and closer.

"Relax." I grab the handle. "Sure, no problem."

I focus on the frozen hall again. Picture the buried doors, the frosted balconies, the icicles twinkling in the candlelight and my puffing-chimney breaths. But just as I'm about to open the door I see the Specters, too, waiting for me, reaching out to Grip me with those white-fire tendrils of light. "No . . ." I whisper. Just like in my nightmare, they can see I'm gonna fail. They're trying to scare me away. "Leave me alone. We're on the same side."

"Um, I know," Hickory says behind me. "Why do you think I'm trying to—"

"Not *you*," I say, "the Spec—ugh, never mind."

I try the door again and again, shifting my stance, taking deep breaths, focusing on the hall and banishing the Specters. I pretend I'm back there, sinking knee-deep in the snow. I remember the suffocating silence, try to chatter my teeth, but nothing works. Because the Leatherheads have fired a few warning shots across the hall. Because I can't stop thinking about Elsa. Because Roth would've clawed his way out of the lava by now, and he's coming. Because I'm sure the Specters are waiting for me, and I'm afraid.

"Jane," Hickory says. "Hurry."

Open, shut. Open, shut. Always fire, never ice. I open the door with my good hand and my bad, with the bandage and without, but it just won't work.

Violet runs back. "No doors down that way."

314

Yaku's here, too. "Nothing."

A warning shot blasts the wall above the door, showering us in stones. We can see the Leatherheads now, a whole battalion marching in formation, stalking between the pillars.

Come on, come on.

Open, lava, shut. Open, lava, shut.

"Maybe all the doors around the hall you're trying to shift to are busted or blocked up with snow," Hickory says. "Focus on a different room. The booby trap with the crushing columns. Or what about where I found you—the balcony near the snowy gateway."

"I can't do that."

Another gunshot blasts the pillar to our right.

"*Why not?*"

"Because I was lost, okay?" I'm panicking, sweating, about to cry. "Wandering around for hours. We could trek through the snow for days and never find the frozen hall. We have to head straight there. I can see it so clearly. There are loads of doors and balconies, and the spike pit's buried under the snow. It was the first big hall I entered after I left—"

I freeze. My heart skips a beat. I turn around and stare at the others. "Bluehaven."

Return, the voice said in my dream.

Violet grins. She knows exactly what I'm thinking. "Do it, Jane."

I turn back to the door. Close my eyes, take a deep breath, and grip the handle once more, but this time,

I don't focus on the snow. This time, I focus on the Sacred Stairs, Outset Square, White Rock Cove and the Museum of Otherworldly Antiquities.

This time, I picture home, and there isn't a Specter in sight.

"Return," I whisper, and when I open the door, the lava has disappeared.

There are people—hundreds of them—packed into a Manor chamber, armed with guns, swords, and pitchforks, bathed in golden sunlight shining through an open gateway. And leading the crowd, standing right in front of me with a crossbow in hand—

"*Winifred!*"

"You're late," she says. And to the crowd behind her: "Bluehaven . . . attack."

THE BATTLE OF BLUEHAVEN

The townsfolk stream around us, screaming at the top of their lungs, gushing through the door like water through a burst dam, rushing headlong at the Leatherheads with their shields and weapons raised. The Leatherheads charge to meet them, screeching up a storm, and the two sides clash, filling the pillared hall with the clang of blades and the echo of battle cries.

We're ushered into the sunlit chamber. The remaining townsfolk gawk at me and gasp at Aki. Someone grabs Yaku's hand and shakes it, and he snatches it back. Looks like he's about to pummel them.

"Team A," Winifred shouts, "storm the fortress. Mind the lava, free the prisoners, and bring them back to Bluehaven. Eric Junior!"

"Yes, ma'am." A white guy in his twenties steps forward. Takes me a second to realize it's Mayor Atlas's son. No snot-nosed little turd, but an actual man with an almost-beard and all. "Hey, Jane."

"Um . . . hi?"

"You're in charge, Eric," Winifred tells him. "You know what to do."

He clenches his square, stubbled jaw, nods at Winifred, and pats my shoulder as he squeezes by, like we're old pals. "Good luck, kid. You really haven't aged a day, huh? Violet, good to see you. Hang in there, John. Hey, wow, Hickory Dawes. Sir!"

Hickory gives him an awkward salute.

Eric Junior's eyes light up. "I literally have a thousand questions for you." Is he *blushing?* "But first, I've gotta form the stortress—I mean, storm the . . . yeah, I'll just . . excuse me." He hurries from the chamber with the rest of Team A, red as a tomato.

"That was weird," Hickory says.

Violet hugs Winifred tight. Winifred hugs her back, tears swimming in her eyes. I just stand here like a chump, watching them, slack-jawed and speechless.

"How long has it been?" Violet asks.

"Since you left? Four very long years, my dear girl," Winifred says. "Alas, the battle has only just begun, and we don't have much time." She straightens up and turns to me. "Jane."

I nod hello. Narrow my eyes. "Hali-gabera." I leave her hanging for a moment, but I can't deny I'm relieved. I shake my head and smile. "I can honestly say I'm glad to see you."

Winifred smiles back. "Then let's go, shall we? Team B, you're with us. Move it!"

"So *that* is Hali-gabera," I hear Yaku mutter to Violet. "I thought she would be taller."

Gunshots echo through the pillared hall. Something explodes and the chamber rumbles, raining dust and debris. The townsfolk rally, ushering us toward the golden light of the open Manor gateway, the top of the Sacred Stairs. They hug Violet and welcome her home. They point at Hickory and whisper to each other: the legend of old returned at last. One of them tries to take Dad from Aki and shies away when he snarls.

"Winifred," I shout over another volley of rifle-fire, "we have to get to—"

"The tunnel beneath the crypt," she says, "I know. We've cleared the path. The second gateway's ready and waiting." She nods at a group of men and women standing guard nearby. "Signal the retreat in ten. Roth's on his way."

A stiff sea breeze swirls around us as we rush outside. It's blessedly cool, the midmorning sky clear. I've never been up here before—not since I was a baby, anyway, when Dad and I first came to Bluehaven. I take in the sparkling ocean, the steep hillside and the terraced farms. The town lying in ruin around the shore, and the crumbling Sacred Stairs.

The island seems so small.

"There's a view I never thought I'd see again," Hickory says, staring at the ocean.

Violet shoves him. "Get a move on or it'll be the last thing you see."

We scramble down the steep steps, leaping over missing chunks, keeping as far from the edges as we can. It's a deadly drop to the fields below. I see what Violet meant when she said Bluehaven was dying. The crops are barren. The coconut palms look like tall, swaying sticks, the fruit trees like skeletons. The Manor's been sucking the life out of the island.

Winifred runs alongside me. "I'm sorry I kept so many secrets from you, Jane. I don't expect forgiveness, but I want you to know you've done remarkably well."

Another explosion from inside the Manor rumbles down the Sacred Stairs. A portion of stone breaks away just after we've passed it, plummeting to the mango orchard far below.

"How about we save the kudos till we finish this, huh?" I shoot Winifred a sharp glance. "We *are* gonna finish this, right? We *are* gonna win? I mean, you saw it, right? Back when you touched the symbol under the catacombs. You know what's gonna happen."

"Jane—"

"Before we went to Arakaan, Violet told me you'd only do all this if you saw something good—if you saw a happy ending—so tell me. No more lies. What did you see?"

"Don't worry," Winifred says, "everything is proceeding as Nabu-kai planned."

"That isn't an answer," I say. "What happens next?"

"I can't tell you, Jane."

"But if you know how this ends—"

"That's just it, Jane," Winifred says, "I don't."

I nearly stop in my tracks. "*What?* How can you not know?"

"Because my part in this story is about to come to an end."

"Meaning what, exactly?"

"You know what it means. I'm an old woman with a score to settle and debts to repay." She glances back at Violet and Hickory. "You cannot tell the others, but my journey will come to an end where so many have begun. I will face Roth in Outset Square."

"And what? Let him *kill* you?"

"I will die, yes," Winifred says, matter-of-factly, "and take him with me. When we reach the square, you will hand me the arrow and continue to the Cradle with Violet and Hickory. That is the path Nabu-kai laid out for us— laid out for *me*. We cannot stray from it now."

"Screw Nabu-kai!" I shout. "Screw the path!"

A volley of gunfire. A chorus of screams. Some of the townsfolk are retreating from the Manor, following us down to Outset Square. A Leatherhead leaps through the gateway and tackles a man over the edge of the landing. A Tin-skin howls at the top of the Stairs.

"It's okay, Jane," Winifred says. "It's my time."

We reach the bottom of the Stairs. There's a small crowd gathered in the square. Mayor Atlas, Peg, Old Barnaby Twigg, and some others. Everyone's older, skinnier, wrinklier. They ogle Aki as he gently lays Dad on the cobblestones, but they also look at me. Stare in a way they never have before. There's no fear, no loathing. They actually look *happy* to see me.

Very disturbing.

"Hullo," I say.

Violet scans the crowd, looking for her parents, but they're not here. Predictable, really. She holds her head high, like she doesn't care, but I can tell she does. It's heartbreaking.

"Welcome back, Doe." The mayor strides up to me, a shotgun resting on his shoulder. Aki snarls at him. Atlas hesitates but pushes on. "Seems you've had quite the adventure." No insults. No threats. He actually wants to shake my hand. "Truce?"

The nerve of this guy.

"*Truce?*" I say. "You threw me in a cage and tried to kill me. Right over there on the Stairs."

Atlas clears his throat. "Yes, well, I apologize. That was . . . a long time ago."

"Not for me, it wasn't." I leave the guy hanging, turn back to Winifred. "There must be another way."

"Another way to what?" Violet asks.

Winifred ignores her. "Give me the arrow, Jane."

I take it from my sleeve. The battle's spilling down the Sacred Stairs now. Townsfolk. Leatherheads. Tin-skins. It's all-out war, but there's no way I'm giving Winifred the arrow.

"Jane," she says, "we don't have time for this. Roth is going to charge through the gateway any moment now. Give me the arrow and run. The way is clear."

"Listen to her, Jane," Hickory says. 'We have to go."

"It's my destiny," Winifred says fiercely, but with a note of pleading in her voice as she holds out her hand. "Everything has been leading to this. Please, you have to let me do this."

Life is a series of sacrifices.

But it isn't Winifred's sacrifice to make. It isn't the townsfolk's. It shouldn't have been Elsa's. This is my fight.

"Okay, then." I hand Winifred the arrow. "Give him hell."

"Oh, I intend to," she says, fitting the arrow into her crossbow. "Now go. Run." As expected, she turns to face the Stairs. Turns her back on me. Big mistake.

I snatch the shotgun from Atlas and whack Winifred in the back of the head. She drops like a sack of clams.

Everyone stares at me, open-mouthed. Not even Violet knows what to say.

"You just knocked out Hali-gabera," Yaku gasps.

"Yeah, well"—I ditch the shotgun—"now we're even." I pick up her crossbow and toss it to Hickory, tuck the hood of Winifred's cloak under her head. "Sorry, old girl. You said it yourself, way back when: I'm the hero of this story, whether I like it or not."

"Jane," Violet says, staring up at the Manor. "He's here."

The townsfolk streaming from the gateway are clutching their chests, their faces, their mouths. Roth's striding among them, a new half-mask fixed to his face, taking his first few steps down the Sacred Stairs into a brand-new world. I can feel him staring at me.

"Good," I say through gritted teeth. "Let him come."

RETURN

First things first.

"Atlas," I say, "take Winifred and get out of here. Hide her. Tie her up. Whatever happens, don't let Roth see her." I turn to the others. "Run."

I don't need to tell them twice. Roth's already leaping down the stairs.

"Um, Jane?" Violet says, backing toward the museum. "We need to go."

"One sec." I kneel over Dad, tap his cheeks. "Wake up. Please." I shake him. "Dad! If you wake up right now, I . . . I promise I'll never sing to you ever again." His eyes flicker open. I sit back. "Wow, okay. I was kinda hoping for a *little* hesitation there, to be honest."

"Jane!" Violet says.

"Right. Sorry. The hall with the spike pit floor, Dad. The entrance to the Cradle. Which door is it?" He slow-blinks. Tries to talk, but he's fading. "Come on, Dad."

"Look," he mutters under his breath.

"Look for what?"

"Light . . . of the Specters. Blood . . . of the innocent . . ."

"What does that mean? Dad—"

But he's gone again, passed out.

"*JANE!*" Violet and Hickory shout together.

"Okay!" I turn to Yaku. "Can you take him? Keep him safe?"

"Of course." He picks up Dad almost as easily as Aki would. "Good luck, Jane."

"Thanks. If he wakes up before we're back, tell him I love him. If I don't make it back—"

"You will," Yaku says with a nod. "Now *go!*"

I take a final look at Dad, kiss him on the cheek, and bolt across the square with Violet, Hickory, and Aki. The Museum of Otherworldly Antiquities looms before us, its double doors open wide.

"I assume you have a plan," Hickory shouts.

"Roth has no keys," I say. "No prisoners. We get him off Bluehaven—draw him down through the catacombs, through the second gateway and back into the Manor. If we can slip into the Cradle without him, he'll be stuck in the snow."

"And once we step *out* of the Cradle again?"

"No idea. Haven't thought that far ahead."

"Oh, good." Hickory slings the crossbow round his shoulders. "Just checking."

Roth isn't even bothering with the Stairs now. He's sprinting and leaping from terraced farm to terraced farm, making a beeline for the museum. At least we've got his attention.

We burst into the museum foyer. Every stained-glass

window has been shattered. A beam of light shines through a hole in the ceiling. Hickory skids to a halt, gaping at the semi-naked statue in the middle of the room. "Is that *me*?" He smiles. "I look good."

I grab his arm and drag him on. "You can perv at yourself later, *Great Adventurer.*"

"This way," Violet shouts, leading us to the stairwell in the far left corner.

Down the stairwell, through the big wooden door, into the Great Library we go. Violet plucks a torch from the wall and leads the way. Even Aki's dwarfed by the towering bookshelves. Roth's garbled screech echoes through the library and we step up the pace, legs pumping, hearts racing, headed for the archway at the end of the aisle. We don't need to go through Winifred's study this time. Don't need to take the secret passage behind the painting on her wall. Violet leads us down the main stairs to the catacombs instead.

"There's a chasm down the tunnel, so be careful," I say. "The gateway's at the end."

"You sure you'll be able to open it?" Violet says.

The gash in my palm tingles at the thought.

The catacombs are dark, dank, and deserted. The ceiling's so low, Aki has to duck. Barrow-loads of rock and rubble are scattered around the tombs.

"That way," I say, leading us down a skinny passageway. The Scrolls of the Dead have been removed from the tiny alcoves. Spiders scurry over the walls as we run, their cobwebs flapping like dusty flags.

I can't believe I was here with Winifred only a week ago, setting off into the Manor for the very first time. It feels like a different place altogether. But here's the dead end. Here's the dirty great hole in the ground and the stale breeze brushing past my cheeks. Winifred's left us a ladder. Some torches, too, judging by the warm glow way down there in the dark.

"Down," I say, pushing Hickory toward the hole. "Aki, you—ugh." His gob's already crammed with spiders. "Get in the hole!"

We scramble down the ladder, sprint through the tunnel, and climb around the chasm, squishing and swiping away spiders. Winifred left us another torch in the chamber at the end. The flames flicker as we dash inside. Our shadows play over the walls. The not-so-secret stone gateway looks a little worse for wear compared to the last time I saw it—like a dirty, rotten tooth. I unravel the bandage from my palm and catch my breath.

"Go on," Hickory says. "What are you waiting for?"

"Last time, the gateway opened and shut pretty quickly," I say. "We have to time this right."

Violet turns back to the tunnel. "Is he coming? Maybe he got lost."

Not a chance. Aki taps his earholes. A second later, the rest of us hear Roth, too, storming down the tunnel, grunting through his half-mask, getting louder, closer, until his footsteps cut out suddenly, replaced with a swift *whoosh*. He's leaping across the chasm.

"*Now!*" I shout, and slam my hands onto the stone.

The chamber rumbles. The gateway rises. We scramble inside, sinking ankle-deep in snow. The Manor candles flicker to life down the hallway, lighting up the broken door at the other end—open, just as I left it.

The wall of snow's still there. So is the hole I burrowed up top.

"The hall's through there," I shout. "Go, go, go!"

Violet clambers up through the hole and reaches back down to lend me a hand, and that's when the air in the hallway thickens—when my skin crawls—when my eyes water and burn and the gateway slams shut with a deafening *thud*. Roth made it just in time.

"Jane!" Violet shouts.

"Stay there," I shout back.

Roth glares at us, breathing hard and fast, rippling the air between his porcelain lips. He points at me, staking his claim. *You're mine.*

"Not a chance, boss," Hickory says, unshouldering the crossbow, taking aim.

I grab his arm. "Don't. Look at his chest." The metal plate's stuck to his skin.

Roth lunges at us, quick as lightning, but not as quick as Aki. One punch, one kick, and Roth goes flying into the wall.

Aki whirls around, grabs me and Hickory and tosses us through the hole in the snow, one after the other, up into the frozen hall.

To Dad and Elsa's spike pit, buried under feet of snow.

"Aki, no!" I untangle myself from Hickory and leap

back to the hole, but Aki's already turning around, snarling, advancing on Roth to give us the time we need.

"We have to go, Jane!" Violet pulls me back through the snow. "We have to find—"

A bright, white light shines on her face.

The color drains from Hickory's. "No . . ."

Time slows. Violet shouts something, but I can't hear her. Can't hear Aki and Roth fighting down in the hallway, either. As I slowly turn back to the hall—teeth chattering, feet numb—all I can hear is the sound of my own breathing and the thudding of my heart.

There are the columns and flickering candles.

There are the balconies and frosted doors.

There are my old footprints in the snow.

And there's the archway at the other end of the hall, no longer black, but filled with that burning, white-fire light. I was right. They're here. The Specters really have been waiting for me, ever since I set foot on Arakaan.

Ever since I found out I'm the third key.

They float through the hall like two monstrous ghosts, out-glowing every torch and candle, making the icicles sparkle and shine. Just like in my nightmare, they roar so loud it hurts. Just like in my nightmare, I know they can see it. I know they can feel it.

They think I'm gonna fail.

They think I'm a threat to the Manor.

Sure, I'm afraid. Hell, I'm this close to turning the snow at my feet a violent shade of yellow. But I can't let the Specters Grip us. Not when we're so close to the end. Not when Roth's breathing down our necks, and Aki's put his life on the line.

The Specters launch at us in a burst of furious light—shattering every icicle, shedding snow from the upper balconies—and I do the only thing I can. I leap in front of Hickory and Violet with my arms out wide, and shout at the top of my lungs.

"*NO!*"

I stand my ground.

I stare both Specters down.

THE FINAL TRIAL

It works. It actually works. The Specters stop. They just sit there—*float* there—towering over us, so close we could reach out and touch them. They're looking at me, waiting.

"Um . . . *stay*," I say.

Hickory yelps behind me. Violet makes a weird little gulping sound.

Back in the hallway, the fight's raging on. Dahaari versus Gorani. Roth's gurgling into his mask. Sounds like Aki's got him in a headlock. He rattles his throat.

By all means, I imagine him shouting, *take your time up there.*

"Uh, right." I hold out the Cradle keys to the Specters. Try to stop my hands from shaking. "Look, I—I know I'm not what you were expecting. I may not be the brightest kid around. I may not be the strongest or the fastest or the wisest, either, but I'm *here*. I'm all you've got. I'm all the Manor's got. One of you helped us back by the river. I need your help again. Okay?" To my surprise, the Specters nod. They can understand me. Whoa.

I point to the hallway. Roth's broken free of the head-lock. Even manages to get an arm through the hole in the snow before Aki pulls him, snarling, back again.

"You can't Grip Roth, can you?" I ask the Specters. "The big bad guy with the mask?" They shake their heads, swaying their tendrils of light. "His mind's too strong?" They nod. "Hmm. No offense, but as far as guardians go, you're not exactly the cream of the—"

Hickory clears his throat. "Please don't insult the scary nightmare beasts, Jane."

"The Cradle," Violet whispers. "Ask them about the—"

"Cradle," I say, "yeah." I nod at the Specters. "We know the entrance is here somewhere. It's about time we took you two home, don't you think?"

The Specters shoot back across the hall and disappear through a gap above the snow to our left, leaving a trail of their foul-smelling gunk in their wake. The top of another broken, mostly-buried-in-snow Manor door. My old footprints wind right past it, so close it makes my stomach squirm. The Cradle was right here all along.

Roth bursts through the hole behind us, growling like a rabid dog. He leaps for me, but Aki's hot on his tail. He tackles Roth into the snow, snarling and rattling his throat.

Click-clack-click, he goes. That's Gorani for *Get out of here*, I assume.

We dash after the Specters. Squeeze through the gap in the broken door and slide down into another candlelit hallway. The Specters are waiting for us in the chamber at the other end, floating on either side of a stone plinth.

The pedestal where Dad and Elsa found the keys.

We run, slip and slide along the frosty floor.

The Cradle entrance isn't here.

"What now?" I ask the Specters. They're just floating there, useless as a couple of ghost-turds, facing the back wall, but there's nothing there.

"Hit the pedestal," Hickory shouts, standing guard by the hallway, crossbow at the ready.

I slide back to it. Throw my weight on it. Slam my fists on top. "It isn't working!"

"Try turning it! Clockwise!"

Violet joins me at the pedestal. We grab one side each, grit our teeth and heave. Kick away the ice around the bottom and try again. The pedestal budges an inch. And another. And *another.*

"I think we've . . . almost"—*clunk*—"got it!"

The chamber rumbles. The pedestal starts sinking into the floor.

"This is it." I slip Masaru's chain from around my neck and grip the keys tight as a section of the wall ahead rises up into the ceiling, revealing a pale, smooth door. But there aren't two keyholes. There are dozens. A hundred of them spaced evenly around the stone.

"Which ones do we choose?" Violet asks.

And that's when the walls start closing in.

"Oh, *come on!*" I snap Masaru's chain, give Violet a key. We run our hands over the stone, checking for Cradle symbols, but apart from the keyholes, it's blank. "Any ideas, Hickory?"

"Yeah," he says, backing toward us, eyeing the compressing walls. "Hurry."

"Did Elsa give you any clues?" Violet asks. "What did your dad say?"

"He said something about . . ." I glance back at the Specters. "Light! Look for a light!"

The walls are a few yards apart now, getting closer by the second. We only have a minute, tops. We peer into each keyhole as quickly as we can, trying to catch even the faintest trace of light shining from within, but it's hopeless.

"Aki!" Hickory shouts. "Get in here!"

I glance over my shoulder. Aki's trying to get to us, trying to squeeze through the gap in the door down the hallway. "Where's Roth?" I ask. "Aki couldn't have killed him."

"Don't worry about that!" Hickory drops to his butt and shoves his weight against the wall, trying to slow it down. But the floor's so slippery, so icy, that he can't even brace himself properly. "You get that door open, now!"

"Here!" Violet cries. "White light, like the Specters!"

She shoves her key into a lock near the top, ready to turn. I peer into keyhole after keyhole, but they're all dark inside.

We're about to be turned into pancakes.

"I can't find any—wait!' I catch a flicker of white in a keyhole near the bottom. "Got it!" I shove my key in, too. "Turn on three. One . . . two . . . three!"

We turn the keys. The walls stop closing in. The chamber falls silent.

"Take the keys out," Hickory whispers, staring at the door, rising to his feet.

We pluck the keys from the door—*click*—and that does it. The white light shines from every keyhole. The chamber rumbles again. The walls retreat, and with an almighty wrenching sound, the great stone door rises into the ceiling. White light shines beneath the door, so blinding we have to shield our eyes. The two Specters fly inside, reunited with the others at last, but when the door's fully open, they vanish.

Only darkness remains.

The Cradle is open.

A pained yelp behind us. We spin around in time to see Aki freeze, halfway through the hole in the door. His black-beady eyes bulge wide. *I'm sorry*, they're saying. *Go.* There's a terrible wrenching sound, a pitiful squeal, and Aki's jerked back into the frozen hall.

"Aki," I scream, but it's too late.

Roth's slipping through the hole. Charging down the hallway, his metal armor glinting.

"Inside!" Hickory shouts.

The hundred-keyhole door starts to close the moment we step through. Violet instinctively raises her crossbow, but there's no point in shooting it while Roth's heart is protected. We back into the darkness, watching the gap shrink and Roth get closer, willing the door to descend faster.

But again, Roth dives and slides under the door just in time. It shuts with an echoing *boom*, and we're plunged into darkness. He growls. Violet cries out. There's a scuffle. I leap forward to help, but I'm shoved to the ground by Hickory. I spin around, ready to leap into the dark again, when—*thwat!*—the crossbow fires.

We freeze, all of us, waiting.

The torches on either side of the door flare to life.

My heart sinks.

Roth has Violet in a headlock with one arm, the crossbow held aloft in the other.

And Hickory's standing before the Cradle Sea, clutching the arrow embedded in his stomach, falling to his knees, collapsing at the black water's edge.

"Jane," he gasps, and falls utterly, terribly still.

Hickory Dawes is dead.

THE CRADLE OF ALL WORLDS

The Sea stretches on into the darkness, well beyond the flickering light cast by the torches on the walls. It isn't ordinary water, I realize. Not exactly. It moves differently—like silk, like oil—and it's rippling now, trembling like the stone beneath my feet. I want to cry. Scream. I want to tear open the wound in my hand and rip this entire cavern apart. I can feel the furious tide coursing through my veins, ready to burst, but I know that's what Roth wants.

He wants me to lose control.

I step closer to Hickory. Maybe he's just injured. Faking it. If I tend to his wound, maybe he'll come back to us. But no. Roth won't allow it. He ditches the crossbow, brings a sickle blade to Violet's throat. I freeze.

"Jane," she gasps, "swim!"

But she knows I can't. This place is so big I can't even see the foundation stone out there in the Sea. I'd never make it. How the hell are we supposed to get to the center?

"Let her go, Roth," I say, trying to ignore the throbbing in my palm, the itch on my skin, the hot tears welling in my eyes. "I swear, if you hurt her—"

He tightens his grip on Violet, she drops her key and cries out, and the furious tide within me stirs in response. The quake intensifies. The Sea ebbs and flows. Roth's already got me tangled in his strings. Already dangling me like a puppet, making me dance.

I drop my key, too. Play nice.

"You don't need to do this, Roth. I'll go with you. Just let her go, and we'll head out to the stone. Me and you." I nod at the Sea. "Assuming you know how."

He takes the blade away from Violet's throat and taps the tip to his temple. He knows, all right. Probably gleaned the secret from Dad's mind.

He drags Violet to the edge of the Sea. Forces her hand out over the water and cuts it. She grits her teeth and winces as her blood drips into the black water.

Blood of the innocent. Just like Dad and Elsa were way back when. The blood of someone who doesn't want to claim the Cradle.

The silken water bubbles and churns. Roth drags Violet back a step as it laps at their feet. An ancient stone bridge rises from the depths, long and thin, stretching out into the Sea. It stops an inch or two above the surface. Waves lap over it as the water swirls and settles. Violet stares at me, imploring me to make a break for it, but I can't leave her. I won't.

Roth points his blade back at the door before pressing it against Violet's neck again. He wants me to grab one of the torches.

I force my legs to move. Pluck a torch from its bracket and hold it up high. Thousands of symbols are painted onto the walls of the Cradle. Millions of them. They're rust-red. Dried blood, I think. The blood of a god. Seer blood. *Nabu-kai engraved the fate of all worlds into the walls of the Manor itself,* Dad told me, *and the destinies of those who would shape them.*

What would happen if I touched one? Would I be granted a vision, just like Winifred? Would I be shown someone's life from beginning to end? All their trials and triumphs? I can tell Roth wants to find out, too. He's staring at the symbols with a sick look in his eyes. A kind of overpowering hunger. But now isn't the time.

He nods at the bridge. *Walk.*

Torch held aloft, I step back past Hickory. For a second, I'm sure he moves. Certain his mouth just twitched. I'd give anything for him to sit up, flash his stupid dimples at me and tell me he has a plan, but he doesn't. It was just a trick of the light. A cruel tease.

What do I do? What do I do? What do I do?

The arrow's sticking out of his stomach. The crossbow isn't far, but I'd never make it in time.

I wipe away a tear and pause at the edge of the Sea. Shoot Roth a death-glare, nod at Violet. I want to tell her everything's gonna be okay, but we both know that isn't true.

Roth marches us onto the bridge, farther and farther out to Sea. It's terrifying, being surrounded by this much water. This place has plagued me all my life. How many times did I drown in those dreams, tossed around by those waves, dragged through the depths?

I can't believe I'm here. This is where I was born.

Where the Makers made and left me. Where I stayed for millions of years while life sparked and spread in the Otherworlds. While people lived, loved and died. While empires rose and fell, and Roth tore Arakaan apart.

"It's like mercury," Violet mutters, gazing out at the rippling Sea.

My quake's still trembling. The Cradle sounds like it's growling. I bet I could snap the bridge like a twig if I wanted to, but then what? Roth can't drown. We can.

Tiny waves break out across the Sea, splashes of white foam flashing gold under the torchlight. The bridge dips below the surface now and then, so it looks as if we're walking on the water itself. We walk and we walk, sickened by Roth's stench. Weakened.

I wonder where the Specters are. They've gotta be out there somewhere, lurking in the deep, deep dark. Waiting for something, but what?

I think about Hickory, lying on the stone. I think about Aki back in the frozen hall, injured or worse. I think about the Tin-skins and Leatherheads streaming down the Sacred Stairs, storming Bluehaven. Yaku carrying Dad to safety, the townsfolk in retreat. I think about Eric Junior and his team, headed toward Roth's lair to rescue the other prisoners.

They were counting on us—on *me*—and I've failed them all.

"Jane," Violet whispers. "Look."

Step by step, the foundation stone emerges from the gloom at the end of the bridge, jutting from the Sea like a giant shark fin. A misshapen pyramid. A massive triangle of stone with one inward-curving side, just like the symbol on the keys.

Roth flicks his blade and wrenches Violet's arm. *Keep going. Don't try anything stupid.*

"Take it easy." I stifle a coughing fit. "I get it."

The foundation stone's the size of a house. I don't know if it's the rumble of the quake, the ugly pockmarked stone or the Cradle Sea splashing at its base, but there's something menacing about it. Something sinister. Maybe it's the smell. Like before a storm. It's getting stronger the closer we get, cutting through Roth's stench, as if the air itself is alive with invisible lightning, ready to explode. It makes the hairs on my arms stand on end.

"This doesn't feel right," Violet wheezes.

"Roth," I say, "'it isn't too late. You can still turn around. Walk away."

He chuckles. *Not a chance.*

The wound in my palm itches and throbs again as I step up to the trembling stone.

Roth flicks his head up at the steep, rotting slope. *Climb.*

"I know," I say. "Keep your shirt on." Then I do a double-take, recognize Masaru's cloak hanging from his shoulders. "Wait, is that—" Roth grunts. "Okay, okay. I'm going."

I hold the torch out wide and climb one-handed. Roth follows, forcing Violet up, too. The quake gets worse the higher we go, the wound in my palm itching so much it feels like a nest of ants are burrowing out of my skin. I try to block it out, but it's maddening.

We reach the top in no time. The air bites and bristles.

The waves swell, surge, and crash. It's as if we've wandered out of the Manor to some lonely, forbidden Otherworld. A watery realm with starless skies. It's just us, the quaking stone and the roiling Cradle Sea.

There's a smooth patch of rock at the tip of the foundation stone. This is where Dad and Elsa must've found me. I wonder what I did when I saw them, what they said.

I shove the torch into a hole in the rock and turn to Roth. He forces Violet to her knees.

"Please," I say. "I'll do anything. The Cradle's yours. You don't need to hurt her."

But that's the only reason he's kept her alive. He wants her to suffer so I suffer. Break her so I break. Bend me to his will. Violet knows it, too. I can see it in her eyes and it kills me.

"You're not gonna be able to control me, Roth," I shout. "I can't even control myself. Trust me, I've *seen* what's about to happen—the Cradle Sea flowing through every gateway, destroying every Otherworld. If you do this, there'll be nothing left for you to rule!"

He grabs Violet's hair and tilts her head back. She coughs and splutters, struggling to breathe. The furious tide swirls inside me. A phantom wind rises. A wave crashes into the stone, bursting like liquid fireworks. I clench my fists and the rock cracks at my feet.

"Stop, Jane," Violet gasps. "You're giving him what he wants."

"I can't let you die," I shout. And at Roth: "Let. Her. Go."

The torch snuffs out, and that's when I see the glimmers of white light, way out in the Sea. That eerie underwater moaning I heard so often in my nightmares fills the Cradle, reverberating through the electric air. The Specters are here at last: great swirls of white fire swarming and shimmering near and far, lighting up the dark so brightly we can see the towering walls inscribed with symbols and the domed ceiling of the Cradle high above. For a second, I'm sure I see Hickory, too—stumbling along the stone bridge, coming to save us—but then I blink, and he's gone.

Wishful thinking.

The Specters rise around us. Twelve beastly wraiths of light spinning slowly in a perfect circle. They don't roar. They don't attack. They don't even try to Grip Roth or me. They just float and spin, trailing those tentacles of light, their white-fire eyes burning.

Roth chuckles. He isn't afraid. Not one bit.

Hell, he's enjoying this.

"Jane," Violet shouts, "look at me! Focus on my voice! It's okay. We're gonna be okay.'"

But I know that isn't true.

The phantom wind howls around us. The Specters circle faster and faster till they merge into one blinding blur. A white halo shining over the stone. The air crackles. The wound in my palm hurts so much I can't help scratching at it, drawing a stream of blood. The quake responds in kind, the foundation stone shaking so much that Roth and I lose our footing.

And Violet makes her move.

She breaks free. Leaps up, twists Roth's arm around, kicks the backs of his leg and brings him to his knees. Without thinking, I slam my bleeding palm onto the stone and make the connection at once. I feel every crack and quiver, and shove my other fist up into the air. The stone responds like an extension of my arm, shooting a column of rock up at Roth, which slams into his side and sends him flying. But Roth's too quick, too nimble. He flips through the air, lands on all fours like a cat, and charges right at me.

"Violet," I shout, "don't—"

Too late. She leaps between us, takes the full brunt of his attack. Roth knocks her out in an instant, but he doesn't stop there. In one swift motion, he picks her up, lifts her high over his shoulders, and tosses her from the stone.

I scramble to the edge. See her disappear beneath the surging waves. Fall to my knees and scream.

The spinning Specters roar so loud it hurts.

And that's when the furious tide really overflows.

THE KEY OF ALL SOULS

The foundation stone splits in half, right down the middle. A cleft one foot wide. Feels like my head splits, too, cracked like a coconut. I feel a crackle in my fingertips, as if lightning's running through my veins, as if my whole body's on fire. Worse still, I can feel the void opening deep inside me, just like in my nightmare, and Roth leaping on top of me, strangling me with one hand and holding my bleeding palm to the stone with the other. This is it.

He fixes his eyes on mine. I want to shut him out, but I'm in too much pain. He forces his way into my mind, and what he finds delights him. The fear. The power. He can feel what I'm feeling and see what I'm seeing. Every crack spreading through the stone. Every fissure snaking deep down under the Sea, up along the towering walls of the Cradle, and across the cavernous ceiling. The stone bridge falling to pieces. The hundred-keyhole door fracturing. The corridor beyond falling apart. The cracks spreading through the frozen hall and out into the Manor. The second gateway to Bluehaven shaking, trembling, collapsing.

He can feel it all, and he's hungry for more.

Violet was right: the foundation stone's amplifying my powers. But the Makers aren't here to guide me. It's just me and Roth and the terrible void. I try to resist it, relax the way Hickory suggested, but Hickory's gone now, and so is Violet, and all I feel is loss and heartbreak. The kind of grief that turned Roth into this walking disease, this monster, this cruel puppeteer. I can feel him trawling through my memories, fixating on the worst. Hickory dying. Violet disappearing into the waves. Elsa plummeting in the truck, and that snippet from my nightmare of Dad sinking in the dark. He forces me to relive them. Like the Grip, it seems to last an age. But he also shows me other things. His dastardly plans. He's gonna choose an Otherworld to test out the power of the Cradle Sea, all right. It was gonna be Arakaan, but now he has a different target in mind.

Bluehaven.

Dad, Winifred, Yaku—all those townsfolk who came to our aid—they're about to feel his wrath. First he'll wipe out the island, then he'll go after the Otherworlds.

I'm the key to enslaving them all.

I gasp. "You can't . . ."

Oh, but I can. His voice feels like knives scraping through my skull.

The cracks keep spreading, snaking deeper into the Manor. Balconies collapse. Columns snap in two. Archways crumble. The hundred-keyhole door explodes. I can feel the Sea now, too, surging and splashing around the stone, pulsing like the blood through my veins. I can't just feel it, though—I can control it. Which means Roth can control it through me.

Take a step back, Hickory said. *Focus on something good.*

I try, but Roth's already taken over. He focuses my mind on the Sea, spins it round and round like the Specters, a raging whirlpool with the foundation stone at its core. The faster it moves, the more it pulls away from the stone, the more it glows, shining that fierce, white-fire light, no longer bound by the life force of the Makers.

Roth's about to unleash the Sea.

He slips out of my mind. Wants me to see the triumph in his eyes before he does it. Wants to see the defeat in mine. He growls at me through his glistening half-mask, burning my face with his breath.

I beat you, I can see him thinking. *I won.*

The Manor is mine.

But I also see something else—a quick shadow behind him, and—

THWAT!

Roth's eyes bulge. He glances down at his metal-plated chest, tries to reach behind his back. There's no triumph anymore, only pain and confusion, a thin trail of black-ish blood seeping from his porcelain lips. He releases me, staggers to his feet and spins around, and I see the arrow, wedged between his shoulders.

Violet stands at the edge of the stone, dripping wet, crossbow in hand. Hickory's kneeling beside her, drenched and wincing, clutching his stomach.

They're alive. Praise the Makers, they're *alive.*

"Told you I was a crack shot," Violet says. And to me: "Now, Jane!'"

A surge of adrenaline. It's now or never. I leap to my feet, grab a strap of Roth's mask with one hand and the arrow protruding from his back with the other and drive it in deeper, angling it to make sure we've hit the mark. The arrowhead pierces his heart.

He gasps. A quiet, pathetic sound, followed by an exhausted sigh. He sways a little, steps back. The mask comes off in my hand, and we see his jawless face in all its gore and glory. The crooked top teeth. The rotting flaps of skin. His open throat like a mushy tomato. He staggers toward the peak of the stone and gurgles something, spit drooling, a blood clot dripping down.

That's when the Specters strike.

One after another, they break free from their spinning circle and shoot toward Roth, seeping into his eyes, his ears, down his mangled, missing mouth, Gripping him at last. With his body dying, his mind is ripe for the taking. His eyes glow as bright as theirs. The veins under his pasty, mottled skin shine like spider webs caught in sunlight. He cries out, screeches, writhes, and twists. Lifted off his feet, he starts floating through the air like the Specters, out over the shining Sea.

I wonder which nightmares the Specters are clinging to, which bad memories they're forcing him to relive. The darkness of his tomb under Atol Na? The queen shoving those bone shards into his lungs? This very moment, right here and now? No. As the Specters flee Roth's body in a blinding flash, only one word escapes his mangled mouth. One name.

"Neeeellaaaaa . . ."

Then he drops into the shining, still-churning Sea, and dissolves like salt in water.

Gone at last. Gone forever.

I collapse back to the trembling stone. Violet runs to me, holds me, runs her fingers down my cheek. "Hey, hey, hey," she says. I still can't believe she's here, she's *alive*. "I hate to say it, Jane, but we're not out of this yet. The Sea . . . the Manor . . . you need to fix it."

I shake my head, exhausted. "We're too late. It's already ruined."

Roth's gone, but I can still feel the gaping void, the quaking stone and the swirling white-fire Sea. Everything's falling to pieces, including the gateways. The Manor's sucking the life out of the Otherworlds in a last-ditch effort to survive, drawing them inside.

"We're not too late," Violet says. "Remember what Yaku said on the plane?"

"That I was his hero."

Violet rolls her eyes. "The other thing he said. *What is broken can be rebuilt.* We saved your dad. We just killed Roth. There's nothing we can't do. Nothing *you* can't do."

"Exactly," Hickory says. "I didn't cop an arrow to the gut just so you can give up now, Jane. Put your hand on that stone and think happy thoughts or I swear to the gods—"

"Threatening her probably isn't the best approach, Hickory."

"I'm just saying, I lugged the crossbow all that way, dodging waves and Specters, and dragged *you* from the water with my intestines hanging out. You're welcome, by the way."

"It's called a flesh wound, moron. A few stitches and you'll be fine."

"Hey," I say, "a little focus, please?"

"Sorry," they say together, and Violet holds my good hand again. "It's time, Jane."

"We're right here," Hickory adds, "and we're not going anywhere."

He's right. The Makers may not be here, but my friends are, and that's all I need. I place my still-prickling hand on the stone. Close my eyes.

"Happy thoughts," I whisper. "Happy thoughts, happy thoughts, happy thoughts . . ."

I think about Dad, back on Bluehaven at last. His smile. His eyes. Sure, he has terrible taste in music, but we can't all be perfect. I think about Elsa smiling at me in the watchtower of Orin-kin as the twin suns rose before us. Sure, she secretly wanted to kill me, but imagine what *could've* been. I think about Aki putting his life on the line to save us and hope to the gods he's okay. I think about the townsfolk marching into the Manor to help us, even though they used to be a bunch of jerks, and some possibly still are. I think about Hickory, kneeling beside me on the stone, placing his hand on my shoulder. And Violet. The girl with the crossbow. The girl who's afraid of scorpions. The girl who'll stand up for what's right no matter what, and who'll always have my back. The pyromaniac with the prettiest eyes I've ever seen. I use them as an anchor to drive the bad thoughts away.

The gaping void closes, replaced by that warm, golden glow. The glow that spreads and swirls inside me, lighting me up like the Arakaanian suns. But it isn't just inside me. The light pours from the wound in my hand, across the stone, *into* the stone, seeping like honey through every inch of the Cradle, outshining the Specters, calming the Sea, healing every crack, cleft and fissure.

"Your eyes, Jane," Violet gasps. "They're shining."

"It's okay," I say, and it doesn't sound like my voice, it sounds like the voice from my dream. The voice of the Manor itself, the Makers combined. "You might want to hold on."

And, just like that, I truly let go and embrace the connection, give myself to the Manor, body and spirit. My mind expands beyond imagining, stretching on and on into infinity. I *become* the Manor. The halls and corridors are the veins in my body, the gateways connective tissue, synapses firing. And this, right here, the Cradle: my furiously beating heart.

I can feel every living thing within its walls, too. Every lost and injured soul. The prisoners in Roth's lair. Eric Junior and his team running to save them. Other, lost people wandering through the Manor far, far away, just trying to find their way home. I feel the townsfolk of Bluehaven still battling the Leatherheads in that sprawling, pillared hall. I feel the Tin-skins, the river creatures, and more. I feel Aki, so close—injured but alive—still trying to reach us from the frozen hall. And beyond the Manor, out in the Otherworlds, I feel Dad and Yaku, Winifred and Atlas. I feel the strangers I used to dream about, regular people going about their lives. I sense their anger, their joy, their fears and desires. Billions of shining lights, like stars in an endless sky.

I'm connected to them all.

I'm at one with the Manor. More connected to the Makers than ever before. I rebuild every broken wall. Every trap, chamber and hall. I seal every gateway. I know I could give it everything, disappear, pour every ounce of my essence into the stone, just like the Makers. Part of me thinks that's what they intended all along. It'd be so easy. But the two brightest souls of all are right by my side: Violet and Hickory, tethering me to the waking world. When the final gateway heals and the last crack seals, I ease back, retreat to my body of flesh and blood—this vessel the Makers made—and lift my hand from the stone.

The connection severs. The quake stops. The Sea calms.

It's over. We've won.

The Specters vanish to the depths without so much as a glance goodbye, leaving us alone at the center of all things, catching our breath, wiping tears from our eyes, bathed in the waning light of the Cradle Sea, shimmering like liquid gold. Like my eyes.

"Well, that was intense," Hickory sighs, falling back to the stone.

Violet and I just stare at each other.

This is what I want to happen: I brush that strand of wet hair behind her ear and tell her she's more than a side-kick, more than a friend. Then I lean in and kiss her.

This is what actually happens: Violet leans in and kisses me.

It's just a peck on the lips—soft and warm and practically over before it begins—but I know I'll never forget this feeling, this thrill, which is saying a lot considering I was mentally and physically connected to an infinite labyrinth between worlds ten seconds ago.

I've kissed a girl.

"Sorry," Violet says. "Figured if there was ever a time to do that—"

"Totally."

"I'm sorry if I—"

"No! I mean, I'm glad you did. I think my brain's just . . . melting."

"In a good way? Like, you're okay?"

"Yeah, I'm okay. Are you okay?"

Violet smiles. "Never better."

Hickory clears his throat behind us. "Um, I'm not. Just in case anyone was wondering. I mean, I'm happy for you two—really—but I'm also bleeding. A lot."

"Crap," I say. We spin around to help him. "Sorry, Hickory."

"I need a healer," he grunts. "And a drink. Seriously, can we get out of here already?"

We help him to his feet and look out over the Cradle Sea, back toward the hundred-keyhole door. I know Aki's waiting for us on the other side. I can still feel him. I can still feel them all, the billions of souls out there in the Otherworlds. The feeling's fading, like the golden shimmer of the Sea, but for now it's comforting, knowing I'm part of something big.

There's loads to be done. So many people need our help. We have to pick up the keys, and get the rest of Roth's prisoners back to their homes. We have to help Yaku get back to Arakaan and march any surviving Tin-skins and Leatherheads back there, too. There are all kinds of strange and deadly creatures still trapped inside the Manor. So many more wonders to see.

Whatever Otherworldly environments were inside when I healed the gateways are here for good, I'm afraid. The snow, the lava, the river, the black sand and crystals—they're part of the Manor now, like me. Hell, the forest's probably tearing it to pieces again already. Repair work's never gonna be done, but that's okay. A new age of the Manor has begun.

First, I want a coconut. And a nap. Most of all, I want some quality time with Dad. I'll have to tell him about Elsa when he wakes up. It won't be easy, but what's new? I have Violet. I have Hickory. As long as they're with me, I can do anything.

"Okay," I say. "Let's go home." And once we've helped Hickory down to the bridge and started the long, slow walk back across the Sea: "It's a pity we don't know the name of it."

"The name of what?"

"Our home."

"Bluehaven," Hickory says.

"Bluehaven's the name of the island," I say. "I'm talking about the world."

Hickory pauses, hand clutching the wound in his gut. "What are you on about?"

"The name was lost long ago," Violet says. "Our ancestors—your people—struck it from their early records. Vowed to never say its name. 'The Unspeakable Plague has destroyed the world beyond the ocean,' Riggs wrote. 'It is no more. We must look to the Manor now. We are the last. We are Bluehaven.' We lost the names of places and peoples, but some things—"

"Earth," Hickory says, looking at us like we've lost our minds. "We called it Earth."

"*Earth?*" I say.

"I may have forgotten a lot of things, but I remember that. You seriously didn't know that? Everyone's been calling the whole thing Bluehaven for two thousand years? That's bananas."

"Earth," Violet whispers. She screws up her face. "No, that doesn't sound right."

"Whatever it's called," I quickly say to stop their arguing, "it's safe."

"For now," Violet says as we set off again. "I'm sure something else will go wrong, sooner or later. The question is, what do we do about Bluehaven? The island's ruined."

I shrug. The answer's easy. "We rebuild."

END OF
BOOK TWO

ACKNOWLEDGMENTS

This book, together with *The Cradle of All Worlds*, took twelve years to write. Nearly a third of my life. There are far too many people to mention individually for all their love and support during this time, so let me start by sending a million hugs and a great big THANK YOU to all my friends and family who have stood by my side since this adventure began. Mum, my number one fan and pseudo publicist, I couldn't have done this without you. Thank you for—well—quite literally everything (and apologies for saying "ain't" in the dedication—I know you hate it). Dad, you're not around to read this, but wherever you are in the great beyond, know that my love and admiration for you imbues every page. Brooke, my purely platonic soulmate, words can't express how much our friendship means to me. Seriously, I'm tearing up. Thanks for the chats, the cheerleading, and simply being there every single day. Bailey the Golden Lab, my lil editing buddy, thanks for distracting me.

To my wonderful agent, Grace Heifetz of Left Bank Literary, and the entire Hardie Grant Egmont team—thank you, thank you, thank you. Big hugs to Emma Schwarcz, Marisa Pintado (special shout-out to little baby Raf), and my incredible eagle-eyed editor, Luna Soo. To Amanda Shaw, Tye Cattanach, Emily Wilson, Lauren Draper, Pat Cannon, Madeleine Manifold, Joanna Anderson, Annabel Barker, Troy Lewis, and the sales team, thank you for helping me share Jane with readers around the world. Thanks also to designer Pooja Desai and illustrator Alessia Trunfio for creating this astonishing, incendiary cover. I just love it.

More shout-outs to my dear cousin, Georgia Lyons Brown (aka Porge), for her aeronautical expertise, Elizabeth Tan for her correspondence and advice, and to my future husband, who still hasn't shown up yet. How dare you.

To my fellow authors everywhere, thank you for making this such an incredible industry to be a (very small) part of. To the booksellers and librarians, thank you for championing adventure, celebrating queer heroes, and supporting Aussie kids' literature. To my readers, I love you all. So many of you have reached out since *Cradle* was released, and your messages of support lift me up every time. Even if I didn't have time to respond, know that you made my day.

Till next time, intrepid adventurers,

—Jeremy

ABOUT THE AUTHOR

Jeremy Lachlan was born and raised in Australia, and he now calls Sydney home. His debut novel, *Jane Doe and the Cradle of All Worlds*, was the 2019 Australian Book Industry Award winner for Book of the Year for Older Children, and he once took home $100 in a karaoke competition, of which he's equally proud. He came up with the idea for The Jane Doe Chronicles while lost in the Cairo Museum.